Hope Chest

GRAND DESIGN

Karen Fox

ZEBRA BOOKS
KENSINGTON PUBLISHING CORP.

http://www.zebrabooks.com

ZEBRA BOOKS are published by

Kensington Publishing Corp.
850 Third Avenue
New York, NY 10022

First Printing: August 2001
10 9 8 7 6 5 4 3 2 1

Printed in the United States of America

To Margaret and Ken Hamilton, who've proven
true love is always timeless
To Deb Stover for asking, "Why don't we do this?"
And as always, to the Wyrd Sisters.

Chapter 1

He was gorgeous.

Cynda Madison stepped back to admire the face finally revealed in all its resplendent glory. She had taken several days to remove the years of grime from just this small portion of the portrait, but the work had been well worth the effort.

The face that emerged had been designed for the word handsome. His chiseled cheekbones, firm chin, and aristocratic features all blended together to create a totally appealing and stunningly sensual appearance. With thick, straight black hair, cut long to the collar, and a mesmerizing pair of dark gray eyes beneath dark brows, this man could give Tom Cruise a run for his money.

Who was he?

She should have asked when she had accepted

this assignment, but at the time she had viewed it as just another way to keep bread on the table while she pursued her true love—painting landscapes.

"Oh my, that's wonderful." Eleanor Del Norte, the head of the Hope Springs Historical Society, gasped as she entered the small cottage where Cynda worked.

Cynda hated dragging her gaze from the face to greet the elderly woman. "Isn't he, though?"

Mrs. Del Norte chuckled. "I didn't mean him, though he is quite handsome, but the colors themselves. I had no idea it was so beautiful beneath all that grime."

"It was pretty dirty." Cynda turned to view the portrait again. Almost life-size, his face stood even with hers. "How old did you say this was again?"

"At least one hundred years. It's one of the few survivors of The Chesterfield's last fire."

That would explain the blackened frame. Unable to look away from the dark gaze, Cynda marveled at the passion and hint of arrogance that smoldered in his eyes. "Who was the artist?"

"I don't know." Mrs. Del Norte came to stand beside her. "Unless you reveal it at some point."

"I'll do my best." The artist did good work. Though Cynda knew how to paint portraits, she had never been able to put such passion into one. "Do you know who the man is?"

"Ah, I can help you there." The patron turned an amused smile on Cynda. "Prince Dimitri Karakov."

"A prince?" That explained it. A face like his didn't dare belong to any ordinary man. But why had his portrait been at The Chesterfield? "Did he stay at the resort?"

"Yes, for some time. I believe he accompanied his grandmother each year when she took the waters." Mrs. Del Norte turned away, and Cynda followed suit. "How long do you think it will take to finish this project?"

Cynda hesitated. Now that she knew exactly what she was working with, the process should go more smoothly, yet she hated to proceed too hastily. "It's hard to say," she said. "Two months, perhaps sooner."

"Excellent." Mrs. Del Norte's face lit up. "We're holding an anniversary celebration over the Fourth of July weekend to honor The Chesterfield, and we want to display this then. Our goal is to raise funds to restore The Chesterfield."

Cynda escorted the woman to the door of what had once been the doctor's home, and they paused outside to gaze at the ruins of the once famous hotel. Many walls lay in ruins, the balconies were broken, and the intricate scrollwork had crumbled beneath years of wet Virginia weather. Though a small bit of its former elegance lingered, Cynda found it difficult to imagine the place alive with wealth and luxury.

There were remnants of the elegance, however, in the simple cottage where she worked. Formerly nothing more than a service building, it still retained signs of when The Chesterfield had been host to the nobility and affluent.

As Cynda worked later that evening, unwilling to stop until the last of the daylight had vanished, she imagined she could hear voices in the distance of hotel guests, the whistle of an arriving train at the station by the hotel, the dancing waters of the now decayed fountain in the overgrown gardens.

But when she paused to listen, she only heard the familiar night sounds—the wind rustling through the pines, the hoot of a distant owl, the gurgling of the spring in the distance.

Just her imagination. The Chesterfield hadn't housed guests in decades, but with luck, Hope Springs Historical Society would change that.

Before going to bed, Cynda took one last look at Prince Dimitri and sighed. They didn't make them like that anymore.

As Cynda snuggled against her pillow, the prince's face continued to haunt her. Why? What was it about him? She had found men attractive before, but none of them had stirred her senses as Dimitri did. But this one was a prince. Cynda smiled and shut her eyes. *Of course.*

The dreams crept up on her—wild dreams, filled with images flashing from one scene to another. The Chesterfield, no longer a ruin, but alive with bustle, music and intriguing guests.

Abruptly, Cynda found herself in a crowd, unable to move in the direction she wanted. As a couple pushed past her, she stepped back onto someone's foot. She turned, an apology on her lips, an apology that vanished as she spotted her victim.

"Please, accept my apologies." Prince Dimitri took her hand and bowed low over it, his accent the only clue that English wasn't his native language.

Before Cynda could do more than stare, the scene changed again. She found herself outside the hotel beside the fountain, facing the prince. "I must talk to you," she insisted.

"You can say nothing I wish to hear." He walked

away, leaving her there as she stared after him. The arrogance, the nerve, the . . .

The scene changed again. This time, Dimitri stood in The Chesterfield's lobby, a smile on his face that sent Cynda's hormones into overdrive. She was there, watching him with a strange sense of satisfaction; then suddenly a loud noise filled her dream, and the prince collapsed to the floor, blood streaming from his chest.

"No!" Cynda bolted up in bed as the cry escaped her throat. Forcing herself to breathe evenly, she oriented herself to her surroundings—she was in the cottage at The Chesterfield. The rest had been a dream, nothing more. Then, why was her heart racing, her chest tight with agony?

The painting. She glanced toward it, silhouetted in the darkness against a window. Could her attraction to the prince bring on such crazy visions? It had felt so real.

She forced herself to roll over, her back to the picture. What kind of man had this prince been? Tomorrow, she promised herself, she would take some time and learn more about the man who filled her dreams.

The Historical Society prided itself on its library, and Cynda had to admit their pride was well-justified. She had no doubt the information she wanted was here. The problem was finding it.

Fortunately, the archives of the local newspaper, the *Hope Springs Times*, were filled with articles on Prince Dimitri as well as other aristocrats who had visited The Chesterfield. Cynda grinned as she scanned the newspaper's society pages detailing the exploits of the famous and wealthy. Even the meals they ate were listed.

These folks could work for the Enquirer. Her grin faded as she spotted a headline with Dimitri's name.

PRINCE DIMITRI KARAKOV KILLED AT THE CHES-TERFIELD.

Killed? Her breath caught as if she were suddenly punched in the chest. True, he was long dead as it was, but this felt worse. Murdered? By whom? Was that what her dream had meant?

Cynda read through the article. For a newspaper that loved to present minutiae, the details of Dimitri's death were sketchy at best. He had been shot and killed on December 12, 1889, while staying at The Chesterfield. His body had been returned to his home country for burial and his younger brother crowned king in his place.

But who shot him? What happened? Cynda's frustration grew as she searched through paper after paper to find no further news. Had someone put a hush on the information?

She frowned. A member of the royal family could have done that. Had Dimitri's brother murdered him to gain the throne?

She returned to her cottage with a heavy heart and stood before the portrait. The eyes that met hers were too full of life to die so young. "What happened, Dimitri?"

For a brief foolish moment, she thought he might answer, but the face didn't change. Or did it? Leaning closer, she caught the glimmer of amusement in his expression. Had that been there all along?

She stepped forward to touch the face, then drew her hand back in surprise. It had felt warm, alive.

No, that was absurd. Cynda forced herself to turn away, but found herself heading for her tools. She wanted to discover more of this man buried for years beneath the grime.

No, more than that. She *had* to discover more.

She worked until exhaustion drove her to bed. And the dreams came again.

Dimitri lived, his eyes gleaming with passion, his arms around Cynda as they danced. There were others present, but she didn't notice them. All she could see was the prince and his hint of a smile as he listened to her, the intensity of his gaze as he looked at her. His hands held her possessively, their warmth branding her skin.

"What is it about you?" he asked, his voice as rich as Irish Cream, his accent layering the words with sensuality.

"Me?" He was the interesting one.

The room and the other people faded away as he kissed her. His lips on hers were heaven—warm, soft, teasing, then turning hot, hard, possessive. He pulled her close, her body melding with his, his desire obvious against her belly. He slid his hand over her breast, caressed the peak with his thumb.

Cynda's moan woke her. Her blood still pulsed, her nipples hard, her belly tight with need. Damn, what was going on?

She slid off the bed to stand before the portrait, searching for an answer. She found him good-looking—okay, more than good-looking—but was that triggering these dreams? The faint light from outside added a dimension to his eyes that made them appear to smile at Cynda. If she closed her eyes, she could almost feel his hands on her.

Her breasts grew heavy, aching for his touch. She wanted . . . she needed . . .

Cynda shook her head and stepped back. *Crazy.* This was a job, nothing more.

As if to prove it to herself, she pushed herself to work harder, to reveal the superb figure in all its original glory as she carefully removed the years of buildup. Slowly as days passed, his broad shoulders and chest emerged, immaculately clad in a red jacket decorated with gold braid and numerous medals, followed in time by the appearance of his slim hips and muscular thighs encased in dark trousers.

She hoped to repair the frame as well once she completed the painting. The rich oak was coated with soot, marring the intricate design, but didn't show any substantial damage, except for the spot below the portrait where a nameplate had obviously rested. Where was it? Maybe that could reveal the unknown artist.

Cynda did nothing for the next few weeks but work by day and dream by night . . . dreams that continued to leave her shaken, desire throbbing in her veins when she awakened.

Cynda stood before Mrs. Del Norte and the rest of the Historical Committee as they passed around photos of the portrait in its various stages of revelation. "I should have the finishing touches done within the week." Which was more than a week ahead of schedule. Her interest in Dimitri had made the work fly by.

"Wonderful." Mrs. Del Norte beamed at her. "I can tell we made the right decision in selecting you for this job. The prince almost shimmers with passion."

Cynda shook her head. "The passion was already there. I'm anxious to discover who the artist was. With luck, I'll reveal that soon."

"Excellent work, Miss Madison. This will fit in perfectly with our Fourth of July plans." Mrs. Del Norte stood, signaling the end of the meeting. "We'll look forward to seeing the completed project."

Cynda started to leave, then paused. "Do you have the nameplate that goes on the frame?"

Mrs. Del Norte's expression showed her confusion. "I've never seen a nameplate. I'm sorry."

Oddly restless, Cynda paused in the town square. She had walked to town that morning, almost as if delaying her report would give her more time with the portrait.

It was now June 21. She was almost finished and hated to be so. As much as she wanted to discover the artist and reveal the prince in all his splendor, she didn't want to leave him.

With a sigh, she trudged up the steep hill to where the ruined resort and its outbuildings stood.

Maybe leaving this project would be a good thing. She was reaching the point of obsession.

The prince's passionate gaze coupled with her heated dreams drew her to him. *Ridiculous.* He was only a man in a portrait, long dead. And it was highly unlikely she would ever meet his descendants. Cynda grimaced. No matter what the era, she and the prince would always move in different circles.

So why the dreams? Had she honestly <u>fallen</u> in lust with a painting? She shook her head. Probably more a matter of going too long without a serious relationship. Heck, without any relationship.

Which was fine. She didn't need anyone to take care of her. The years following her father's decision to make his life elsewhere had toughened her, sealed her in a protective cocoon away from needing or wanting.

She had spent the last year concentrating on her mother's care. Since her mother's death, Cynda had tried to sell her own landscapes and make a living. Too bad the two didn't go together.

At least she had her restoration skills to fall back on. Gifted at uncovering the emotion other artists put into their paintings, she always had steady employment. If only she could manage similar passion in her own work. Maybe then she would sell or at least get a showing.

She passed the resort's main building en route to her cottage. Pausing, she gazed at the decaying structure. *What a shame.* It never should have been allowed to deteriorate so badly.

At one time it had vibrated with life, with the rich, the famous, dignitaries and royalty . . . and Dimitri. She could almost hear laughter from inside and, over the noise, his voice as smooth and seductive as in her dreams.

As if drawn, Cynda pushed against the massive front doors, the wood still solid beneath her palms. They swung open with barely any resistance. Strange for doors that old. Evidently, they had once been well cared for.

The large lobby was dust-filled with wallpaper hanging down in strips and a portion of the ceiling lying on the faded carpeting. A wave of sadness washed over Cynda. She could imagine how exciting the resort had once been.

Shaking her head at her fancy, she went to leave,

then stopped as a shaft of sunlight glinted off an object at the far corner of the room. She squinted, trying to make out details. What was it?

She stepped inside, testing the floorboards cautiously. They didn't even creak, and she ventured forward toward the gleaming object.

It was an antique maple chest, the sunlight bouncing off the brass handles. Judging from the flowers carved into the front, sides and top, she guessed it to be a hope chest. Three initials sat below the flowers on the front panel—EMS. Who was that? How did the chest get there? Everything of value had been removed from the resort some time ago.

Was there anything inside?

Impulsively, Cynda touched the lid, the wood warm beneath her palm. Definitely quality material. Would the chest hold something of equal quality? Jewelry, gems, clothing?

She lifted the lid and peeked inside. "I don't believe it." Instead of some ancient treasure, the chest held only five items, most of them darkened with time.

Two objects were in better condition, and Cynda reached inside to stir the pile, revealing a dueling pistol in mint condition and a shiny sheriff's badge. Odd things to find in a hope chest.

The other items showed more wear. Caught around the barrel of the pistol was a gold chain that might have been valuable at one time, only now the links were broken. Resting against the side of the chest was a pair of handcuffs, the wristbands severed into two separate pieces.

Cynda frowned. *What an unusual bunch of junk.* Something glinted at her from the bottom, and she pushed aside the badge to reveal a tarnished brass plate etched with words, one edge of it dented as if hit by something.

She leaned forward to pick it up, excitement bubbling inside her. It was the same size as the space on the portrait's frame. Could it be . . . ?

The words were difficult to read, but she easily made out the most important of them—*Dimitri Karakov*. It was the nameplate for her prince.

She pulled her hand down in a victory gesture, then swayed as the room abruptly spun around her. Closing her eyes, she brought her hand to her forehead in an attempt to still the dizziness.

Noises filtered in, broken words punctuated with laughter. Cynda looked around, trying to place the sound, then blinked. The lobby appeared to waver, rich colors seeping in over the dust and ruin.

She shook her head as the dizziness grew worse. The nameplate dropped from her hand as she reached out to steady herself against the chest.

But it was gone.

She staggered forward, stumbling finally against the wall. Her knees wanted to collapse; her head pounded. With an effort, she held herself upright by pushing against the wall.

The material beneath her hands vibrated as if alive. The grimy wallpaper became smooth beneath her palms. Cynda jerked her hands away in alarm and fell to the floor. The voices grew louder. She crossed her arms over her knees and buried her head on them, alarm mingling with her dizziness. What was happening?

For one instant the noise stopped and the room quit spinning. Cynda started to raise her head, then winced as sound returned in a cacophony of voices. Looking around, she blinked in astonishment.

This wasn't possible.

The lobby of The Chesterfield was filled with people all dressed in antique clothing. Was that man wearing spats?

In addition, the disrepair had given way to thick, elegant carpeting, green textured wallpaper offset by rich oak trim and brightly colored stained-glass windows on either side of the massive entry doors. Cynda swallowed the lump in her throat, unsure what to think. What was this?

"Miss, are you all right?"

She turned at the inquiry to see a young man bending over her. Dressed in a navy blue bellhop uniform, he reached down to take her arm.

"Let me help you."

She rose to her feet with his assistance, still trying to believe her senses—the boy's hand felt real, the carpet beneath her feet was soft, the voices resounding in the room mingled with a variety of accents. "Where am I?"

The bellhop straightened, tugging his waist-length jacket into place. "The Chesterfield, miss. Best resort this side of the Mississippi." He grinned, and Cynda wouldn't have been surprised if he had saluted. "I'm Rupert. Anything you need, I can help."

"Thank you, Rupert." Cynda forced her gaze to the young man, digesting his words slowly. "The Chesterfield?" Her heart gave a sudden thump against her breast. *This* is The Chesterfield?"

An odd gleam appeared in Rupert's eyes. "You're the latest visitor, aren't you?" He turned, motioning her to follow him. "Come with me. Miss Sparrow can help you."

He didn't give her a chance to respond, but worked his way through the crowd.

Visitor? Miss Sparrow? He didn't make sense, but Cynda was reluctant to lose the one friendly face she had found. Hurrying after him, she tried to take in more of the surroundings—the dated clothing, the hint of pipe tobacco and cigars in the air, the lilt of a Scottish accent. Was this another dream?

Yet this was different . . . so different from her dreams.

"Miss Madison?"

Cynda turned to see a young woman, perhaps in her early thirties, in a wide hallway with Rupert standing beside her. The woman wore her brown hair in a bun with the top in a poofy style that reminded Cynda of old westerns, no make-up, and a full-length white apron over her navy blue dress with a white collar and cuffs contrasting the dark color. A small gold pendant was pinned to her bodice. "Me?"

"Yes, over here." The woman extended her hand as Cynda approached. "How do you do? I'm Miss Sparrow. I've been expecting you."

"What?" Cynda stared at the woman in surprise. Expecting her? For what?

"I'll show you to your room. Your uniforms are already there." Miss Sparrow laid her hand on Cynda's arm, her expression sympathetic. "I know this is confusing, Miss Madison."

How did this woman know her? What was going on? "Why should I go anywhere with you?"

"Please trust me. I'm here to help you."

Help her? How? Hesitantly, Cynda fell into step with Miss Sparrow, trying to make sense of the conversation. Her room? Her uniform? "Uniform for what?"

"Your waitress uniform, of course."

"Waitress?" True, she had waited tables once long ago during her teenage years, but she had sworn never again. "I'm an artist."

"Perhaps. In time." Miss Sparrow smiled, then paused before wide lead-rimmed windows and motioned outside. "Wonderful, isn't it?"

Wonderful . . . and unbelievable. Instead of the overgrown weeds and crumbling walls Cynda remembered, this landscape looked new. The grounds were filled with people. In the midst of well-trimmed gardens, a large fountain spewed water to the sky. The grounds were immaculate, lined with exotic flowers, the grass green and lush, and the roads smooth and unbroken. Everywhere Cynda turned, she saw activity—people walking, talking, porters carrying baggage.

"It can't be," Cynda murmured. Even in her dreams she had never seen such detail.

"It is." Miss Sparrow spoke quietly but firmly.

A sinking feeling filled Cynda's stomach. "But how? What?"

Miss Sparrow hesitated, then gently touched Cynda's shoulder. "Welcome to The Chesterfield, Miss Madison, in the year of our Lord 1889."

"1889?" Cynda couldn't keep the panic out of her voice. "That's impossible."

"All things are possible, Miss Madison."

Cynda looked from the woman to the scene outside. This couldn't be true, couldn't be happening.

She had come back in time? Wasn't that the kind of thing that only happened in movies?

Shaking her head, Cynda stepped backward. This had to be a dream.

She abruptly collided with someone behind her. "Oh." Turning to offer an apology, Cynda's words died as she spotted the gentleman.

Prince Dimitri Karakov gave her a half smile and took her hand. Bending low, he pressed his lips to the back of her hand. "Please, accept my apologies."

Cynda nodded, unable to answer. Without another word, he turned away to join a dark-haired young man and an elderly woman, leaving Cynda to stare after him, her heart racing.

Raising her hand, she cradled it to her chest. She had dreamed this, but in her dream she hadn't felt the warmth of his lips against her skin or smelled the compelling scent of masculinity that surrounded him.

Her chest tightened as she looked back at Miss Sparrow. The woman met her stunned expression with a warm smile. Cynda swallowed. Dear Lord, it was true.

She had traveled back in time.

And her prince was alive.

Chapter 2

Cynda hesitated only a moment, then started after Dimitri. She had to warn him. Before she had taken two steps, Miss Sparrow gripped her arm. Cynda glanced back. "That's my prince."

Miss Sparrow arched her eyebrows. "I'm not certain Prince Dimitri would agree."

"You don't understand." Cynda released her breath in exasperation. "I have to warn him. He's going to die."

"There will be time for that later." For such a petite woman, Miss Sparrow had surprising strength in her hold. Not giving Cynda a chance to pull free, she led her through the wide hallway. "For now, you need to change your clothing."

Cynda glanced down at her jeans and T-shirt. Both items were well worn, though she could still read the inscription on the shirt—*Artists do it for the strokes.* Probably not the latest fashion for this time. But what did that matter? She wasn't staying here.

She shook her head. Was she really in the past? Her insides felt as if she had ridden the Tilt-a-Whirl at the fair one too many times. This wasn't possible. Yet everything was so real. Her prince was real.

As she trotted to keep up with Miss Sparrow, Cynda tried to absorb the vibrancy of the hotel around her. Part of her brain insisted she had to be asleep, that this was another vivid dream. How could it possibly be 1889? How had she ended up here?

More importantly, how could she get back?

"There must be some mistake." She gasped, barely able to catch her breath as they climbed a narrow set of stairs to the second floor. "I can't be back in time."

"There's no mistake. You are very much in 1889." The crisp certainty of Miss Sparrow's words destroyed Cynda's last fragile hopes.

To Cynda's chagrin, tears welled, and she blinked them back furiously. "But I can't . . . I . . . this is impossible."

Miss Sparrow paused and turned to face Cynda. Placing her hand on Cynda's shoulder, the woman produced a reassuring smile. "I know this is all a bit of a shock right now, but once you settle in, things will be right as rain. You'll see."

Settle in? Cynda inhaled sharply. Stay here? Forever? No way.

Before she could ask, Miss Sparrow had her in motion again, not stopping until she reached a door halfway down the hall and pushed it open.

"This is your room." She stepped back to allow Cynda to precede her inside.

The room was clean and of fair enough size, though the two beds and wardrobes made it appear smaller. A small washstand nestled in a corner near the window.

Cynda stared at it, trying to grasp its significance. A washstand? She looked around. Where was the bathroom? The sink? Oh, dear Lord, the toilet? As awareness dawned, she whirled on Miss Sparrow. "Please, oh please, tell me you have flush toilets. I can bathe in a sink, but I refuse to visit an outhouse." She had never lost her childhood fear that snakes lingered in the smelly pits, just waiting for Cynda to sit so they could attack her exposed bottom.

Though Miss Sparrow didn't smile, amusement danced in her brown eyes. "We have commodes. You will find them as well as bathing tubs down the hallway on your left."

"Thank God." Cynda sagged to a bed in relief. She could handle anything but outhouses. What was she thinking? She was in the past. How could she handle that?

"No sitting. Up now." Miss Sparrow clapped her hands, and Cynda stood, feeling for a moment like a small child. Close enough. With the disbelief still whirling in her brain, she definitely felt like a lost child.

Miss Sparrow held a blouse and skirt against her. With a shake of her head, Miss Sparrow tossed them on the bed and picked up another set. "Ah, these should fit." She thrust them at Cynda, then swiveled to grab more clothing that she layered on top.

Cynda gaped at the items. "I'm supposed to wear all that?" Spying a corset on the top of the pile, she frowned. "You are aware that it's June? In Virginia? Eighty degrees in the shade on a cool day?"

"Come now. Spit, spot." The woman's set expression didn't change.

"I am not wearing all that clothing. I'll die of heat stroke."

"You will adjust, Miss Madison." Miss Sparrow crossed her arms, her gaze steely. "You will wear this or I will be forced to remove your present clothing and leave you naked."

Cynda eyed her dubiously. She wouldn't do that . . . would she? Miss Sparrow's no-nonsense look didn't encourage her. "Why do I have to change at all?" She heard the whine in her voice. "I just want to go home."

"I'm afraid that's impossible at this time."

Impossible? Cynda latched on to the qualifying phrase. "What do you mean—at this time?"

Miss Sparrow hesitated, then met Cynda's gaze. "It is possible for you to return on the next solstice."

"The next solstice?" That was six months away. No way could Cynda endure this type of lifestyle that long. "There has to be another way."

"I'm afraid not. Besides . . ." Miss Sparrow's voice faded away as she turned back to the pile of clothing.

"Besides what?" Cynda moved to face the woman. "What?"

"There is something you must do first."

"Do?" Cynda would perform the chicken dance and paint her face blue if it would get her out of here.

"There is a reason you are here, Miss Madison."

Cynda released a rude retort, then paused. Did her strange dreams have anything to do with this? She had seen Dimitri alive. She inhaled sharply. Miss Sparrow had said it was 1889. Was Cynda supposed to save Dimitri's life? "Dimitri?"

"Perhaps." Miss Sparrow's expression was unreadable. "In addition, you must touch the item that brought you here on the day of the solstice in order to make the journey back."

Item? What item? The hope chest? Cynda frowned, trying to recall what had happened. She had found the chest, opened it, picked up the nameplate and . . . "The nameplate?"

Miss Sparrow gave her the briefest of nods.

"Where can I find Dimitri's portrait?"

"To the best of my knowledge it has not yet been painted."

A cold chill wound around Cynda's spine. "Then, how can I possibly find the nameplate?" Was she doomed to be here forever?

A hint of a smile touched Miss Sparrow's lips. "Time will tell."

Time? Cynda wanted to scream. Time was screwed up to start with.

Miss Sparrow lifted the blouse again. "Now you will change your clothes. I cannot allow you outside this room otherwise."

With sickening certainty, Cynda knew the woman meant her words. "Those clothes are awful." She made one last protest, but it was weak. If she wanted to find the nameplate, she had to leave her room.

"You're fortunate that the bustle is going out of style and the Major no longer insists the staff wear one."

"Bustle?" The mental picture of a birdcage sitting on a woman's butt appeared in Cynda's mind, and she shuddered. *Thank God for small favors.*

She wanted another fashion to go out of style as Miss Sparrow laced her into a long-waisted corset, tying it so snug Cynda doubted she could sneeze without hurting herself. Glancing down at her elevated chest, she gave a wry smile. "Well, at least I have boobs now."

Miss Sparrow sniffed delicately. Obviously she didn't get the joke. Cynda sighed and struggled into the remainder of the outfit—a white high-necked blouse starched so heavily it could have stood in the corner by itself, a floor-length dark blue skirt, and a long white apron trimmed with blue braid that covered her clothing. The entire thing had to weigh twenty pounds by itself.

When Miss Sparrow traded Cynda's well-abused Nikes for sturdy black shoes, the weight climbed another five pounds. Cynda took several hesitant steps across the room, the skirt's voluminous material nearly tripping her.

"This is ridiculous." How did people move in this stuff? She felt like a trussed pig ready for the spit. As she crossed the room again, she swiped her hand across her forehead. Forget that—a pig *on* the spit. The day's fading heat added to her discomfort, and it was almost dark. How would she ever survive high noon?

"Nevertheless, it is what you'll wear while employed by The Chesterfield." Miss Sparrow opened the door and motioned Cynda through. "Come now. If we hurry, I can introduce you to the Major before you start in the dining room."

"The Major?" Cynda found herself forced to

take shorter steps in order to keep from tumbling on her face, allowing the other woman to get several paces ahead of her.

"He's the manager of the resort. He has to approve your hiring." Miss Sparrow waited for Cynda to reach her side.

"And what if he doesn't?" Cynda asked.

"That is not an option." Miss Sparrow started away again, forcing Cynda to follow. "After all, you must have employment while you are here."

Cynda tried to take a deep breath, but couldn't as the corset squeezed her lungs. "I guess I'll have to," she muttered. "It's not like I have any money with me." Her purse remained on the floor of the future ruins.

Six months. Six months in the past. The unreality of it swirled in her brain. If only she would wake up and discover this was all a bad dream.

"Here we are." Miss Sparrow rapped sharply on a heavy wood door, then pulled it open at a growl from inside. "Good evening, Major."

"If you say so." A deep voice answered her. "The entire place has been in chaos since the Karakovs' arrival."

Cynda peeked around Miss Sparrow. A man stood behind a large desk, his back so straight he could have been wearing a brace. His salt-and-pepper hair placed him in his mid-fifties, but his large waxed and curled mustache was completely black, a match for his dark eyes.

His gaze fell on Cynda, and she swallowed, offering him a tentative smile. He didn't return it. "Who is this, Miss Sparrow?"

Her manner even more brisk than before, Miss

Sparrow tugged Cynda up to stand before her. "A new waitress to replace Miss Evans."

"Seems to me all the new staff you've brought me lately have been here just long enough to snare a husband and get married."

"That does happen with young women, sir."

"Hrrumph." The Major motioned Cynda forward. "What's your name, girl?"

She resisted the urge to curtsey. "Cynda Madison."

"And are you husband hunting?"

Her laugh broke free before she could stifle it. "That's the last thing on my mind right now." Getting home was far more important.

"Fine. Fine." He eyed her up and down, and Cynda resisted the urge to flick off a tiny piece of lint from her skirt. "You'll do, I suppose." Returning his gaze to Miss Sparrow, his expression became even sterner. "I'm counting on you to ensure that no more of these ladies leave to get married. It's our busiest season right now. Plus we have Prince Dimitri and his brother here."

"I'll do my best, sir." Miss Sparrow gripped Cynda's arm and led her from the room. "Thank you."

Outside the room, Cynda found herself facing a hallway filled with people, their clothing and mannerisms unfamiliar. The interview had made her feel even more lost. Her chest ached, and she swallowed back rising tears. "This can't be real," she whispered.

"It *is* real." Though Miss Sparrow's voice was stern, her face showed concern. "You must believe it."

Believe it? Cynda blinked to clear her eyes. Believe the impossible? "Now what?"

"I'll show you the dining room, and you can begin work. The evening shift has just begun."

Once again Cynda was left to follow after Miss Sparrow's brisk steps. Upon reaching the massive dining room, Cynda paused. "Dear Lord." The room easily seated several hundred diners at round tables covered with white tablecloths trimmed with the hotel's colors of maroon, navy and gold. The floor was solid wood, and ornate trim bordered the ceiling. Tall, narrow windows lined one wall, allowing for an impressive view of the lower mountains and valleys. "It's incredible," she murmured. She had seen pictures of this room from the past, but they had never captured the true grandeur of it all.

Her stomach lurched. She *was* in the past. To avoid the truth any longer was foolish. Somehow she would have to endure until she could return home.

"Come along, Miss Madison." Miss Sparrow glanced back at her. "No dawdling now." She led the way to the kitchen entrance and pointed out where the food would be served and introduced Cynda to several other waitresses.

As a voice rose from inside the kitchen, Miss Sparrow sighed and pushed through the doorway, Cynda following. The kitchen was clean yet busy with pots steaming on the stoves. Several young cooks bent over countertops, diligently working, as if trying to ignore the young man being soundly scolded by a tall, round man with brilliant red hair.

Cynda did a double take. *That hair can't be real, can it?* Judging from the man's thick accent, he had to be Russian, though he spoke with his hands in a very Italian fashion.

"Cynda, this is Chef Sashenka. He rules the kitchen." As Miss Sparrow gained the chef's attention, the young man before him quickly melted into the background.

Chef Sashenka threw up his hands. "Another new girl? You bring another new girl *now*? I haf no time to train. My meal . . . my special meal for the prince is ruined. This imbecile—" He turned to indicate the previously maligned young man, then raised his eyebrows at finding him missing.

"I'm certain you'll be very pleased with her." Miss Sparrow spun on her heel and led Cynda from the kitchen.

Cynda glanced back into the kitchen. "I definitely don't want to be on his bad side."

"If you do a good job, you won't have to worry." The older woman pointed out a section of the dining room. "You will handle that area tonight. I see Mr. and Mrs. Burton being seated. Hurry along."

With a gulp, Cynda complied. At least she had done this once before, even if it was many years ago. Though Cynda was obviously nervous, the Burtons were very pleasant, bolstering her courage. More guests arrived, and Cynda entered the continuous cycle of ordering and delivering meals.

Her skills returned quickly. She grinned as she waited for an order to appear. Remembering how to wait tables must be like riding a bike. A person never forgot . . . no matter how much she wanted to.

As the evening grew later, more and more guests arrived. Apparently it was fashionable to dine late. As Cynda delivered a fifth course to one table, she winced at her aching feet. She might not have forgotten how to wait tables, but she had forgotten how sore her feet could be.

A new party was seated in Cynda's section, and she sighed in resignation before she realized who it was. Dimitri. Accompanied by the elderly woman and young man who had been with him earlier.

Her pulse took a sudden leap as she approached their table, her gaze locking immediately on Dimitri. He had been sexy enough in the portrait, but real life was even better. His dark hair and dinner jacket were immaculate, his features more sharply defined, and his gray eyes alert.

Noticing Cynda's attention, he frowned at her.

She quickly turned her gaze on the table's other occupants. The woman appeared to be in her sixties, dripping with jewels—was that goose-egg-sized ruby real?—and dressed in a gown highly fashionable a hundred years ago. Cynda bit back a smile. Well, that would be now. The woman's white hair was caught up in a tight bun, but her eyes danced with merriment.

"Good evening." Cynda abruptly remembered why she was there. "May I get you something to drink?"

"Good evening." The other man at the table gave her a bright smile. He resembled Dimitri in features and coloring yet lacked the same aura of masculinity and sex appeal. "How wonderful to have a lovely young woman to serve us."

His accent was heavier than Dimitri's, but his charm more than made up for it. The way he looked at her brought a flush to Cynda's cheeks. Good Lord, was he flirting with her?

She smiled in return, unable to help herself, until she caught Dimitri's dark scowl directed at her. Its impact acted as a slap, and she sobered at once. What was his problem? "Your drinks?"

Dimitri ordered for all of them, and she hurried away, her pulse still unsteady. The prince certainly didn't have much in the way of personality. For some reason she had thought him warmer than that. Of course, her dreams could have given her that illusion.

Just remembering the passion they shared during her erotic dreams brought heat to her cheeks. She pressed her palms against her face until the skin cooled. The reason she was here wasn't to pursue a sexy prince, especially one so obviously arrogant. However, she could save his life. She had to warn Dimitri. If he, at least, knew about his impending death, he might be more careful or leave before December.

If he believed her.

She didn't broach the subject during the several courses she served his table over the evening. This wasn't the time or place. She would have to wait until she could find him alone.

As she carried the dessert of fresh fruit to his table, she found both Dimitri and the other young man standing in discussion with two women, obviously a mother and daughter.

Cynda caught the end of the older woman's words as she arrived. ". . . so pleased you're here. Perhaps the staff will take notice of my suggestion and offer more dances now."

"I fear I am not one much for dancing." Dimitri glanced at Cynda, then turned back to the women. "If you'll excuse us, we should rejoin Grandmère."

"Certainly." The older woman held out her hand, and Dimitri bowed over it. "I do hope we'll see you again, Your Highness, Prince Alexi." She turned her overbright smile from Dimitri to his brother.

"I am sure you will, Mrs. Winchester." Dimitri bowed toward the younger woman. "Miss Winchester."

They departed with constant looks back, and the men sank into their chairs. "And so it begins," Dimitri muttered. He didn't look at Cynda as she set his berries before him.

"You should enjoy it, Dimitri." Alexi grinned. "Most men would love to have women throwing themselves at them."

"I am not most men."

You can say that again. Cynda bit back a sigh. Gorgeous but rude.

"Then, I will have to circumvent these women to protect you." Alexi turned to Cynda and winked at her. "You, however, have been very quiet throughout the evening. You didn't fawn over my brother even once."

"I didn't know I was required to." She gave Dimitri a mischievous glance. "Forgive me."

He met her gaze for the first time all evening. "Your name, miss?"

"Cynda Madison." She didn't look away. A woman could drown in those dark depths and be happy about it.

Dimitri found himself entranced by this young woman's brilliant blue eyes. So few actually dared to stare at him so openly. Should he be offended or amused? "I will make note of your restraint to your supervisor."

"I'm sure she'll be pleased." The young woman

gathered their dishes and whisked them away with quiet efficiency.

He would speak to Miss Sparrow and request Miss Madison serve them in the future. He had enough problems avoiding young women who viewed him as a prize. Finding one who didn't was refreshing.

"A very nice young woman." Grandmère smiled after the waitress. "You boys should not tease her."

"I wasn't teasing her." Dimitri gave his grand-mother an indulgent smile. "I meant it."

"I would like to tease her." Alexi turned in his chair to watch Miss Madison enter the kitchen. "She is different from most other women."

Dimitri shook his head. "You, my brother, need to curb your impulsiveness. She is nothing but a servant."

"But a very pretty servant, you'll admit."

That was so. Miss Madison was taller than most women of Dimitri's acquaintance, but instead of appearing as a towering amazon, she walked with grace, her form lithe, her golden hair twisted in a smooth coil on top of her head. Her face was unremarkable, yet something in it made a man look twice. It had to be those sparkling eyes—a deep blue rimmed with a faint circle of gray.

They made a man want to keep her talking to see the dancing sparks within them.

Grandmère startled him out of his reverie by touching his hand. "I am fatigued, my dear. I would like to retire."

"It has been a long day." Eager to dismiss his unnerving thoughts of a simple servant, Dimitri pushed back his chair at once and took her arm to help her stand. The trip here had tired her, though this was the first she had admitted it. He nodded at his brother. "Come, Alexi."

Left to wander, Alexi would soon seduce every woman at the resort. Since Grandmère intended to stay for several months to see if the baths helped her swollen joints, Dimitri did not want to spend all that time bailing Alexi out of trouble.

With a drawn-out sigh, Alexi joined him and took Grandmère's other arm. Together they escorted her to their suite of rooms in the elegant tower. Dimitri had no qualms at using his grandmother's fatigue as an excuse to brush past the status-seeking mothers eager to marry their daughters with a prince. Already he could tell his time here would be the same as always—tedious and boring and filled with matchmaking mothers.

Grandmère retired at once, and Alexi moved to the balcony to smoke his thin cigar and stare out over the shadow-covered hills, but Dimitri couldn't relax. Despite traveling most of the day, he was strangely restless.

Perhaps a walk would ease his restlessness. The gardens at the rear of the hotel sported a path designed for just that.

After descending to the main floor, he entered the gardens. The hour was late, and he was alone, a blessing in itself. The night air was still warm, though a breeze wound its way through the bushes to toss his hair. Ah, he felt better already.

The sound of falling water in the distance intrigued him, and he moved in that direction until he found the small circular fountain, rising three tiers high with water cascading from one level to the other. He climbed a few steps to reach the platform surrounding the fountain and paused to watch it. The soothing rush of water eased the tension in his neck.

Perhaps he would endure his boring, predictable stay here after all.

Cynda dragged herself through the hallway toward the staircase near the rear of the hotel. Every muscle in her body ached. How could she possibly do this for six more months? She would die.

At least she had met Dimitri and his family. Seeing the man in flesh and blood only added to her attraction. It wasn't bad enough that she had fallen for a portrait; now she was lusting for the real thing. Even with his less-than-stellar personality.

With luck she would see him in the dining room each night and find the right opportunity to warn him of his untimely death. If only she knew how it had happened . . . would happen. He had been murdered, but by whom? And why?

After meeting Alexi she didn't see how he could be the culprit. No one who smiled like that could be a murderer. Except on *Murder She Wrote*.

Passing the large windows that lined the walkway to the baths, Cynda caught a glimpse of movement outside and paused to focus. Dimitri.

She hesitated only a moment. He was alone. She might never have a better time to approach him.

Hurrying outside, she listened for him, but he had vanished into the dark night. Where had he gone? True, he had been moving with purpose, but she would have seen him if he had come inside. He had to be here somewhere.

The murmur of the fountain accompanied the crickets chirping, and Cynda headed in that direction. She had always loved the water. Maybe he did also.

She found Dimitri there, watching the spilling water, and she climbed to the platform quietly. "Dimitri, I need to talk to you."

He whirled on her. "I beg your pardon. Do you know whom you're addressing?"

His tone made her hesitate. She hadn't thought about the fact he was a prince. He was merely a man she wanted to help. So, how did one address a prince? "Your Highness?"

"What is it?" His irritation came through clearly. "Did Grandmère leave something at the table?"

"No, I need to talk to you, to warn you—"

He held up his hand, cutting her off. "Perhaps in America you are allowed to be more forward, but in my country servants do not speak directly to royalty."

Cynda gaped at him. What arrogance. "I bet it makes it hard to get things done, doesn't it?"

His eyes narrowed. "Good night, Miss Madison." He turned to leave.

She stepped toward him. Even if he was a jerk, he still deserved to be warned. "I must talk to you."

"You can say nothing I wish to hear." He started away from her, and Cynda clenched her fists.

The arrogance, the nerve, the audacity. Who did he think he was? Maybe she should let him die.

Whirling around, she misjudged her footing on the platform and tumbled down the steps with a sharp cry. She tried to catch herself, but landed hard, skinning her palms and knees, even through the thick skirt.

But the majority of the pain centered in her ankle. Fiery needles shot through it. "Damn."

"Are you all right?"

She glanced up to find Dimitri standing over her, his expression masked by the darkness. "What do you care?" she muttered. She waved him away, completely embarrassed. Talk about screwing up an exit. "I'm fine."

Ignoring her, he knelt beside her and glanced to where she gripped her ankle. "If I may be so forward?"

Cynda grimaced. He wanted to look at her ankle? "Gee, I don't know." He acted as if he was about to undress her. "Should I be worried?" She didn't bother to hide her sarcasm. "I don't want to overly excite you." Like that was even possible. When he gave her a dark glare, she grinned. "Go ahead."

He pushed her skirts up until he could examine her foot. "It is difficult to see." He probed gently with his fingers, and she winced, jerking her foot away. "There is much pain?"

"Some." Cynda levered her hands against the bottom step and tried to push herself up. Lying on the ground left her at a definite disadvantage. "I'll be all right."

He gripped her arm, his lean fingers wrapping completely around, and helped her to her feet. The moment she put weight on her sore ankle, she nearly fell, agony burning a path up her leg.

"I think not." Before Cynda could respond, Dimitri lifted her into his arms, his hold firm.

Cynda flung her arm around his neck, her heart rising into her throat. "This isn't necessary."

"Let me be the judge of that." Dimitri turned to the path, and Cynda swallowed.

Okay, *now* she was worried.

Chapter 3

"You don't need to carry me. I'll be fine." Cynda's pulse accelerated with each step as Dimitri's warmth seeped into her, creating rivulets of fire in her veins. His dark hair brushed her hand where she had it thrown over his shoulder, the strands soft yet as noticeable as flames.

This was *not* a good idea.

"You are injured." Dimitri kept a steady pace through the garden.

Cynda released an exasperated breath. He was too unnerving. Especially with flashes of her dreams invading her mind. Already her breasts swelled above the constraints of the corset. She would do better to remember his previous arrogance. "Won't you contaminate yourself by touching a *servant*?"

He paused at that and glanced down at her, his face hidden in the night shadows. For several long moments he said nothing, and Cynda swallowed the lump in her suddenly dry throat.

"This is an extraordinary incident." Without another word, he resumed walking.

You can say that again. Cynda sighed and tried to peer ahead. "Where are you going?"

"The doctor has a cottage near the baths."

"I don't need a doctor. It's just a sprain."

He ignored her. Typical male.

"It's the middle of the night." Couldn't this hunk understand she didn't want to do this? Maybe if she punched him. She grimaced. Then he would probably drop her, and she would break her back. This being in the past stuff sucked rotten eggs.

"His job is to assist the guests."

"But I'm not a guest." A point he had made quite clear not so long ago.

"But you *are* hurt." He paused before a small cottage and kicked at the door.

Cynda closed her eyes and bit back a frustrated scream. This was just getting better and better. Why did she have to be such a klutz?

The door opened to reveal an older man, obviously awakened from his sleep as he was still tying the belt of his dressing gown. "Yes?" He blinked once, then stood back, holding open the door. "This way."

Dimitri carried Cynda inside and placed her on a chair indicated by the doctor. At the loss of Dimitri's touch, Cynda wanted to cry out in dismay. *Stupid girl.* Wasn't this what she had wanted?

"What have we here?" The doctor stood before Cynda, looking down at her as if she were a young child.

"I slipped and twisted my ankle," she replied.

"It's nothing, really. I just need to put some ice on it and keep it elevated for a while, and it'll be fine."

The doctor lifted one eyebrow, his gaze intent on Cynda. She grimaced. Was she not supposed to know that stuff? How did folks handle sprained ankles in 1889?

"Let's see for ourselves." He pushed up her skirt just the minimal distance to expose her foot and removed the shoe from her already swelling foot. As he probed her ankle, she winced and jerked away. Instead of giving up, he continued to examine it until, apparently satisfied, he straightened.

"I have to agree—a twisted ankle. Ice will bring down the swelling, and you will need to keep it propped up for a week."

"A week?" Cynda couldn't keep the panic from her voice as she bolted upright. "I just started today. The Major will fire me if I'm off a week." Then what would she do for money and a place to live?

"I will ensure he understands the situation." The doctor smiled for the first time. "I'm Dr. Ziegler. I don't believe we have met."

"Cynda Madison. I just arrived today." And what a day it had been, too. To her surprise, tears welled in her eyes.

Dr. Ziegler touched her shoulder. "I'm sure it's been difficult adjusting."

She gave him a wry smile. "You have no idea." Was it just this morning that she had been walking home from the Historical Society and stupidly entered the ruins of The Chesterfield? It felt like years ago.

"I'll check on you later in the week." The doctor

looked toward Dimitri as if seeing him clearly for the first time. "Your Highness, this is a surprise."

Dimitri bowed slightly. "I was nearby when I heard Miss Madison cry out."

Dr. Ziegler stood a little straighter. "Very good of you to look after her. I'll have someone take Miss Madison to her room. You needn't bother to stay."

"I'll take her." Dimitri offered a smile that changed his entire expression, making Cynda's heart skip a beat. God, he really was gorgeous.

"It's late, and I must return to the hotel," he continued. "It would be impractical to disturb someone else."

"I do not wish to impose on you, Your Highness."

"It is no bother." Before the doctor could object further, Dimitri approached Cynda and scooped her into his arms again.

She grabbed his neck, her eyes wide in surprise. Why was he suddenly being a nice guy? She would have expected him to get rid of her as fast as possible. "Are you sure?" she whispered.

His gaze fastened on her face as if searching her soul. "Allow me to assist you, Miss Madison."

How could she respond to that? She gave him a brief smile and nodded at the doctor as they left the office.

"I'll could come by tomorrow," Dr. Ziegler said as he stood in the doorway.

"Thank you." Cynda barely had time to give him a quick wave before Dimitri entered the night, his stride as brisk as before. "My room is on the second floor over the west wing," she told him.

"Very well."

Cynda resisted the urge to lean her head against

his shoulder. He held her with firmness and no apparent effort—as if she were as petite as she had always longed to be. But she knew better.

When he reached the bottom of the narrow stairs leading up to the servants' rooms, she grasped the edge of the door frame to stop him from taking the steps. "Put me down." She met his gaze. "I'm not going to have you kill us both by carrying me up those stairs. If you'll help me, I think I can climb them."

Dimitri lowered her slowly to her feet, and Cynda inhaled sharply when she tried to put weight on her sore ankle.

He seized her arms, a frown on his brow. "Are you certain?"

The concern in his voice made her pause and stare at him. Did he honestly care about her well-being?

"I can do this." She smiled, then eased from his hold and grasped his arm for balance. Using that and her other hand against the wall, she could hop up the steps.

They had only taken two stairs when Dimitri slid his arm from her hold and wrapped it around her waist, nestling her against his side. "I think this will work better."

Better for whom? His closeness threatened to steal her breath away, and she needed all she could get right now. To maintain her balance, she put her arm around his waist, then gave a jerky nod, not trusting herself to speak.

This method did make her upward trek easier—at least externally. Internally, her hormones were jitterbugging the entire way. His crisp masculine scent teased her, and his muscles moved against her with each step. She wasn't sure she was going to survive this. She glanced up the steps. Just a little farther.

Relieved to finally reach the top step, she removed her arm too soon only to lose what little balance she had. She wavered, but Dimitri caught her close before she could do more than teeter.

Crushed against his chest, Cynda could only stare up at him. Talking . . . breathing was out of the question. A rapid pounding filled her head. Was it her pulse or his?

Dimitri's eyes darkened to pewter as he looked at her. He didn't release her, and for several long moments they stood that way in silence. His glance dropped to her lips, and Cynda swallowed to ease her constricted throat. Was it her too tight corset or his hold that stole her breath?

The precise clip of heels on the stairs broke the spell, and Dimitri released Cynda, both of them turning to see Miss Sparrow join them.

"Miss Madison, Dr. Ziegler notified me that you've been injured."

"I fell and twisted my ankle." Cynda grimaced. "I feel like an idiot."

"What's done is done." Miss Sparrow led the way down the hall. "If you would be so kind as to bring her, Your Highness."

Was Miss Sparrow giving orders to a prince? Cynda blinked, then gasped as Dimitri once again lifted her close to his chest. Heat warmed her cheeks, and she didn't dare look at him. Surely he could see the effect he had on her. She felt certain she wore a banner across her forehead that read "severe case of lust."

Miss Sparrow opened the door to Cynda's room,

then stood back to allow Dimitri to pass through. As they entered, a young woman sitting on the other bed dropped her jaw and the brush in her hand.

"Land sakes," she exclaimed.

Dimitri ignored her and lowered Cynda to her bed, then stood back. He gave a precise bow. "I hope your recovery is swift, Miss Madison."

"Thank you, Di—Your Highness." Cynda glanced at him, only to find his expression veiled. Without another word, he left the room, pausing only to bow slightly toward Miss Sparrow.

Cynda released her pent-up breath with a sigh and lay back on her pillow, closing her eyes. Well, she had met her prince all right. And fought with him *and* had him carry her to bed. What more could a girl ask for?

"Come, Miss Madison, let's remove your clothing before you wrinkle it." Miss Sparrow approached the bed, all efficiency. "Miss Sullivan, if you will assist us."

As the other girl joined them, she gave Cynda a shy smile. Cynda returned it. The girl was the epitome of the petite sweet nothing Cynda had always envied, with dark eyes and dark chestnut hair falling halfway down her back.

"Miss Madison, this is Molly Sullivan, your roommate. I expect she will be of great help to you in the next few days." Miss Sparrow planted her hands on her hips. "Now then. Your apron, please."

Cynda grimaced. And this was only day one of her visit to the past.

* * *

At one time Cynda had thought lying around with nothing to do sounded heavenly, but by the second day of her confinement she was ready to scream with boredom. She had already read the books Miss Sparrow loaned her, including the latest by Mark Twain, *The Adventures of Huckleberry Finn*. Which Cynda had read in sixth grade.

She had asked for a pair of crutches, but Miss Sparrow had refused. However, she had relented slightly by the third day and allowed Cynda to be taken in a stretcherlike chair to the bathhouse to soak her injured ankle.

"How do you feel today?" Molly breezed into the small room at the bathhouse where Cynda sat soaking her foot. A maid at The Chesterfield, she worked from early morning until late afternoon, but her evenings were usually free. "How is your ankle?"

Without waiting for an answer, she crossed over to the pool and lifted the towel over Cynda's soaking foot. "It still looks awful."

"Thanks, Molly." Cynda wiggled her toes, then winced. Her ankle was still swollen and painful, no matter how she wished it otherwise. "I can't wait to walk again."

Molly rolled her eyes. "You say that now. Wait until you're serving the vittles again."

"I'm just so bored." Cynda didn't remember the last time she had had nothing to do. As it was, she ached to draw. "Is it possible to get some paper and a pencil?"

Molly's eyes widened. "I don't know. I'll have to ask Miss Sparrow."

"If you would, I'd be eternally grateful."

With a grin Molly turned back to the entrance.

"Never know when I might need someone to be eternally grateful to me."

Before she could step through, she collided with a man entering and drew back with a gasp. Alexi made a sweeping bow before her. "I beg your pardon."

"Land sakes," she said, frozen in place.

"I've come to check on the invalid." Alexi gazed past Molly to Cynda and smiled. "I presume that is permitted." He trained his smile on Molly. "As long as you chaperone us."

"I . . . ah . . . yes." Molly staggered backward, and Alexi entered the room with a flourish. Pausing by Cynda, he held out a large basket of fruit— apples, pears, even oranges.

"May I offer my own personal remedy for swift recovery?" he said.

"Thank you." Cynda returned his grin as she took it, still surprised to see him. Of all the people in the hotel, Alexi Karakov was the last one she would have expected to visit her. Fortunately, he looked enough like his devastating brother that she could pretend Dimitri had come to call.

As if.

"What brings you here, Your Highness?"

"When Dimitri mentioned you were injured and that he was to blame, I felt I should assure myself you were given good care."

"He said he was to blame?" Impossible. Dimitri would never take the blame for her carelessness. "I'm sure you misunderstood."

"Perhaps." Alexi didn't press the point. Instead, he leaned forward, his eyes gleaming. "But it does give me an excuse to see you again. We have had to endure a silly girl as our waitress in your absence."

Cynda doubted Miss Sparrow would allow any "silly" girls on the staff. "I'm sure she's very efficient."

"She fawned all over Dimitri." Alexi released an overly dramatic sigh. "Which, of course, he hates."

No doubt Dimitri hated anything outside of his small royal world. Cynda bit back a grin. "I'll do my best to heal faster."

"See that you do." The twinkle in Alexi's eyes belied the order in his voice. He suddenly glanced at Molly, who still stood beside the entrance. "Did I interrupt? Forgive me."

"It was nothing important." Cynda waved at Molly. "Don't worry about it, Molly. If Miss Sparrow comes by, I'll ask her myself about the paper."

"Paper?" Alexi asked.

"I am losing my mind from boredom." Cynda absently readjusted the fruit in the basket to a better arrangement for painting, then caught herself. "Molly was going to try to find me some paper and pencils so I could draw."

"Do you draw?"

"I used to . . . before I came here." *Not that it paid the bills.*

"Excellent." Alexi straightened, enthusiasm bubbling. "I will see you supplied within the hour." He dashed to the doorway, pausing only long enough for a short bow, then vanished from the room.

"My goodness," Molly said, her eyes wide. "He is certainly . . . energetic."

"He is that." Cynda liked him. He was so completely opposite from his dour brother. Opposite enough to kill Dimitri? No. It had to be someone else.

But who?

Dimitri ducked into his suite and closed the door behind him. No tap followed at the door, and he eased a sigh of relief, loosening his tie from around his throat. Thank God, he had managed to lose Mrs. Harrington and her too many, too eligible daughters.

Tossing his tie on a nearby chair, he followed it with his coat. The day was too hot for formal attire. His collar had been heavily starched at the beginning of the day—now it sagged around his throat much like he wanted to sag into a chair.

He crossed to the balcony doors and stood in the opening, eager to catch what little breeze passed by. He had barely spent a week at The Chesterfield, and he was ready to leave. True, he had known what to expect from previous visits when he had accompanied Grandmère here, but the reality of evading husband-hunting females was wearisome. Would they be so eager to marry him if he were a poor, average man?

He ran his fingers through his hair. They were all the same no matter where he went.

Except for Cynda Madison.

She was completely different from any woman he had met—much too forward for a servant, yet intelligent, quick-witted and far too attractive for his peace of mind. Though she had approached him as many other women had in the past, she hadn't flirted but had spoken directly. She had spoken his name as if she knew him, her voice reaching . . . something . . . deep inside him.

His attempt to evade her company had been disastrous. Instead, he had ended up even closer to her. He rubbed his hand against his chest, still surprised that her warmth hadn't burned an imprint into his skin.

The door to the suite opened behind him, and he turned to see Alexi enter. His brother also tugged off his tie and removed his coat as he approached. "Are you afraid to go out?" he asked, a teasing glint in his eyes.

Dimitri grimaced. "There are far too many single women at this resort."

"I'll be glad to take care of them for you." Alexi grinned. "Maybe they'll settle for the second son even if I won't be king."

At least Alexi would know the woman wanted him for himself rather than his position. Unfortunately, he also showed little discrimination in his choices.

"None of the women here are for us. You know that."

"That doesn't mean I can't enjoy them." Alexi crossed to the bar and poured himself a drink. "I especially like Miss Madison. Did you know she is an accomplished artist?"

Dimitri's gut knotted at the mention of the servant's name. "And how did you learn that information?"

"I knew you wouldn't visit her while she's incapacitated, so I did two days ago. I found her some drawing supplies, and she's produced some excellent sketches for me, much better than most. I'm impressed." Alexi watched Dimitri for several long moments, then tossed back the contents of the glass.

"You've visited her? In her room?" Sudden anger made Dimitri's voice sharp. "I would think even you knew better than that."

Alexi set the glass carefully on the bar. "It was at the bathhouse, and we were chaperoned. I am not a fool, brother." He came to stand before Dimitri, his expression defiant. "I like her. I look forward to when she once again serves at our table."

He disappeared into the adjoining room, and Dimitri groaned. Miss Madison was far more intelligent than most women of their acquaintance. If she intended to trap Alexi in marriage, she would, and his brother would fall willingly. He was too easily swayed by a pretty face.

With reluctance, Dimitri donned his tie and coat. He would have to visit Miss Madison himself and ensure she understood his brother was not to be trifled with. A member of the Karakov royal family would never marry a commoner.

Yet he found himself strangely disquieted as he made his way toward her room in the west wing. Now that he had broken his vow to see Miss Madison again only when she served his meals, an uncharacteristic eagerness rose within him. He scowled and walked even faster.

It wasn't until he reached the end of the hallway that he realized he should take some token on his visit. Spying one of the vases of fresh flowers that adorned many of the tables in the resort, he plucked out a perfect daisy. It reminded him of Miss Madison—beautiful and resilient despite its commonness.

Not allowing himself to question that thought, he hurried the remainder of the way. He hesitated by the steps leading up to her room, disgusted with his impetuousness. It would not be proper to visit her in her room. Perhaps he could ask Miss Sparrow to arrange something.

Before he could turn away, Miss Sullivan, the maid who shared Miss Madison's room, descended the stairs. Her eyes widened at spotting him, and she dropped a curtsey. "Your Highness."

Ah, here was a solution. "I would like to speak with Miss Madison. Can you arrange that?"

"She is at the bathhouse again, Your Highness. Miss Sparrow insists she go twice a day to soak her ankle."

"Very good." Dimitri headed down the west wing toward the bathhouse. At least there, some rules of propriety could be observed. The place was constantly filled with people.

Outside her small room, he paused and drew in a deep breath. Ridiculous. He was going to be king of his country. One woman should have no effect on him.

Dimitri stepped inside, then froze at spotting Miss Madison. She was bent over a pad of paper propped against her bent knee, her hand moving quickly, her blond hair loose, falling past her shoulders, covering her face, and her figure clothed in a blouse and skirt. A towel dangled over the edge of the pool, covering her bare foot.

She looked up, and her eyes widened in surprise. At once, she overturned the paper on her lap. "Di—Your Highness, what are you doing here?"

Dimitri hesitated. How should he broach this? "I wanted to see how you are progressing."

"Very well, thank you." Her response was very formal for a woman who hadn't hesitated to say what she thought before. She motioned toward her ankle, soaking in the spring water. "I'm hoping to return to work within a couple days. The swelling is down, and the bruising is fading."

"I'm glad to hear that." Realizing he still clutched the daisy in his fist, he presented it to her.

Her face lit up, and the smile she gave him made his breath catch. "Thank you so much. How did you know I loved daisies?"

"I . . . it reminded me of you." Dimitri stopped suddenly. He hadn't intended to say that.

Her cheeks grew pink, and she bent over the flower so he couldn't see her expression. "Thank you for taking the time to visit. I appreciate it."

The sincerity in her voice made him hesitate. "I understand my brother has been to see you," he said finally.

Her smile appeared again as she met his gaze. "Yes, he's been very kind."

Her expression appeared innocent, but Dimitri had met other women who had appeared equally innocent in the past. "He said you are a competent artist."

"I have some talent in that area." A question flickered in her eyes. "He's been very supportive."

"I noticed you were drawing as I entered." Dimitri stepped closer to her side. "May I see?"

To his surprise, her cheeks flushed again. "I . . . I'd rather not."

"I insist." Why should she hesitate? As a rule, women liked to display their work.

Though obviously reluctant, she picked up the

pad of paper. "It's not much. I was just sketching a picture of"—she stopped and gazed at him, an emotion deep in her gaze that he could not name—"of Alexi."

Ah, this would give him the opening he needed. "Please." He took the pad from her hand and examined the sketch. The face staring back at him was familiar, very familiar. Yes, it could be Alexi, yet . . . He frowned. If he did not know better, he would think the sketch was of himself.

And it was very good. He had assumed Alexi had exaggerated about her talent as most women dabbled with painting, but she truly did possess the skills of an artist. He glanced away to find her watching him intently. "Very good." He returned the pad, suddenly aware of their close proximity.

Her breasts swayed slightly when she reached for the pad, and he realized she wore no corset beneath her clothing. Her wide eyes drew a man closer, and her full parted lips begged for a kiss. For a moment he was tempted to do just that.

Inhaling deeply, Dimitri backed toward the door. He had to leave. "I look forward to your recovery, Miss Madison."

"You can call me Cynda if you like." She grinned. "This Miss stuff gets tedious, doesn't it?"

He didn't dare allow such familiarity. "Miss Madison," he repeated with a nod of his head. He turned for the doorway.

"Wait, Dimitri."

At her call, he looked back. She had her hand extended as if to stop him, to pull him back to her. A rush of desire surged through him, surprising him. He found he wanted to return to her side.

"I . . . I need to warn you," she said quickly. Her

words surprised him. Warn him? "I think someone is going to try to kill you."

He laughed. Kill him? "I sincerely doubt that. My country is at peace. I have no enemies, especially here. I could not be safer."

"But—"

His amusement vanished at her continued seriousness. "Have you heard something?"

"No, but you're in danger."

Her concern was real, and he reexamined her words. Who would want to harm him? As he had said, he had no enemies. "You have nothing to fear. I am quite safe."

He bowed slightly. "Good day, Miss Madison." He stepped into the wide hall, then paused outside her room.

Why should she fear for him? Odd. He could honestly say no other woman had approached him in that manner.

Forcing himself to walk away, he grimaced. Yet the danger was very, very real.

From Miss Madison herself.

Chapter 4

Cynda rejoiced when the doctor finally allowed her to rejoin the resort staff, though later that evening as her shift in the dining room drew to a close, she wondered why she had thought it a good thing. Her ankle ached from the hours on her feet, and all she wanted was to collapse back into the bed she had sought to escape.

Leaning against the wall inside the kitchen, she paused to massage her ankle. The ache wasn't horrible, just enough to make itself known.

"You are all right?"

She straightened quickly as Chef Sashenka approached. "I'm fine." After witnessing an earlier display of his volatile temperament, she wasn't about to risk setting it off.

"If you are in pain, I excuse you early." Genuine

concern appeared in his eyes, and Cynda risked a smile.

"Just a long day," she replied. Maybe the fierce Russian chef wasn't so fierce after all. "I'll finish my shift."

He eyed her for several long moments, then nodded. "You have problems, you come to me, *da?*"

"*Da* . . . uh . . . yes." Noting her order was ready, she turned toward it. "Thank you, Chef Sashenka."

"Sasha."

She looked at him in surprise.

"Is better than hearing name butchered by Americans." He turned abruptly and resumed shouting orders to the cooks as Cynda blinked.

Okay, Sasha it was.

After loading the order onto her tray, she returned to the dining room to deliver it, noticing at once that Dimitri, Alexi and their grandmother were sitting at their usual table . . . in her section.

Her pulse leapt at the thought of seeing Dimitri again. *Foolish girl.* After he had visited her at the bathhouse, she had dared to hope that perhaps he had some interest in her. But that hope had quickly died when neither Dimitri nor Alexi had visited again. No doubt they had considered their obligation to the invalid completed.

However, Dimitri hadn't believed her warning. Somehow she had to convince him the danger was very real. But how? He would never believe the truth.

She offered them a smile as she approached their table. Alexi returned it with enthusiasm, but Dimitri went to the opposite extreme, avoiding her gaze deliberately.

Cynda's smile faded. *So that's how it is.* Once

again, she was relegated to the role of servant . . . too far beneath the majestic prince for notice. Did he really believe that?

Raising her chin, she recited the specials and waited for everyone to order, determined to reveal no emotion at all. Was this the same man who had given her a special daisy . . . a flower she still kept by her bed and had sketched from every possible angle?

"And I would like the roast pheasant," Dimitri said, completing the order.

Cynda nodded with as much disinterest as she could muster. "I will be right back with your drinks." She turned, smartly, and hurried toward the kitchen, her heels echoing her irritation. And she knew just what she would like to do with those drinks when she delivered them.

As if to counter Dimitri's aloofness, Alexi oozed charm each time Cynda tended their table until she couldn't help but return his smile.

"That's better," he exclaimed. "Your smile is far better than any of Chef Sashenka's desserts."

"It is a pretty smile," Grand Duchess Karakov added, a twinkle in her eyes. "But I find myself more partial to Chef Sasha's custard."

Cynda nodded. "I'll bring it right away." She glanced at Dimitri and raised her brows. "And for you, Your Highness?"

He met her gaze, and she started at the dark gleam illuminating his eyes. "Nothing, thank you."

"Very well." She delivered the dessert quickly and breathed easier once the family finished their meal and departed the dining room. Every muscle in her body was pulled tight with tension. Thank goodness her shift was nearly over.

She smiled wryly. At least she had forgotten about her ankle.

But the relief was temporary, and she limped as she headed for her room later. She longed to drop onto the bed and not move for hours.

The hallways were nearly deserted, her footsteps loud in the night silence. Cynda eased a sigh when she reached the bottom of the staircase to her floor. Soon she could get off her throbbing ankle.

"Miss Madison."

She turned to see a man approaching and caught her breath. Dimitri? No, Alexi. Though similar in appearance, Alexi lacked the sensuality that oozed from his older brother.

"Your Highness." She smiled at him. "Is there a problem?"

"Indeed." Alexi stopped beside her and produced his charming grin. "I must apologize for my brother's behavior tonight. While he does tend to withdraw into himself, I've never seen him as rude as he was tonight."

"Perhaps he wasn't feeling well." Cynda resisted the urge to laugh. *She* was making excuses for Dimitri?

"No matter what the reason, a future king should behave better." He caught her hand in his, and Cynda blinked in surprise. "My deepest apologies, Miss Madison."

She inhaled deeply to calm her racing pulse, unsure which disturbed her more—Alexi's censure of his brother or the possessive way he held her hand. Why couldn't it be Dimitri touching her instead?

"No apology is necessary." She tried to ease her

hand free, but found his grip too strong. "And call me Cynda, please."

Alexi's eyes brightened. "If you will return the honor and call me Alexi."

Cynda grinned. "Are you sure I won't be hanged at dawn for such familiarity?"

His laughter echoed down the corridor. "I assure you, you are quite safe."

"Alexi." The word reverberated down the hall, filled with condemnation.

She knew that voice. Glancing over Alexi's shoulder, Cynda spotted Dimitri in the hallway, his long strides bringing him closer.

Alexi sighed, then raised her hand to his lips. "I must go. Good night, Cynda."

Drawing her hand away, she forced her gaze back to the younger prince. "Good night, Alexi." She stepped up onto a riser as Dimitri joined them, his glare centered on her. "And good night to you, Dimitri."

Before he could respond, she scurried up the stairs. He wouldn't like her using his name. Well, too damn bad.

She paused just inside her room, listening to Molly's even breathing. Why had Alexi felt it necessary to apologize for Dimitri? From what she had seen thus far, Dimitri had rude down to a fine art. Was he like this all the time or was he being a jerk just for her?

". . . a future king should behave better." Recalling Alexi's words and her own mission, Cynda frowned. Did he feel himself better suited for the title? Enough to kill for the position?

She shook her head. Not Alexi.

Still, she was going to keep her eye on both the Karakov brothers.

During the next two weeks, Cynda continued to find Dimitri and his relatives seated in her section, yet he remained distant while Alexi flirted openly. Unable to remain cool around Alexi and his grandmother, Cynda responded in kind, bestowing her warmest smiles on Dimitri and grinning at his obvious irritation.

She felt rewarded for enduring Dimitri's rudeness when she received her first pay in cash. Money, at last. Cynda wasted no time in catching the train down the mountain to Hope Springs. With only her uniform to wear, she needed new clothing . . . now. Her jeans and T-shirt had mysteriously disappeared after her arrival in this time period, and she didn't need to be a genius to figure out who had taken them.

She stepped off the train and paused, taking in the 1889 version of the town. Much smaller than in the present, yet quaint . . . like something on a postcard. She grinned as she walked along the narrow street. Maybe she should buy a postcard and send it to Mrs. Del Norte. *Visiting The Chesterfield in 1889. Having a great time. Wish you were here.*

Great time. *Yeah, right.* No air-conditioning, long sleeves, eighty-some degrees, and humidity of at least a hundred and ten percent. Her uniform, minus apron, already clung to her skin. What wouldn't she give for a tank top and shorts?

Locating a dress shop with ready-made clothing took a while, but Cynda quickly settled on a short-sleeved gown in a pale blue and changed into it before she left the store. *Better already.* A breeze helped as well, easing the sticky humidity. Now to explore.

The town bustled with life. People walked the streets and exchanged formal greetings as they passed one another. Horses were tethered before the shops, and several buggies occupied an area by the stables. Cynda smiled. She had no difficulty picturing the entire scene as a Currier and Ives painting.

And couldn't she paint it as well? A wave of longing washed over her as the idea took hold. She longed to paint again. The paper and pencils Alexi had found for her provided some outlet for her yearnings, but she had nearly used the entire supply. Where could she find what she needed?

Spotting a gentleman strolling nearby, she hurried to join him. "Excuse me. Can you tell me where I can find art supplies?"

"Art supplies?" He glanced at her. "Probably Hadley's Emporium."

"Where is that?"

He smiled. "You must be new in town."

Nodding, she extended her hand. "Cynda Madison. I work at The Chesterfield."

"Police Chief Jess Garrett." He shook her hand quickly, then pointed along the main street. "Head that way for two blocks. You can't miss it."

"Thanks." Cynda fought the urge to run along the road. Any place named Emporium had to have the stuff she needed.

"Oh, my." The police chief had been right. She couldn't have missed Hadley's Emporium. Besides the large sign perched over the long front porch, an assortment of items hung from the beams and filled the window, swinging in the wind. Pans, hats, material, even candy. Evidently the Emporium was an everything store.

Just so long as it had paints and brushes.

"Good afternoon, ma'am." A man turned to greet her as she entered, his smile as wide as the rest of him. "Can I help you?"

"Actually, yes." Every inch of the interior was filled with merchandise. She definitely needed help. "Do you carry art supplies—paints, brushes, canvas?"

"Back this way, miss." The man led her into the crowded depths of the store. Pausing beside a shelf, he bent to search through a box on the floor. "Here we go. This what you want?"

Excitement bubbled through Cynda as she spotted the array of brushes. "Yes, exactly."

He continued to pull things from the box and set them on the nearby shelf. Spotting several tins, Cynda opened one. Though she recognized the colored powder at once, she hesitated. With pre-blended pigment available in tubes, she hadn't mixed it in years. Did she still remember how?

"Do you have linseed oil?" she asked. She did need that for sure.

"Sure do." The man swiped his hands on his pants as he stood. "Anything else?"

"Canvas backgrounds?"

"Hmm, that may be a problem. Seems to me I sold the last one a while ago. Let me check." He vanished into the rear of the building, then reappeared moments later with a single canvas. "This is all I could find. I can order more if you want."

"That would be great." Cynda followed him to the front and paid for her purchases, grinning at the total which was far less than she was used to paying for art supplies. Of course, her pay was a lot less, too.

She skipped the first two steps as she left the shop. Now she could paint again, and she intended to start with the town and resort. When she returned to her own time, she would have unique paintings of this area to show. Maybe then she would finally make a name for herself.

As she rounded a corner, the tantalizing aroma of roasting meat stirred her taste buds, and she followed the scent to a small restaurant—Café of Dreams. Not a name she would expect to find in this time period.

She entered, then froze, blinking in surprise. The small room was filled with tables and chattering diners, but the decor reflected a modern restaurant with plants hanging in every available nook and a cultured ambiance. If not for the period clothing worn by the diners, Cynda would have sworn she had returned to her own time. A wave of homesickness washed over her. God, she missed home, even if it had been nothing more than a tiny apartment.

A young black man came to meet her with a friendly smile. "May I help you, ma'am?"

"One, please. No smoking." The words emerged automatically.

He jerked, obviously startled. "There's no smoking at all in this place, ma'am. Mrs. Corrie don't allow it."

"Oh, good." Surprising actually, considering the year. Evidently, this Mrs. Corrie was a forward-looking type of woman.

Once seated at a small table adorned with a vase

containing one perfect flower, Cynda examined the menu. Another surprise. While it contained simple fare such as red beans and rice, it also offered beef bourguignonne and cheese soufflé, more in line with the food at The Chesterfield. The menu even boasted spinach salad with strawberries. Cynda did a double take and surveyed the room again. Yep, she was still in 1889. What was going on here?

Cynda's stomach growled. What she really wanted was a fat juicy hamburger. "Too bad there isn't a Big Mac," she said with a wry grin.

"I beg your pardon?" A young woman paused by the table, her expression startled.

Oh-oh, she was caught. Cynda shook her head. "It's nothing."

"I thought I heard you say 'Big Mac.' "

"It's a hamburger," Cynda said. "Two all beef patties, special sauce, lettuce, cheese . . . oh, forget it. I'm being silly."

A slow smile crossed the woman's face. "I haven't seen you here before. Are you new in town?"

Cynda nodded. "Cynda Morgan. I'm working at The Chesterfield. I just arrived about three weeks ago."

"Yes, of course. In June." The woman extended her hand. "I'm Corrie Garrett. This is my restaurant. I'm the chef."

"I love it here." Cynda clasped the woman's palm. "If the food is as good as the decor, I'll be in heaven."

"It's better." Corrie grinned. "Let me prepare a chef's special dinner plate. I promise you won't be disappointed."

Something in Corrie's confidence reassured Cynda. "Okay. Surprise me."

An impish light danced in Corrie's eyes before she turned toward the kitchen. "Oh, I will." Cynda watched her disappear into the kitchen, suddenly realizing what else looked odd. Corrie wore a chef's coat and trousers. Did women do that in this time? If so, Cynda damn well wanted trousers, too.

As Cynda waited for her food, she watched the other people in the room as they talked and enjoyed their meals. *Nice to be able to do it sitting down for a change.*

A couple brushed past her as they left, and at seeing a tall, dark-haired man she jerked her head around to watch them. Dimitri? No. A second glance confirmed the man to be no one she knew. More likely, it was wishful thinking.

Cynda propped her chin on her hands. What was she going to do about Dimitri? His life was in danger whether he believed her or not. Somehow she had to prevent his death; but the only suspect she had was Alexi, and she found it difficult to believe the younger brother could harm the older.

Who else would want to kill Dimitri? And why? She had less than five months to find out.

A smartly dressed waiter delivered her meal, and Cynda smiled at him. "Thank you."

A huge sandwich filled the plate—two thick patties of meat sat between warm bread, layered with tomatoes and lettuce and a familiar-looking sauce. Cynda dabbed her finger in the sauce to sample it. Much better than any "secret sauce" she had ever had. Better yet, genuine, authentic French fries accompanied the sandwich.

Grasping the 1889 hamburger in both hands,

she managed to take a bite. This sandwich put any other to shame. Barely taking time to breathe, she downed the burger and all the fries. She was definitely coming to this place again. It was almost like being back home.

Cynda paused, a thick knot in her chest. Home.

Corrie appeared by the table. "Did you like it?"

"I loved it." Cynda studied the other woman. She looked the same as everyone else, yet . . . "How did you know? About the Big Mac?"

Corrie hesitated. "I—" Before she could continue, the police chief approached and pulled her into his arms for a thorough kiss. Laughing, Corrie looped her arm around his waist when they finally parted. "Cynda, this overzealous lug is my husband, Jess."

"We met earlier," Cynda said.

Jess glanced at her and smiled. "Ah, right. You were asking for directions. Did you find what you needed?"

"Yes, everything. Thank you."

"Good." Tightening his arm around Corrie's shoulders, he pulled her toward the kitchen. "Where's that baby daughter of mine?"

Their voices faded as they left, leaving Cynda's question unanswered. How had Corrie known about the hamburger? If Cynda remembered correctly, hamburgers weren't introduced until the early 1900s, and Big Macs a lot later.

Was it possible Corrie was from the future, too?

Yet Corrie was married, ran a restaurant, had a child. She had obviously been here for some time. Would someone who came here from the future decide to stay? Cynda shuddered. Not likely. The corset alone solidified her conviction to go back.

After settling her bill, she emerged outside to find the afternoon sky clouded over with dark clouds and the wind even more fierce than before. The air held the scent of rain. She needed to get back to the hotel before it started.

The train's shrill whistle rang out as she was halfway to the station. Oh, no. Was it that late already? Lifting her long skirt, Cynda ran the rest of the way, but arrived to see the train puffing its way up the track to The Chesterfield.

Damn. That had been the last one for the day, too.

Shouldering her bag, she grimaced and headed for the narrow dirt road leading up the mountain to the resort. It was only about two miles.

Uphill.

Cynda cast a nervous glance at the sky as thunder rumbled through the hills. Just so long as the rain held off.

As if sensing her thoughts, the clouds burst open, spilling enormous raindrops, soaking Cynda in moments. *Great.* Her new dress clung to her, and mud coated the hem as well as her shoes.

Well, this is fun. Life in 1889 was one joy after another.

Hearing a noise behind her, Cynda turned to see a covered buggy approaching, and she stepped aside to let it pass. Instead, it stopped and Alexi waved. "Get inside before you're soaked."

"I'm already soaked." Cynda hesitated, unwilling to track mud and water into the buggy.

"Get in." When Alexi acted as if he was going to come get her, Cynda hurried to take his hand and climbed up beside him. Though the slight roof didn't keep all the rain away, it provided more shelter than she had had before.

"Thank you." She swiped the water from her face. "I missed the train."

"My pleasure. If I had known you wished to visit the town, I would've been glad to take you."

"That's all right. I had several errands to run."

Alexi nodded as he guided the horse slowly up the deteriorating road. "Then, we are well met."

"Well, a few minutes earlier would've been nice." Cynda swiped at her dripping dress, then examined her bag. Everything was wet, but not seriously harmed. "I found the best restaurant today. Café of Dreams."

"Yes, I've been there. It is a unique place. Mrs. Garrett is a most progressive woman." A hint of admiration filled his voice.

"Do you like progressive women?"

"I am greatly in favor of progressiveness altogether. My country is very much in need of it." A more somber note colored his words now.

"Is it that bad?"

"There is much to be done to better our standard of living. My people are not as well off as those in America." He sighed. "And my father is unwilling to change."

"But Dimitri will once he's king, won't he?"

To Cynda's surprise, Alexi scowled. "We both see the way of the future for our country, but Dimitri insists we must move slowly. I don't understand. The change is required now. The people need this." He sliced his hand through the air to emphasize his point, and the horse danced nervously, forcing Alexi to steady him.

"I am sorry," he added. "I feel strongly about this."

"I can see that." In fact, Alexi demonstrated the most honest passion she had seen in him yet. Passion enough to harm his brother? "But won't Dimitri do the right thing? Doesn't he care about the people, too?"

"Perhaps." Alexi sat in silence for several long minutes. "Dimitri has spent his life preparing to become king," he said finally. "I have been the one among the people. I am the one who knows what is really needed."

Cynda touched his arm. This really mattered to him. "Then, you'll be a big help to your brother."

His smile emerged slowly. "Yes, I will be there to tell him, whether he prefers to hear it or not."

"Now *that* sounds like a brother."

He laughed as they approached the front entrance to The Chesterfield. "I am that." A groom came to hold the horse's head, and Alexi jumped out, then hurried around to help Cynda descend.

Keeping his arm around her waist, he rushed them into the shelter of the front porch. They paused there, and Cynda smiled at him. "Thank you for the ride, Alexi. I appreciate it."

"The pleasure was all mine." He removed his arm slowly. "I have the buggy at my disposal if you ever need to go to town again."

"I'll remember that." Cynda turned to enter the hotel, then froze when she saw Dimitri by the doorway. His eyes were the color of steel and equally as cold.

Acutely aware of her haggard appearance, Cynda lifted her chin. "Good afternoon, Your Highness."

His jaw worked before he finally replied. "Miss

Madison." He looked beyond her to his brother. "Alexi, Grandmère was looking for you."

"I purchased the items she asked for. Don't worry." Alexi joined them, his gaze darting from one to the other. "Shall we go see her?" He led his brother inside, and Cynda eased a sigh of relief.

Dimitri had wanted to say more. She could tell. And none of it was likely to be pleasantries.

Her spirits sank. Somehow she had the feeling he wasn't quite through with her.

Cynda Madison might be different from other women, but she was playing the same game. Dimitri clenched his jaw as he left the dining room that evening. She hadn't been working tonight. No doubt she was busy planning her marriage to a prince.

Alexi was smitten with her, but he had been smitten with the wrong kind of woman before. There would be no marriage to such an unsuitable person. Dimitri would put a stop to this now.

After seeing his grandmother and Alexi to the tower, he returned to the back hallway and the stairwell leading up to the servants' rooms. Cynda had diverted him last time he meant to speak with her. She wouldn't do so again.

As a waitress descended the steps, he ordered her to have Cynda come see him. She bobbed a curtsey, then shook her head. "She's not there, Your Highness. I think she went for a walk."

Dimitri nodded. Why hadn't Cynda walked home instead of riding with his brother in a small buggy . . . unchaperoned? He had told Alexi about the foolishness of his actions. If Cynda held true to form, she would be declaring that Alexi had compromised her, insisting they be married at once.

Anyone who had seen her arrive would believe her story, especially with her disheveled appearance. She had looked like a drowned muskrat, yet still intriguing. Dimitri couldn't blame Alexi for wanting her. Tendrils of her hair had escaped their coil and draped along her neck, accenting the fine line of her throat. For one insane moment, Dimitri had wanted to trace that line.

Her cheeks had been flushed yet damp, and her dress had clung to her womanly curves, the swell of her breasts, and the gentle roundness of her hips. He had had to clench his fists to keep from touching her, thankful for his rigid training.

If only Alexi had endured some of that training, Dimitri wouldn't be constantly saving his brother from his improprieties.

Reaching the back walk, he chose a path and hurried along it. The sooner he could dispense with this duty, the sooner he could put Cynda Madison out of his life.

But would she be as easy to remove from his dreams?

Chapter 5

Cynda dangled her fingers in the small fountain as she absorbed the night sounds of crickets and owls mixing with the trickle of the water. The rain had stopped, leaving a fresh scent in the air.

Normally, she had no trouble sleeping, but after the day off and the ride with Alexi, her brain was too active to quiet down. Was Alexi the one destined to kill Dimitri? His passion regarding the way his country should be run had surprised her, along with the revelation that he disagreed with Dimitri about it.

In the news article she had read, Alexi had become king of his country following Dimitri's death. Other men had killed for far less. She sighed and splashed the water. She needed to learn more. Dimitri would never believe his brother guilty of violence unless she had some kind of proof.

"There you are."

She jumped as the deep, accented voice erupted from the darkness, and she stared until Dimitri came into view. Though the night cloaked most of his expression, she could see the anger blazing in his eyes. Slowly she rose to her feet to face him.

"I didn't realize you were looking for me," she said. "I thought you preferred to avoid me as much as possible."

Dimitri hesitated for a brief moment. "I need to talk to you."

"So, talk." She crossed her arms, pretending an insolence she didn't feel. "I might listen."

"I know what you're up to, and you will not succeed."

"Excuse me?" He knew she was here to prevent his murder?

"I've met your type before. No matter what accusations you make, I will never allow Alexi to marry you."

"Marry Alexi?" She nearly choked on the words. Accusations? What accusations? "I don't want to marry Alexi, and I have not made one accusation of any kind."

"You—" Dimitri broke off. "I beg your pardon?"

"I don't want to marry your brother. Not now. Not ever." She liked Alexi, but he didn't stir her senses as Dimitri did. Even with him telling her off, her skin tingled with awareness, her pulse skipped beats, and her chest grew tight. "Why would you think that?"

His gaze narrowed. "What kind of ploy is this?"

She released her breath in exasperation. "Why don't *you* tell *me*?"

"You were alone with my brother today in a very improper state."

"Oh, give me a break." Cynda stabbed her finger against Dimitri's chest. "I was walking home in the pouring rain, and Alexi stopped to offer me a ride. I accepted. That's all there is to it."

Dimitri glanced down at her finger, then to her face. "Then, you do not intend to accuse Alexi of impropriety and insist he do the right thing?"

"Lord, no!" Cynda stepped back, her eyes wide. "You guys take this propriety stuff much too seriously in this time."

"What does that mean?"

Realizing what she had said, Cynda grimaced. "Nothing."

"Very well." If anything, Dimitri's demeanor grew even stiffer. "I apologize for my behavior. However, I insist you stay away from my brother in the future."

Cynda barked a short laugh. This guy was way too full of himself. "You are something else. Forget it, princey. I think your brother is old enough to decide for himself who his friends are."

"Then, you refuse?"

"You betcha. I like Alexi. Why can't you accept that I can be his friend and not be interested in him romantically?"

"In my experience, women exist only to make a good marriage."

"Well, that's not *my* experience." She had to stick around Alexi, no matter what Dimitri wanted. How else could she find out if he intended to harm his brother? "I have no intention of marrying your brother, but I will be his friend."

Dimitri caught her shoulders and held her in front of him. "You will do as I say."

"This is America, Dimitri." She glared at him. "Created on the foundation of freedom. You're not *my* prince. You *can't* tell me what to do."

They stared at each other. For a moment, Cynda imagined the storm had returned, for surely that was lightning crackling around them. Dimitri's grip tightened, then relaxed, and he lifted one hand to trace the line of her face.

"You are a most unusual woman, Cynda Madison."

Her closed throat made speaking difficult. "I'm just the first woman who's refused to kowtow to you."

A slow smile spread across his seductive lips. "I believe you are."

Cynda's stomach knotted. She couldn't have looked away if she had wanted to. "Trust me, it's good for you."

He caught her chin in his hand and lifted her face. "Can I trust you?" His voice was husky as he bent closer to her mouth.

"Oh, yes," she breathed, anticipation igniting in her veins. She closed her eyes, eager to see if his kiss matched the passion of her dreams.

Abruptly, he released her, and her eyes flew open. He stepped back. "Forgive me. Good night, Miss Madison." He hurried down the few steps leading to the fountain.

"Call me Cynda," she said, not sure he would hear her murmur, her heart heavy with a sense of loss.

He hesitated, but didn't turn around. "Cynda," he said finally, then vanished into the darkness.

Cynda sank against the fountain wall. That was incredibly stupid. Now Dimitri would think she was chasing *him*.

"Damn."

Dimitri brushed past the shrubbery, only vaguely aware of the branches snapping at him. How could he excuse such behavior? He had almost kissed her . . . had *wanted* to kiss her. After just warning her away from Alexi, he didn't want to consider where the logic was in that.

She did something to him . . . made it difficult for him to think clearly. The foolishness of his impulsive action provided clear proof of that. He would have to stay away from her.

"Dimitri." Alexi waited by the entrance, his expression for once devoid of amusement.

Dimitri raised one eyebrow. "You were looking for me?"

"I wanted to speak with you about Cynda, but you already provided the explanation."

Dread raised its hackles. "And what explanation is that?"

Alexi stepped forward to face him. "You don't want me around Cynda because you want her for yourself."

"That's ridiculous." Dimitri didn't want her. He couldn't. She was nothing but a servant . . . an untitled American. The effect she had on him was temporary. "Even if I did want her, I couldn't have her. I must remember Anya. You know that."

"That doesn't stop the wanting." A coldness appeared on Alexi's features that stunned Dimitri. "After all, Father has a mistress."

Dimitri scowled. "And you know how Mother feels about that." His parents provided the appearance of marital bliss when social and political events called for it, but they hadn't shared a bed in years. Dimitri didn't want his marriage to be in the same mold. "I will not take a mistress."

"Then, tell me why you want me away from Cynda."

"Because she's wrong for you. She's nothing but a servant. I don't want you to make a mistake."

Alexi shook his head. "You are a . . . what is the word? . . . snob, Dimitri. The woman is beautiful, intelligent, fun to be with, yet you dismiss her because she has no wealth or title. Who is the loser there?" Whirling away, Alexi entered the hotel and stalked down the hall.

Dimitri sighed. His brother didn't understand. He hadn't been raised with the weight of a kingdom on his shoulders. And often—far too often—duty came before personal pleasure.

And that included Cynda Madison.

"Drat, drat, drat." Cynda hurried down the staircase, tying her apron behind her. She was going to be late for her shift. The battery in her watch had died two hours ago, and she just now realized it. Blast and double blast. She wasn't likely to find a replacement battery here either.

As she reached the hallway, she spotted Dimitri's grandmother in the corridor leading to the bathhouse. No doubt, she was off to take the waters. Cynda had to admit they were soothing.

She had only taken a few steps when she heard a cry behind her and turned to see the older woman on the ground. "Oh, my God." She ran to the woman's side. "Grand Duchess? Are you all right?"

The woman was conscious, but in obvious pain. She spoke rapidly in her native language.

"I don't understand." Cynda wished she did. "Where does it hurt?"

The grand duchess paused, then drew in a deep breath. "My leg."

Cynda glanced around for assistance. She didn't dare move the elderly woman. Spying Rupert at the far end of the hall, Cynda stuck her fingers in her mouth and produced a shrill whistle. It captured Rupert's attention at once, and he came running.

"Go fetch the doctor right away," Cynda ordered. "I'll stay with the grand duchess."

"I'll be right back." The young porter raced away as Cynda located the blanket the woman had been carrying and wrapped it around her shoulders.

"You'll be fine," Cynda said, kneeling beside her. The angle of one of the grand duchess's legs said broken to Cynda, but she was far from being any medical expert. "Lean against me if it will help."

The woman eased her weight against Cynda with a small cry of pain.

"We have an excellent doctor here." Cynda wrapped her arm gently around the woman to hold her steady. "He'll take good care of you."

Rupert returned shortly, followed by Dr. Ziegler, who knelt beside the grand duchess to examine her. "I believe your hip is broken." He glanced at Rupert. "Fetch the stretcher from my office."

The young man nodded and ran off again as Dr. Ziegler turned to Cynda. "You've done well. Can you stay a little longer?"

"Of course." A tongue-lashing from the Major was far less important than this.

"What happened?" The doctor addressed the question to both of them.

Cynda answered first. "I saw the grand duchess on her way to the bathhouse; then I heard her cry out. When I turned around, she was on the floor."

The elderly woman squeezed Cynda's hand as she struggled to speak. "I caught toe. Fell."

He nodded. "We'll have you feeling better soon." He projected a positive manner, but Cynda had a feeling the woman would endure more pain before the better part started.

When Rupert arrived with the stretcher, he and the doctor eased a sheet beneath the grand duchess, then lifted her onto it. She cried out, her face white, and Cynda held her hand tightly. "Can I do anything for you?" she asked.

"My . . . my grandsons," she gasped.

"I'll get them right away." Cynda glanced at Dr. Ziegler. "Where are you taking her?"

"To her room. Run ahead and have her grandsons prepare her bed."

She nodded and hurried toward the tower, where the truly elite stayed at The Chesterfield. She knew which suite the Karakovs occupied from the gossip that swept the resort and rushed to rap on the door.

Dimitri answered her knock and scowled at her. Before he could reprimand her for trespassing on his territory, Cynda spoke. "Your grandmother fell. The doctor is bringing her here."

Concern replaced Dimitri's scowl. "How badly is she hurt?"

"I believe her leg is broken. The doctor will be able to tell you more."

He nodded and reached in his pocket for some coins. "Thank you."

Cynda stepped back. "Oh, please." She allowed derision to color her voice. "I don't need money for helping your grandmother." Not waiting for his reaction, she spun around and dashed for the dining room.

The Major leapt on her in reprimand as soon as she arrived, but changed his tone upon hearing about the grand duchess. While Cynda went to her usual area, he hurried to check on the elderly lady's status, Miss Sparrow accompanying him.

The evening passed slowly as Cynda waited for word on the woman. When Miss Sparrow didn't return, Cynda assumed the worst. Maybe the grand duchess had been injured more than a broken bone. Maybe she was in serious danger. What if she died?

Would Dimitri and Alexi return to their homeland? Of course they would. Then, perhaps, Dimitri wouldn't be killed in December. But even that thought didn't alleviate the depression Cynda suffered on thinking of Dimitri gone. He was only a man from a painting, who had been far more rude than nice to her. Why should she miss him?

Good question.

When Dimitri and Alexi showed up late in the

evening, she hurried to their table. "How is your grandmother?" Surely they wouldn't be here if she was in any danger.

Dimitri's gaze met hers. "In pain, but resting now."

Alexi took Cynda's hand and placed a kiss on the back. "Thank you for assisting Grandmère."

"I'm just glad I could help." Withdrawing her hand, Cynda avoided looking at Dimitri as she took their order. No doubt, he would be scowling again.

They were among the last to leave the dining room, shortly before it closed for the night. When Cynda finally finished her duties, she was surprised to find Dimitri lurking in the corridor near her stairwell. What now? Another reprimand?

She approached him with hesitation, then started when he bowed low before her. As Alexi had earlier, he brought her hand to his lips and placed a gentle kiss upon it. "Thank you for helping Grandmère. She said you were of invaluable service."

Cynda didn't rush to pull her hand away as he straightened. With her nerves sizzling, she could barely move. "I only did what anyone would do."

To her surprise, Dimitri didn't immediately release her hand. He glanced down at it, pale and small within his tanned broad palm. When he lifted his gaze to Cynda, she inhaled sharply at the fire burning there. "You have my deepest gratitude. My grandmother is very important to me."

"I didn't do it for you." Despite the trembling within her, Cynda found the words to respond. "I did it for her."

Dimitri gave her a smile that sent white heat

through her blood. "Yes, you probably did." He brushed his thumb over her hand, his touch electric against her skin, then released her and bowed again. "Good night . . . Cynda."

She turned to watch him depart, cradling her hand against her chest. "Good night, Dimitri."

For the next few weeks she didn't see either of the princes, not even at dinner. Evidently, they were spending time with their grandmother while she healed. Cynda had heard that the grand duchess's hip had been broken and she was confined to her bed for several weeks.

At least Dimitri wouldn't be leaving anytime soon.

Cynda devoted her free time to painting, starting with the majestic Chesterfield. Setting up her easel across from the main entrance, she sketched the outlines of the expansive hotel and its single tower.

Learning how to mix the powders into paint took a lot of experimentation and produced creative, but unusable results until she finally created pigments she could use. The hours flew by as the rough outlines of the hotel came to life, gaining depth and soul as she added the color. More than once, she had to hurry to make her shift in the dining room.

Her life took on a rhythm—paint between shifts, wait tables the rest of the time. Though she searched for Dimitri whenever she walked the halls, she never saw him and consoled herself with a world of canvas and pigment.

She was adding the fine details to the balconies on the tower when she glanced up for another look and froze. Dimitri stood on his balcony, his face turned her direction. Was he watching her?

She raised her brush in a salute and experienced a quick rush of excitement when he nodded in return. However, he then turned and vanished into his suite.

How long had he been watching her? Minutes? Hours? Days?

"You have great talent."

She jumped as a voice spoke beside her, and she looked around to see Alexi standing by the easel. "Thank you."

She examined the half-finished painting with a critical eye. It was some of her best work. The resort radiated splendor and vitality. Of course, the different pigments helped in achieving that depth. Maybe she needed to live in 1889 to finally learn how to paint.

And here she figured she had come back in time to save Dimitri's life.

Smiling at Alexi, she set down her palette and wiped her hands on an old towel. "I haven't seen you in a long time."

"Grandmère has been in much pain. Dimitri and I fear to leave her for long." Concern shadowed Alexi's eyes.

Cynda ached for the elderly woman. "Is she doing better now?"

"Much better. In fact, Dimitri said we don't both need to stay, so I am making good use of my free time." Alexi gave her a disarming grin, and Cynda laughed.

"Checking on my painting?" She shook her head. "I can think of many other things you might be doing."

"I have seen you out here day after day working with such dedication. I could not rest until I saw the result for myself." He frowned. "I did not mean to make you stop. Please continue."

Cynda hesitated. She did want to paint while the light was still good. "You don't mind?"

"Will it inhibit your work if I watch?"

The last time anyone had watched her paint was years ago in art school. "I don't think so." Lifting her palette, she quickly became absorbed in the nuances of The Chesterfield. She forgot Alexi was nearby until he spoke again.

"Have you had formal training?"

Slightly startled, she turned to smile at him. "I have a degree in art from . . ." Her college hadn't been founded yet. "I have a college degree in art."

"Amazing. For a woman to have a college degree is truly rare."

Cynda laughed at the awe in his voice. "Not that rare. Besides, it hasn't helped me sell my work."

"I would be proud to purchase this painting when you have it completed."

Purchase it? She almost dropped her jaw. "I . . . I don't need charity, Alexi."

He scowled, resembling Dimitri even more. "I think the painting is superb. It will be a nice memory for us all when we return to our home."

His earnestness touched her. "Very well. The painting shall be yours."

"Excellent." He bowed his head. "I am truly grateful."

"And I am thrilled." Returning to her work, Cynda lifted her brush with renewed excitement. Though she still suspected Alexi of making his offer out of kindness, she couldn't deny the heady feeling of finally selling a painting. Maybe someday, she could actually make a living at this.

After all, she had sold to a prince.

Dimitri repeated Alexi's scowl as he watched his brother hover over Cynda's shoulder while she worked. He clenched the balcony railing. As usual, Alexi chose to ignore Dimitri's warnings about Cynda. She was not the type of woman either of them could consider a future with nor was she the type to dally with.

When Cynda laughed at something Alexi said, Dimitri tightened his grip even further until the metal bit into his palms. She attracted him, intrigued him more than any other woman of his acquaintance. Secrets lingered in the bright blue depths of her eyes . . . secrets he wanted to discover.

With Alexi, this was a game. No matter where they went, he found a woman to charm. Usually an unsuitable woman.

Dimitri sighed. He would be the first to admit that being the second son was a difficult position. Yet the responsibilities were not the same either. While Dimitri had spent most of his life preparing for his eventual position as king, Alexi had run wild among the people, developing an affinity for them that worried Dimitri.

The years ahead would be difficult.

Glancing back at the front lawn, Dimitri discovered both Cynda and Alexi gone. He stiffened.

Where were they? Pushing back from the rail, he entered the suite, determined to find Alexi and drag him back if necessary.

"Dimitri?" His grandmother's voice brought him to an abrupt halt. He couldn't leave her.

"Yes, Grandmère?" He entered her bedroom, hating how she appeared so pale and fragile amidst the pillows. She had come here to strengthen her health in the rejuvenating baths. Instead, she was confined to her bed while her bones healed. "Do you need anything?"

"I'm afraid my water pitcher is empty. If you don't mind . . ."

He bowed. "It is my pleasure." Taking her pitcher, he filled it from the water tap of her sink, a modern convenience he already appreciated. After returning it to the table beside her bed, he poured her a glass and handed it to her. "Madam."

She drank, then smiled at him, a hint of her former sparkle in her eyes. "You make an excellent servant, Dimitri."

"I live to serve, madam." Hearing the door to the suite open, he straightened. "Please, excuse me."

Hurrying into the main room, he found Alexi pouring a drink, his expression satisfied. "Where did you go?" Dimitri asked.

"Worried about me, brother?" Alexi downed the drink. "Cynda needed to get ready for her shift, so I decided to return here. Were you thinking the worst of me?"

"I've told you to stay away from her." Dimitri struggled to keep his voice low so that Grandmère wouldn't overhear.

"And I don't feel inclined to obey."

Dimitri curled his fists tight against his side. "She is only a waitress, Alexi."

"And a fine artist. I plan to buy the painting she's working on now. It's good." Alexi settled into a nearby chair. "I wonder if I should sponsor her and give her the time she needs to paint." He glanced at Dimitri, his gaze amused. "She really is talented."

"You don't have the means to sponsor anyone." Dimitri bit out the words. They were cruel, but true. Alexi had no fortune of his own. Their father's estates and income were entailed to Dimitri.

Alexi's lips twisted in a wry smile. "Trust you to put it so bluntly. Of course, I cannot afford to sponsor an artist or even myself without the kindness of our father."

Dimitri sighed. "Alexi, I don't—"

His brother waved aside Dimitri's words. "I know who I am . . . what I am. I will never have anything unless it is given to me." He jumped to his feet and headed toward his bedroom. "What would you do if I decided to stay here and start a new life for myself?"

Of all the nonsense Alexi had spouted during his life, this was the most insane. "That's ridiculous. You have no skills, no way to support yourself."

Alexi paused by his door. "You might be surprised." He entered his room, closing the door behind him.

Dimitri ran his fingers through his hair. Where had Alexi come up with this madness? Dimitri would never allow his brother to remain here in this foreign land.

It had to be Cynda. She must have said something to encourage Alexi.

Glancing through the open balcony doors to the vacant lawn outside, Dimitri sighed. He had to find out.

Soon.

Chapter 6

Damn and double damn. Cynda rushed along the hallway toward the main entrance. If she didn't hurry, she would miss the train to town. Not having a watch was a real problem.

She nearly plowed Dimitri over when he stepped into her path. He caught her arms to steady her as she regained her footing. She gave him an apologetic smile. "Sorry."

"You're in a hurry."

"I want to catch the train to town."

"I believe you're too late." Dimitri tilted his head toward the front doors. "Yes, there's the whistle."

Cynda grimaced. Another long walk to town. At least it was downhill this time. "Oh, well. One of these days I'll make the train."

"I am planning to visit town today. Would you care to accompany me?"

"Excuse me?" Cynda searched his face, but saw no signs of guile in his expression. "Who else is going?"

A slight frown creased Dimitri's forehead. "Alexi is sitting with Grandmère if that is what you wish to know."

"I was wondering more about a chaperone." She grinned. "Aren't you afraid of me?"

To her surprise, he nodded. "Sometimes." He suddenly broke into a radiant smile. "But not today." He motioned toward the door. "Shall we?"

"It would be my pleasure." Pleasure was the right word. Any time spent in Dimitri's company, whether passing in the hallway or serving him dinner, sent a tingle through her veins. The man's effect on her was headier than two bottles of wine.

He had a buggy waiting out front and assisted her into it. The day was brilliant with a just-washed blue sky and gentle breeze to ease the heat and humidity. Cynda wore her blue dress and a simple hat she had purchased during her last trip into Hope Springs.

As she sat beside Dimitri, she stole a glance at his profile. His chin was firmer than Alexi's, she decided, and his eyelashes slightly longer. The structure of his face, though similar to his brother's, was a little more rugged, and his mouth was— she sighed—to die for. Those full, sensual lips were made for kissing, and from memories of her dream, he knew how to put them to fine use.

He turned and caught her staring, and she looked away quickly, then back. "How is your grandmother doing?" she asked.

"She is healing, though not as rapidly as the

doctor would prefer. It appears we will have to stay longer than planned.''

"Oh?" When was he leaving? Soon?

"We had hoped to return by September before winter affected our voyage across the ocean, but the doctor says Grandmère will not be able to travel until November at the earliest.'' Dimitri tightened his hands on the reins. "At that date it is too late to make the trip. We shall have to wait until spring.''

Drat. So much for getting him to leave before December. Dimitri would never desert his grandmother. "Won't your people miss you?''

"My parents are there. I am not needed yet.''

He didn't sound too upset about having to remain. If not for his looming murder, Cynda would love him to stay. Now she *had* to discover his murderer before that time.

Realizing that Dimitri expected a response, she forced a smile. "Everyone will be pleased.''

He started to speak, then stopped and concentrated on the road. The wind caught strands of his black hair and tossed them across his forehead and into his eyes. Without thinking, Cynda reached up to brush them back into place.

When Dimitri turned to her, his gaze surprised, she jerked her hand back. What was she doing? "I'm sorry." Her earlier dreams made her feel a closeness with this man that didn't really exist. His kisses and lovemaking had been a vivid dream, nothing more.

He lifted one eyebrow in a questioning gesture, but remained silent until they reached Hope Springs. The train had already arrived, and guests from The Chesterfield filled the streets of the small town.

Taking her hand, Dimitri helped her dismount from the buggy. Cynda smiled. "Thanks for the ride. I'll catch the train back."

He didn't release her hand right away, but held her in place when she would've fled. "That's not necessary. I had thought to accompany you."

Now that's a switch. Why would he *want* to spend time with her? "I plan to run several errands."

"That's fine. I have no pressing engagements." Letting her hand slide from his, Dimitri fell into step beside her as she maneuvered her way through the streets. This was only her fourth visit to Hope Springs, but she already knew where she wanted to go.

First stop, the Emporium. While Dimitri gawked at the multitude of merchandise, Cynda purchased more pigment and canvas. She was almost finished with her first painting of The Chesterfield and couldn't wait to do more.

"You have need of more paints already?" Dimitri asked as they left the store.

"The Chesterfield is a big place." Cynda grinned. "Plus the leaves will be changing soon, and I want to start a new painting then."

"Alexi mentioned that you were formally schooled in art." Though Dimitri's voice was casual, something in his tone caught Cynda's attention.

"That's right. It's what I've always wanted to do."

"Instead, you wait tables here?" Puzzlement filled his features.

"I have to sell my paintings in order to make a living at it." She grimaced. "And so far I haven't done a very good job of that."

"I see." He remained silent as Cynda wound

through the streets to the small dress shop she liked.

"I'll only be a moment," she said before she ducked inside. She knew exactly which dress she wanted to purchase this time and went straight to it. Thank goodness it was still there. The style was similar to her plain blue gown, but this one had a v-shaped yoke and was a lovely shade of dark rose.

"I would like to see that on you."

She jumped when Dimitri spoke behind her and turned to look at him. "Since my wardrobe is pretty limited, I'm sure you'll get that chance."

When she lifted her small change purse to pay, Dimitri caught her arm. "Allow me. I am certain you are not paid much at the hotel."

The seamstress's face reflected the shock Cynda felt. "No, thank you." Though the morals of the time should probably influence her decision, Cynda's pride fueled her reaction. "I am paid enough for this." She completed the purchase quickly and hurried outside.

"I have offended you." Dimitri joined her. "My apologies."

"You surprised me," she admitted. "Isn't paying for a woman's clothing a way of implying a relationship?" She cast him a teasing glance. "And I'm certain you don't want that."

His face revealed nothing. "Of course not."

"However, I will allow you to pay for lunch." She caught his elbow and turned him down the street. "I have discovered the most wonderful restaurant."

Every time she came to Hope Springs, she made time to visit the Café of Dreams. Besides the wonderful food, the atmosphere reminded her of her own time and brought with it a relaxing familiarity . . . a rarity since her arrival here.

They were seated immediately at a small table in the corner and given menus. The hamburger Cynda loved wasn't listed, but she only had to ask to get it. "Want to try something different?" she asked.

A glint of humor entered Dimitri's eyes. "You wish to order for me?"

"Yes." She grinned. "You won't be sorry."

"Very well." He closed the menu and sat back, his arms crossed and a hint of a smile around his lips. "Surprise me."

She quickly ordered the awesome burger for each of them, then met Dimitri's gaze. "If you don't like this, I'll . . . I'll slip you an extra helping at dinner."

"Is that possible? Chef Sashenka runs a tight kitchen."

"True." Cynda sighed. The Russian seemed to have eyes everywhere when it came to the dining room and kitchen. "But it doesn't matter because you'll love this meal."

"I admire your confidence." Dimitri relaxed in his chair. "Tell me about yourself, Cynda Madison. Who are you?"

You wouldn't believe me if I told you. Cynda bit her lip. "I'm a woman of many talents," she said finally. "You wouldn't believe all the different jobs I've held."

"Perhaps I would."

She gave him a challenging look. "I've run a dog-walking service, sent people around the world for a travel agency, popped corn in a movie theater, waited tables, and painted houses. Before I came here, I'd completed several jobs restoring old paintings. Turns out I have a knack for it."

Dimitri frowned. "Travel agency? Movie theater?"

Oops. That would teach her to let her tongue outrace her brain. She waved her hand. "Don't worry about it." Leaning forward, she met his gaze. "What about you?"

"I have spent my life in preparation for my future role as king."

"And that's it?" She imagined him sitting through lectures and enduring rigorous training on etiquette. How boring.

"It has taken most of my time." The humor left him, and Cynda grimaced.

Damn, she had finally had him loosening up and blew it. The arrival of their meal saved her from further mistakes, and she laughed as Dimitri eyed his burger dubiously.

"What is this?" he asked.

"A hamburger. It's wonderful. Trust me."

The glance he gave her contained doubt, but he picked up his knife and fork and started to saw at it.

"No, no, no." Cynda reached across the table and lifted his burger in both hands and lifted it to his lips. "You eat this with your hands."

"Pardon me?" Dimitri backed away. "It's rather messy."

Okay, so it has the dressing dripping from it. "It's supposed to be messy. That's how you know it's good." She moved the burger closer. "Come on. Take a bite. Just one."

A small glint of humor returned to his eyes, and he leaned forward to take a bite, nearly pulling it from Cynda's hands. He brought his hands up over hers to catch it, and she caught her breath with a sharp inhale. The electric chair couldn't hold as much charge as his touch.

He chewed slowly, then broke into a devastating smile. "It's different, but I like it."

"Good." Cynda lowered his burger to his plate and picked up her own. Lifting it in a mock toast, she grinned. "Enjoy."

Watching Dimitri devour his meal was more fun than eating her own. He didn't have her years of experience of handling sloppy burgers, so he tended to spill more onto his plate and his chin.

When Cynda giggled, he cast her a sharp glance, then slowly broke into a low chuckle as he wiped at his face. "I don't think one napkin will be enough."

"We can get more."

She finished first and sat back to enjoy the show. His pleasure obvious, the highborn prince lost his arrogance as he ate the sandwich. The animation and high spirits changed his appearance. Though still handsome, he looked younger, more at ease with himself and the world.

Was it the pressure of becoming king that made him the way he was? As the thought occurred to Cynda, so did another. She would just have to show him how to have fun. Even kings deserved that.

"Excellent choice," Dimitri said as he finished his meal. He suddenly did a double take and lifted his napkin to dab at the corner of her mouth. "You missed some." Mischievousness danced in his gaze.

Cynda's heart somersaulted. "Thank you." The words emerged in a breathy whisper as she suddenly found it difficult to speak.

He drew his hand away slowly, but didn't lean away. "You're welcome."

Neither moved until the waiter stopped by their table. "Any dessert today?"

"No." Dimitri spoke abruptly as he sat back. "Thank you. The reckoning will be fine."

He didn't look at Cynda as he paid for their meals and stood to pull back her chair. However, at the entrance, he froze and gripped her arm. "We can't go out there right now."

"Why not?" Cynda peered outside, then grinned. Several of the Harrington girls were outside the restaurant. In fact, they gave every sign of entering. "I believe they're coming in."

Dimitri groaned, and Cynda could see him pull his isolated, arrogant royal persona around him. No, dammit. She didn't want to lose this more relaxed prince.

She caught his hand in hers. "Come on. There has to be a back entrance."

He looked startled, but followed her between the tables and into the kitchen. Corrie glanced up and quirked an eyebrow.

"Sorry, Corrie." Cynda smiled. "Do you have a back door?"

The chef pointed to the opposite end of the room. "There. It leads into the alley."

"Thanks." Keeping her grip on Dimitri, Cynda pulled him through the kitchen and out into the narrow alley and toward the street.

Unfortunately, the Misses Harrington were still perusing the menu outside the restaurant, and Cynda jerked backward, falling into Dimitri. He caught her as he staggered back and ended up with her against the brick wall and his arms on either side of her.

Though her pounding heart made it difficult to speak, Cynda grinned. "Not quite safe yet."

Amusement filled his features as well as something else—an emotion that darkened his eyes to pewter. "You are an extraordinary woman, Cynda."

"Nice of you to notice," she quipped, hoping he wouldn't hear the heavy thudding in her chest.

He reached over to trace the outline of her lips with his thumb, sending a rush of pure longing to her very center. "Am I . . . am I still messy?" she asked.

"No." His voice held a huskiness that brought a knot to her stomach. He moved closer until the warmth of his body mingled with hers, his gaze glued to her face, his thumb resting beside her mouth. He curled his fingers beneath her chin to tilt it upward.

Cynda couldn't look away . . . didn't want to look away. She ached for his kiss, her hormones threatening to take control from her. "Dimitri," she whispered.

His mouth bent toward hers.

"Don't be silly, Sarah. What would the prince be doing in town?" The shrill voice of one of the Harrington daughters pierced the alley quiet, and Dimitri froze, then drew back, dropping his hand.

"Forgive me," he murmured, turning away.

Forgive him? Never. She *wanted* his kiss. How dare he stop? Cynda had to take several deep breaths before she could speak.

"Don't worry about it." Moving to the alley opening, she peeked around. "They've gone inside. It's safe now."

They left the alley and hurried past the restaurant. "Is there anywhere else you need to go?" Dimitri asked. His good humor was gone, his tone formal once again.

"No." She sighed. "We can go back."

Upon reaching the buggy, he assisted her up, his touch impersonal, then jumped up to join her. As they turned toward the road to The Chesterfield, Cynda finally voiced the question nagging at her. "The Harrington girls aren't servants. What's wrong with them?"

"They are still common."

He spoke so matter-of-factly that Cynda gasped. "So only royal blood is good enough for you?"

"Yes."

She stared at him in disbelief, then shook her head. "Sheesh."

"I take it you disapprove?"

"I just don't understand what makes your blood better than mine. I bet you still bleed red."

"It is a matter of upbringing." He cast her a sidelong look. "No woman of breeding would be sitting here without a chaperone."

"I imagine." Frustration at his about-face in attitude gnawed at her. How could he be ready to kiss her one moment and then disparage her character the next? "She would probably be sitting in a parlor somewhere, her back rigidly straight as she politely entertained the *right* kind of people while in reality she was bored out of her mind."

"I wouldn't expect you to understand." His tone implied she was far too *common*. "Which is why I need to talk to you."

"You need to talk to me?" No wonder he had

offered her a ride. It was always easier to lecture a captive audience. "And what have I done now?"

"I do not like your influence on Alexi."

She lifted her eyebrows. That again? *"My* influence on Alexi? What influence?"

"He came in after talking to you and declared he wanted to remain in America and make his own way in life."

Which, of course, was probably tantamount to suicide as far as Dimitri was concerned. "I don't see that as a bad thing, but I have never discussed that subject with him."

"Never?"

Cynda curled her hands into fists. "You may think as little of me as you like, Dimitri, but I am not a liar."

"Then, it must be due to the open affection you show him."

She rolled her eyes. "I am nice to him. I like Alexi, but I am not romantically interested in him. I told you that."

They drew near The Chesterfield, and Dimitri slowed the horse's pace. "I do not want you to talk to him anymore."

Did Alexi know how much his brother tried to control his life? Probably. No wonder he rebelled. Cynda shook her head. She still didn't know if Alexi would be Dimitri's killer. "Forget it. If he wants to talk to me, I'll talk to him."

Dimitri frowned. "I can make your life very unpleasant."

Cynda stared at him. "Are you threatening me? What do you plan to do? Throw me in the dungeon?" The buggy slowed by the front entrance, and she jumped from it, nearly tripping over her long skirt. She whirled back toward him. "Go ahead and try, Your Very Royal Blue-Blood Highness."

With that, she stalked past the staring guests and the drop-jawed Jack O'Riley into the hotel. Why had she thought saving Dimitri's life was important? At the moment, she felt like choking him herself.

She blew out her breath in disgust. December couldn't come too soon. She couldn't wait to escape this place and return to her own time.

Away from the arrogant, pompous, damned sexy prince.

Chapter 7

Miss Sparrow pulled Cynda aside as she reported to work a few days later. "I have a special assignment for you," she said.

"A special assignment?" Cynda gazed at the woman with mild curiosity. What was that?

"You have been specifically requested to deliver and serve meals to one of our shut-in guests."

A slight shiver of apprehension replaced the curiosity. "I—"

"It is not open for discussion."

Cynda hesitated. Since her parting from Dimitri, she hadn't seen any of the Karakovs and still wasn't sure she wanted to. "I'm not sure that's a good idea."

Miss Sparrow frowned. "I'm afraid you have no choice, Miss Madison."

"Even if it will make the guests angry?" The

last thing Cynda wanted was another confrontation with Dimitri.

"Do you have someone in mind?"

"Actually, yes. Dimitri won't like this."

"Are you certain of that?"

That caught Cynda's attention. Had he requested her? Was this his way of apologizing? Or putting her in her place? "Did Dimitri ask for me?"

"I'm not at liberty to say." Miss Sparrow handed Cynda a piece of paper. "Here are the times for delivery and the meal requirements. I feel certain you will behave admirably."

As Miss Sparrow left, Cynda grimaced. "That makes one of us," she muttered.

After glancing at the paper, Cynda hurried to the kitchen. She had less than an hour to get the evening meal together. Apparently, the Karakovs dined earlier in their suite than in the restaurant.

At the designated time she stood outside the suite with the meal tray, her hands cold. Dammit, she wasn't going to let Dimitri intimidate her. Drawing in a deep breath, she rapped on the door.

Dimitri answered the knock, then stood frozen when he spied Cynda. Two emotions instantly raced through him—elation at seeing her again and wariness. He had missed her over the past few days, the time moving by slowly without the energy Cynda always seemed to supply.

At the same time, his protective instinct arose. How had she arranged to be the one to deliver their meals? What trickery was she planning now?

"I have your dinner," she said. Her manner was cool and professional, yet the slight lift of her chin indicated she hadn't forgiven him for their last altercation.

Wasn't that a good thing? He wasn't so certain anymore. Dimitri stepped back and allowed her to enter. "In there." He motioned to his grandmother's bedroom, and Cynda carried the tray inside.

Grandmère greeted Cynda with a warm smile. "Miss Madison, how wonderful to see you again. Please come in." She indicated the table set up near the side of her bed. "We've been taking our meals there. My grandsons have been nice enough to keep an old lady from eating alone."

"Nonsense." Cynda responded with genuine warmth as she set the table and prepared a separate tray for the grand duchess. "I'm sure it's because they enjoy your company."

Dimitri tried to ignore his envy toward his grandmother. Cynda had smiled at him like that once, too. Their closeness in the alley flickered through his mind. She almost made him forget who he was . . . what he didn't dare do.

"How is it you are now our server?" he asked. Did she sense his attraction to her? Was she trying to manipulate him as well as Alexi?

The glance she gave him was anything but seductive. "Miss Sparrow told me I had to."

"Excellent." Alexi breezed into the room, his charm in place. "I've missed seeing you, Cynda. You haven't been painting outside for the past few days."

Dimitri grimaced. Did his little brother have any sense at all? Some women could be flirted with and abandoned, but not this one. He watched Cynda as surprise briefly moved across her face to be replaced by a warm smile. No, this woman was not one for dalliance.

"I'm almost done with it, Alexi," she said. "I've been working inside on the finishing touches."

Dimitri had been watching for her from their balcony also. He had probably noticed before Alexi when she no longer worked on the opposite lawn.

"Wonderful. I look forward to seeing it." Alexi produced a dazzling grin, then swung into a chair at the table. "You do remember that I intend to purchase it?"

"I remember." Her gaze flickered toward Dimitri, then down before he could frown.

Alexi did not have the resources to throw away on an amateur painter. Nearly every woman dabbled with paints and was eager to give her completed projects as gifts. Why should they pay for Cynda's? Was she that much better?

Dimitri went to take the tray to his grandmother, but Cynda whisked it away from beneath his hands.

She delivered the tray, ensuring Grandmère was well situated before she returned to the table, her gaze defiant. Dimitri took his seat. He wanted to shake her. He wanted to hold her. He scowled. The woman was far too insolent to be a servant.

She irritated him almost as much as she attracted him.

Humor lit Alexi's eyes as he met Dimitri's glare. Ignoring his brother, Alexi proceeded to charm Cynda while she worked. To him and to Sophie, she was warm and friendly, her engaging smile appearing often. To Dimitri, she remained cool yet polite.

"I understand the hotel has a ball on All Hallows' Eve. Is that correct?" Alexi asked.

"I believe so. I've heard others on the staff talking about it. The costumes are supposed to be wonderful." A dreamy look entered Cynda's eyes, and for a brief moment Dimitri pictured her in an elegant gown suited to her natural beauty.

Alexi's next words to Cynda shattered that image. "I insist on a dance with you."

"I doubt I will attend." She exchanged their empty plates for a chocolate soufflé.

Alexi covered her hand with his. "You have to be there. My evening will be ruined if you're not."

She laughed and pulled her hand away. "We'll see."

Dimitri pushed back his chair with more force than he intended, rocking it onto two legs. Cynda and Grandmere stared at him in surprise while Alexi merely grinned.

"I am finished. Excuse me, please." Dimitri couldn't listen to another moment of his brother's inane chatter. Or worse, Cynda's encouraging responses.

Stalking onto the balcony, he let the slight breeze cool the boiling heat in his veins. If Cynda wanted to play Alexi's games, he should let her. She would be the one hurt, not Alexi. Dimitri had no intention of letting his brother become entangled with a servant.

"You left suddenly." Alexi leaned against the open door. "Jealous?"

Dimitri schooled his features to reveal nothing. "I told you before I am not interested in Cynda."

"What you say and what you do aren't the same thing." Alexi grinned. "Everyone in the hotel is talking about how you took Cynda to town last week ... unchaperoned. And you lectured me because I gave her a ride back in the rain?"

"I am not in danger from Miss Madison."

"Aren't you?" Alexi's tone implied he didn't believe that. To be honest, Dimitri wasn't completely convinced he did either.

"I have future obligations." Dimitri had to remember that . . . always. "There is Anya."

"Ah, yes, Anya." Alexi sounded uncharacteristically bitter. "Don't forget her." Pushing off the door frame, he crossed the main room to his chamber.

Dimitri sighed and resumed staring into the distance. Many times he didn't understand his brother.

Or himself.

I'm a coward. He had fought alongside his father in the border wars yet dreaded returning to Grandmère's room. Let Cynda have time to clean up and depart first.

The night darkness wrapped its soothing tendrils around the hotel until the surrounding mountains faded into a dark blur on the horizon. Dimitri felt the tension ease from his body. Better. Much better.

Cynda should be gone by now.

Entering the suite, he approached Sophie's room, then stopped beside the open door as he heard Cynda. She was sitting on the bed beside Sophie, reading *Little Lord Fauntleroy,* a book his grandmother had been struggling through for days. Though Grandmère spoke English well, she had far more difficulty in reading it. Had she persuaded Cynda to finish the story for her?

Dimitri found himself caught up in Cynda's voice rather than the story. The rise and fall of her uniquely American accent tugged at him; the emotion she put into the words of dialogue stirred his emotions. What was it about this woman?

She finished the story and closed the book as

Grandmère sighed. "So much better than I was doing." She patted Cynda's hand. "Thank you, my dear."

"My pleasure. I've always enjoyed this book, ever since I was a child."

Grandmere started. "How can that be? This book was only published four years ago."

"Oh, yes," Cynda laughed as if nervous. "Of course." She slid from the bed and went to the cart. "I will see you tomorrow, Your Imperial Highness."

"Call me Sophie, dear."

Cynda froze by the doorway. "Is that proper?"

Dimitri blinked, as surprised as Cynda. Though Grandmère didn't flaunt her title, allowing anyone use of her given name was an honor, indeed. That Cynda recognized it proved once again she was more than he tried to make her.

"If I give permission." Grandmère waved her hand in a royal gesture. "And I do."

"Then, thank you . . . Sophie. I am honored." Cynda resumed her progress. "Good night."

She almost ran into Dimitri as she emerged from the room and stopped suddenly, the dishes clattering on the tray. He jumped back, chagrined.

"I beg your pardon," she murmured as she maneuvered around him toward the door to the suite, not even pausing.

He rushed to open the door for her. "Can I be of assistance?"

"I can manage. The dumbwaiter is just at the end of the hall." She brushed past him without turning her head.

Stepping into the hall, he watched her depart. He couldn't stop himself from calling, "Good night, Cynda."

She went several more steps before she stopped. She didn't look around. "Good night." Without another word, she continued on her way.

Dimitri returned to the suite with a grimace. How could he expect Alexi to stay away from her when he found it nearly impossible to stay away himself?

"Is that you, Dimitri?"

"Yes, Grandmère." He went to stand in the doorway to her room. "Did you need anything?"

"No. I am quite fine." Her keen gaze fastened on his face. "She's a nice girl, isn't she? I'm glad she is still serving us."

Dimitri nodded. "Yes, she's nice."

And trouble for the Karakovs.

With a capital T.

As one week led into the next, Cynda found she enjoyed taking meals to the Karakov suite. Alexi flirted with her outrageously, and Sophie was always kind. Even Dimitri forgot himself occasionally and spoke warmly to her.

But this time when she knocked on the suite door, it wasn't to deliver meals. She shifted the canvas in her arms.

Dimitri answered the door and raised his eyebrows. "Dinner isn't for several hours yet."

"I have my painting finished, and I wanted to give it to Alexi." She entered as Dimitri stood back. "Is he here?"

"He's riding. I expect he'll return shortly." Dimitri took the canvas from her hold. "May I see it?"

Without waiting for her reply, he unwrapped it, then held the painting out at arm's length. For several long moments, he said nothing, and Cynda had to resist the urge to fidget. What did he think?

The painting was good. She knew it. She felt it. Yet his approval was important to her.

Finally, she couldn't stand it any longer. "Do you like it?"

He set the painting against a chair before speaking. "You show definite talent. You should not be wasting it here as a servant."

"I'm not a servant." Would he never understand that? "I'm hired staff. I get paid for what I do."

"That is not important." He dismissed her words with a brush of his hand. "You should devote yourself to this if you wish to improve."

"I spend every spare minute—"

"You need a sponsor." He nodded to himself as if he had just arranged her life to his satisfaction. "I will see if I can find one for you."

"A sponsor?" Images of Vavoline stickers on race cars flickered through her mind.

"Someone to support you while you paint."

"In return for what?" It sounded too good to be true.

"Your artistic success would be his success, and of course, any monetary success would be his as well." Dimitri glanced at her quickly, then paced across the room. "I know some people. In New York. I could make arrangements for you to meet them."

Cynda shook her head. She didn't dare leave The Chesterfield. No matter what happened, she had to be here on the next solstice. "Thank you, but no."

"No?" His tone reflected his disbelief.

"Thank you, but I don't want to leave here. Not yet."

"Are you insane?" Dimitri crossed to her and seized her arms in a fierce hold. "Do you know what kind of opportunity this is?"

"Let me go." Her voice rose as her pulse quickened.

"Quiet." He loosened his grip as he motioned toward the door to Sophie's room. "Grandmère is sleeping."

Cynda released her breath in exasperation. "I realize what a wonderful chance you're offering, but I have to stay here. It's important."

"What can be so important?"

"Saving your life." She met his gaze angrily. "Whether you like it or not."

He dropped his hold, his expression stunned. "Saving my life? You still believe that?"

"I know you're in danger."

"How do you know that?"

She hesitated. "I can't tell you. Just believe me."

Skepticism entered his gaze. "And who should I fear?"

Cynda bit her lip. How to say this? "It might be your brother."

"Alexi?" Dimitri laughed, though the sound held no mirth. "Do not be ridiculous." He narrowed his eyes. "Is this a trick to turn me against my brother? For I tell you now it won't work. I trust Alexi with my life."

"You just might." Though his confidence pricked at her suspicions. What if it wasn't Alexi? Then who?

His gaze never left her face as he came to stand before her. "You look as if you are honestly worried." He cupped her chin in his palm. "Let *me* worry about my life, Cynda."

She needed to tell him the truth, but would he believe her even then? Or would he commit her to a horrible asylum? "Dimitri, I don't want you to die."

"I have no intention of doing so." His smile was gentle, sending a ripple of longing through her veins. "I am in no danger. I have no enemies."

"But . . ." Words failed her. How could she tell him he would die on December 12? Unless she found a way to stop it.

He lifted his other hand to tuck a flyaway strand of hair back into her recalcitrant bun. "I'll be fine," he added.

Her thudding heart blocked her throat as she stared at him. How could he be such a jerk one moment and the man of her dreams another? His eyes darkened even further as he slid his hand to the back of her head, holding her in place.

He didn't speak, but he didn't need to. Surely the fire in his gaze was an echo of her own.

The click of the door opening resounded with all the impact of a gunshot. Dimitri dropped his hands and stepped back as Cynda turned to face Alexi.

"Hi." She gave him a shaky smile. "I brought your painting."

He nodded, his expression veiled, and crossed the room to where Dimitri had set the canvas. "Very nice. Thank you, Cynda. I will arrange payment."

Though his words were polite, they were layered with a definite tension. Judging from Dimitri's rigid stance, he felt it as well.

Cynda sidled toward the door. "It's a gift," she said impulsively. Money wasn't important right now. Especially when all she wanted was out of that room. "For all of you." She opened the door. "To remember The Chesterfield. Good-bye."

She hurried away, half expecting to hear shouts or fighting from the suite. Instead, there was only silence.

And that frightened her even more.

The wind tugged Cynda's hair from its bun and blew it into her eyes as she stood on the slope behind the bathhouse. Using the back of her hand, she brushed the strands away, then continued working.

What a glorious day. And a glorious view.

Cynda peeked over the canvas at the spectacular scenery before her. While The Chesterfield was again the central focus, the surrounding mountains and the changing colors played just as important a role.

Autumn was coming. In two or three weeks, the reds, oranges, and golds would obliterate the remaining green leaves. If she timed it right, she would be ready to paint that portion of the landscape about then.

For now, she concentrated on outlining the resort and its surrounding properties. No matter how many times she looked at The Chesterfield, she saw different things. It fit here, nestled among the Allegheny Mountains—a majestic splendor in itself. How sad that it had fallen to ruin in her time.

"Cynda."

Though she heard her name, it didn't register at first.

"Cynda."

Jerking out of her trance, she glanced around to see Alexi approaching, a warm smile on his face.

"What are you doing here?"

"I wanted to watch you paint," he replied. "If you don't mind."

"There's not much to see yet. I'm just starting."

"I don't mind. I enjoy the company." He came to stand beside her. "You're much prettier to look at than Dimitri."

"But there are many other women in this hotel who would love to spend time with you." Since Alexi had walked in on her and Dimitri in the suite, he had been more charming than before. It bothered her. She liked Alexi, but not when he seemed determined to woo her.

Or was it because Dimitri didn't want him to that caused Alexi to increase his efforts?

"None that I prefer to be with."

"Suit yourself." Cynda returned her attention to the painting. Maybe Alexi would grow bored and leave.

But he didn't. After an hour, he still stood beside her, his silence as unnerving as speech.

After Cynda set down her brush and stretched the kinks from her back, she turned to face him. "This can't be very exciting."

He lifted her hand and held it between his. "I have something to ask you, Cynda."

Her stomach knotted. This sounded like something she didn't want to hear.

"Will you attend the ball on All Hallows' Eve with me?"

Relief relaxed her tongue as well as her muscles. "That's over a month away."

"I did not want anyone else to ask you."

She sighed. "Alexi, I'm going to be honest. I like you, but I'm not interested in a relationship with you."

His surprise filled his face. Had no one ever turned him down before? "If you like me, why won't you attend with me?"

"Because it would lead you to believe something that isn't true." She gently withdrew her hand from his. "I'm not romantically interested, and I don't expect I will be."

He scowled. "This is Dimitri's doing, isn't it?"

"No. I told him the same thing when he warned me away from you. I want to be your friend, nothing more."

"*He* warned you away?" Alexi's expression darkened. "My brother is once again interfering in my life?"

Oops. Cynda grimaced. "He wouldn't if he didn't care about you."

"Caring has nothing to do with it." Alexi paced several steps away from her, then whirled back around. "He is asserting his authority over me, don't you see? He will be king, and he wants to make certain I understand that."

"I'm sure that's not it." No matter how irritating Dimitri could be, Cynda always sensed his love for his brother. "He just wants to keep you from making a mistake."

"A mistake?" Bitterness colored his voice. "I am far less likely to make a mistake than he is."

Cynda blinked. "What does that mean?" Was Alexi referring to her?

A look of resignation replaced his anger. "Nothing." Alexi came to face her again. "I may never be king, but I am still a prince. I am capable of making my own choices."

"I'm sure you are." Cynda spoke soothingly, though she understood Alexi's mind less and less.

"And I refuse to let my brother dictate my life."

Before Cynda could react, Alexi seized her shoulders and kissed her, his mouth firm and his hold decisive.

Though nice as far as kisses went, his did nothing for her. Cynda remained unresponsive, then pushed against his chest when she felt his hold weakening. "Alexi, don't," she said as she broke free. "This is not going to change my feelings."

He looked chagrined. "My apologies. I should not let anger guide my actions." He offered her a charming smile. "Forgive me?"

"Are you willing to remain just friends?"

His sigh was overly dramatic. "If I must."

"Very well then, I'll—"

"What the hell do you think you're doing?"

They both whirled to see Dimitri climbing the hill toward them. Cynda closed her eyes briefly, wishing she could make the sight disappear.

He had the worst timing.

Chapter 8

"I can explain." Alexi intercepted his brother, but Dimitri's focus remained on Cynda.

Oh, great. She lifted her chin. It was going to be all her fault again.

"There is nothing to explain." Dimitri's voice was cold. "Your behavior is no less than I would expect."

"You don't know me as well as you think," Alexi retorted.

That brought Dimitri's gaze to him. "Don't I?"

They glared at each other, and Cynda swallowed the growing lump in her throat. Was this where the end started for Dimitri? Would she be the catalyst for Alexi killing his brother?

She rushed toward them. "Dimitri, it's nothing."

He turned his frozen gaze on her, bringing her to an abrupt halt. "I will handle *you* next."

"You'll leave her alone," Alexi said, his fists curled.

Cynda touched his shoulder. "Why don't you go back to the hotel? I can handle Dimitri." She gave the elder prince a defiant stare. "I'm not afraid of him."

"I'm not going to leave you alone with him."

She returned her focus to Alexi. "It would be better if you did."

Alexi hesitated. "Are you certain?"

"Positive." She produced a half smile, desperate to separate the two brothers.

"Very well." Alexi took a couple steps, then stopped. "It was nothing, Dimitri." He narrowed his gaze. "I don't understand why *you* are so upset."

With those words, he ran down the hill.

Cynda faced Dimitri. If anything, he had grown more stony-faced. "You can rant and rave now and get it out of your system."

"How dare you make light of this situation."

"What situation? It was *nothing.*"

"And what is your definition of nothing?"

"He kissed me, I asked him to stop and he did. End of story."

"It did not appear that way to me." Dimitri's eyes turned to cold steel. "You were enjoying it."

"Oh, was I?" Cynda rolled her eyes. "And how could you tell? Were you in my place?"

"You—"

She jabbed her finger into his chest. "Listen to me, you arrogant lug, if I had been enjoying it, you would've known."

He grabbed her arms, pulling her close, capturing her still jabbing hand between them. "Shall we find out?"

He covered her mouth, his kiss staking a claim—possessive and hot. Although Cynda had experienced nothing with Alexi's kiss, now she most definitely felt something. The instant his lips touched hers, fire raced through her veins, and her pulse set speed records. Behind her closed eyelids, colors exploded—red, orange, white.

As if sensing her response, he gentled his attack, seeking now, tentative, giving as well as taking. Cynda moaned as her insides clenched with wanting. She raised her hand to touch Dimitri's neck and hair, to hold him fast.

He showed no signs of releasing her. Instead, he wrapped one arm around her waist to pull her closer and cradled the back of her head with his other hand.

The kiss intensified as Cynda melted. If she hadn't been holding on to Dimitri, she would have fallen, for her knees no longer supported her. Her breasts swelled against his chest, and she felt an answering bulge against her abdomen.

She wanted him. Lord help her, she craved him.

Forced to come up for air, they stared at each other in silence. Only the hammering of her heart and ragged breathing filled Cynda's ears.

Dimitri's eyes had gone a soft pewter. Did she have that same hungry expression? His gaze dropped to her mouth, and he leaned forward again, then stopped and gently eased away from her.

He didn't apologize. Thank God. She would have hit him if he had. Instead, he gave a short bow, then walked away, his pace brisk.

Cynda bit back a sob. Didn't it figure? She had finally found the man from her dreams—and he was the one man she couldn't possibly have.

* * *

The next morning, Cynda had barely risen and dressed for the day when she received a summons to the Major's office. What did he want? Aside from his nitpicky inspections each morning, she rarely saw the man. Apparently, he left Miss Sparrow to oversee the maids and waitresses.

She rapped on his door and received permission to enter. As she did so, she found Miss Sparrow standing beside the Major, her expression desolate.

Cynda's heart dropped into her stomach. Oh, darn. This wasn't good.

The Major examined her up and down as if she were a bug under a microscope, and her palms went sweaty. When she started to speak, he held up one finger, and she lapsed into silence.

He came around his desk to face her. "Miss Madison, I have received a complaint about you from one of our guests."

"A complaint?" From whom? What had she done?

"It appears you've been making advances toward the young Prince Karakov, which you know is not allowed."

"Excuse me?" Cynda gasped with indignation. "That's a lie."

"Do you deny keeping company with the young man?"

"No, but—"

"Enough." The Major's dark mustache quivered. "We do not and will not allow this behavior from our staff. I'm afraid I have to let you go."

"What?" Panic arrowed through her. "You can't do that."

"I have done that, Miss Madison." He frowned. "You have until tonight to remove yourself and your belongings from this establishment."

"But where will I go? What will I do?" She couldn't leave the hotel. It was her only means of returning to her own time.

"That, Miss Madison, is not my concern." The Major turned his back on her. "Dismissed."

"But I . . ." Cynda turned to the woman beside the desk. "Miss Sparrow?"

"I'm sorry." She didn't look any more pleased with this decision than Cynda.

Cynda gaped at her for a moment, then spun on her heel and left the office. How unfair! She hadn't done anything, yet she had to pay the price. What else should she expect from this chauvinistic time period? Typical male rule.

It had to have been Dimitri who had lodged the complaint. Apparently Alexi's kiss had been the catalyst. Yet Dimitri had kissed her, too—a kiss that still had the power to warm her insides just in memory. How could he do this to her?

She had only stormed down one hallway when she spotted him en route to the dining room. Anger flooded her, and she stormed over to face him. "Damn you to hell, Dimitri Karakov."

Her condemnation drew gasps from the nearby guests. He merely lifted one eyebrow.

"I hope you're happy," she said, not hiding her bitterness. "Now I have no job and nowhere to go."

Surprise briefly flitted across his features. "No job?"

"Yes, your complaint got me fired." She wanted to punch him. "To think I was only trying to save

your life." She exclaimed in disgust, "I wonder
why I even bothered."

Not giving him a chance to spout his usual servant garbage, she hurried away to her room. Once
inside, she sank onto her bed in despair.

What *was* she going to do? Hope Springs didn't
have a lot to offer in the job market, especially for
former waitress/artists. Dear Lord, how was she to
survive the remaining three months until the next
solstice?

A tear slid down her cheek. Damn Dimitri Karakov. She was trying to keep him from being murdered, and he chose to see her as a conniving gold
digger out to snare a prince.

Rising from the bed, she gathered together her
belongings. She didn't have many—the two dresses
she had managed to purchase since her arrival,
undergarments, her hat, and her art supplies.

She changed into one of the dresses and left the
uniform on the dresser. Viewing her pitiful pile of
stuff on the bed, she gave in to a wave of despair.
She didn't even have anything to put her clothing
in.

More tears streaked down her cheeks. She hated
being here. She hated The Chesterfield. And most
of all, she hated Dimitri.

Swallowing hard, she tried to think rationally.
Maybe she could work for Corrie at the Café of
Dreams.

She was rolling her undergarments up in her
dress when she heard a rap on the door. Probably
Miss Sparrow. The woman seemed to know why
Cynda had been brought back in time. Maybe she
could help.

Cynda opened the door, then gasped, unable to

believe her eyes. "What do you want?" she asked
Dimitri.

"I must talk to you."

"I'm tired of listening to you." She tried to close
the door, but he pushed it open and stepped inside.

"Nevertheless, you will hear me."

"Says you." She tried to ignore him and re-
arranged her few belongings into a pile. That took
about a second.

"You're not supposed to be here," she said, seizing the rigid protocol of the period to get rid of
him.

"This is important."

"You always think it's important."

When he remained silent, she finally forced herself to face him. Instead of the gloating she
expected to see on his face, she found him concerned. "So, what is it?"

He brushed her cheek with his broad thumb.
"You've been crying."

She looked away. "What do you expect? I just
lost my job and my place to live, and I have until
tonight to get out."

Turning her toward him, he gripped her chin.
"I'm sorry."

"I can't imagine why. You've been wanting me
gone since we met."

"That's not true."

She made a face, and he grimaced. "I wanted
you away from my brother, but not to the point of
losing your job."

"Are you going to deny you're the one who made
the complaint to the Major?"

"No." He tightened his fingers when she would
have jerked free. "But I only asked him to order

you to avoid Alexi. I thought perhaps you'd obey his orders better than you do mine. I didn't expect him to fire you."

"The Major never does anything in half measures."

"So it appears." He rubbed his thumb over her cheek again as his gaze dropped to her mouth.

Cynda's heart threw in an extra beat. At that moment, she couldn't have moved if her life depended on it.

Abruptly, he dropped his hand and crossed to the window. "I have a proposition for you."

That sounded ominous. "Like what?"

"It is an opportunity for you to paint."

"I'm not going to New York." She had to stay here, at least until December 21.

"This position is here."

"Oh?"

He turned slowly to face her. "I want to commission you to paint my portrait. I will be crowned as king next summer and will need one."

"Paint your portrait?" Had she heard right? Cynda stared at him. He wanted her to paint *his* portrait?

"If I find it satisfactory, I will sponsor you on future endeavors."

"Are you serious?"

He nodded.

"But how?" She still didn't have a place to stay. Perhaps she could find something in town.

"I will arrange for you to have a suite near ours so you can work undisturbed."

"I can't afford a suite. Not everyone is rich, you know."

"I will cover all your expenses for the duration of the sponsorship."

This was too good to be true. Cynda eyed him suspiciously. "What's the catch?"

"Catch?"

"You're not telling me something."

His lips lifted in a half smile. "I believe you will be too busy with this project to spend any time with Alexi." He came toward her. "Do you agree?"

He thought he was saving Alexi from her, when in reality Dimitri was the one she wanted to be with. It would be easier to keep an eye on him— and an eye out for the killer. "I agree."

"Excellent." He nodded. "Come with me and I will take you to your suite."

"You've reserved it already?" Cynda frowned. Pretty damned confident, wasn't he?

"I felt the need to make immediate restitution for my remarks. I hoped you would accept." He went to the door. "After you."

She motioned toward her bed. "What about my stuff?"

"Is that all you have?"

At her nod, he frowned. "I will send someone for it. Come. You are about to become an artist in residence."

Cynda joined him, resisting the urge to dance. She had a place to live, with expenses paid no less, and a job painting. Even better, Dimitri was the subject. This was a dream come true.

As he turned to close the door to her room, she shot her fist into the air.

Yes!

* * *

"This is where you will stay," Dimitri said as he pushed open the door to the suite down the hall from his.

Cynda entered, unable to believe her eyes. It was easily three times the size of the room she had shared with Molly, with a large main room and a bedroom leading off it. Best of all, the suite contained its own bathroom . . . complete with a flush toilet. "It's rather grand," she murmured.

Dimitri shrugged. "It will do."

As she wandered the rooms, Cynda glanced back at him over her shoulder. "I guess we have different ideas of grand."

She paused by the large glass door leading to the balcony and turned to face the room. "I think I'll have you sit there." She pointed to a spot by the wall near the window. "That way we'll have the best light."

"I will leave that in your capable hands."

He sounded as if he meant it, and Cynda gave him a warm smile. "Thank you, Dimitri. Thank you for this opportunity."

"I trust I will not be disappointed."

"I don't think so." She intended this to be the best painting of her life.

"Does this mean I am not damned to hell now?"

She widened her eyes. Was he actually making a joke? "I'll let you off," she quipped. "For now."

As she met Dimitri's gaze, she noticed the molten pewter simmering in his eyes, and her breath caught in her chest. This could be a dangerous move on both their parts. She wanted this man.

Could she work with him day after day and keep her desire locked up?

He took one step toward her.

Could *he*?

Alexi burst into the suite, his features contorted with anger. "I can't believe you're doing this. Are you insane?"

To Cynda's surprise, Dimitri remained calm. "I was responsible for Cynda losing her position. Would you have me leave her to the wolves?"

"If you had left matters alone, this would not be necessary in the first place. I am quite capable of taking care of myself."

"I have yet to see evidence of that," Dimitri said, his voice cool.

Alexi curled his hands into fists. "Perhaps you are too busy being king to notice."

A spark of anger entered Dimitri's eyes. "And what would you know about being that?"

"More than you think." Alexi turned to Cynda. "Beware, Cynda. It's only a matter of time before you end up in his bed, and he won't marry you. I can guarantee you that."

As Cynda opened her mouth to respond, he left the room, slamming the door after him. Why had he been so angry? Was he protecting her? From Dimitri?

"I apologize for my brother. He doesn't think before he speaks." Dimitri didn't look at her as he spoke, his voice quiet.

She wasn't sure whether to be disappointed or relieved. The thought of making love with Dimitri sent fire through her veins, but Alexi was undoubtedly right about one thing. Dimitri would never marry her. After all, she was only a servant.

His servant now.

"We all tend to say things we don't mean when we're angry," she said finally.

He turned to her then, his expression filled with pain. "Yes, we do." He bobbed his head. "If you will excuse me, I will arrange for your belongings to be transferred."

"Thank you." She held his gaze, aching for him. Alexi's words had hurt him. He loved his younger brother.

And she greatly feared his younger brother would be the death of him.

Chapter 9

"Grandmère insists that you dine with us." Dimitri presented the request as an order when Cynda opened the door to her suite that evening.

"Are you sure about that?" she asked.

Dimitri's brief hesitation indicated he understood her underlying question. Her position was tenuous enough without triggering more anger between the brothers.

"You are under my sponsorship," he said. "It is required."

Cynda wasn't sure she believed that, but she went with him anyway. Practicality demanded it. With her meals no longer provided and very little money, she had no choice.

Sophie greeted her warmly. "I am so glad to hear you will be painting Dimitri's portrait. I have been insisting he have it done for months now."

Dimitri raised one eyebrow, but said nothing, going instead to pull out a chair for Cynda. As she took her seat, she glanced around for the missing Karakov. "Where's Alexi?"

"He preferred to dine downstairs tonight," Sophie replied. "He has been so good at keeping me company that I felt he deserved a night of freedom."

Cynda could sense Dimitri's relief. It echoed her own. The last thing she wanted was another argument between the brothers.

The meal went smoothly, served by another waitress who glared at Cynda. Cynda lowered her gaze. No doubt the others saw her as a fortune hunter. If only she could tell the truth. But who would believe her?

She refused dessert, anxious to escape, but Sophie changed her plans.

"I have several new books that young porter Rupert found for me. Would you be so kind as to read another to me?"

How could she refuse the elderly woman who had been nothing but kind to her? "I would be glad to." After all, she had read to Sophie on many other occasions since she had started delivering their meals.

However, on other occasions Dimitri had left the room. Tonight he stayed, settling into a comfortable chair after he had dismissed the waitress.

Cynda looked through the stack of books, then grinned. "This one is perfect." She pulled it out. *"The Prince and the Pauper* by Mark Twain."

"Do I sense a hidden meaning here?" Dimitri asked, his question layered with amusement.

"Could be." Cynda perched on the edge of the

bed and started to read. It had been years since she had enjoyed this story, and she found herself caught up in it as Sophie and Dimitri listened with rapt attention. When she coughed suddenly, her throat dry, Dimitri called a halt.

"That's enough for tonight. You're tired," he said. "You can read more tomorrow."

"I'd be glad to." Cynda marked her place and set the book on a nearby table before she stood. "Thank you for the dinner, Sophie."

"The pleasure was mine." Sophie turned her gaze on her grandson. "Make certain you escort Cynda to her room."

Cynda shook her head. "That's not necessary. It's only down the hall a little ways."

"It is how a gentleman treats a lady." Sophie's tone brooked no nonsense, and Dimitri rose at once to open the door.

They walked in silence to her doorway, and she waited while he unlocked it. "You don't have to do this," she said, acutely aware of his presence.

"As Grandmère said, it is how a lady should be treated."

She cast him a sidelong glance. "I didn't think a servant was considered a lady."

Dimitri's gaze darkened, and he stroked her cheek with the back of his hand. "I am beginning to see there is more than birthright to being a lady." He lifted her hand and placed a light kiss on the back. "Good night."

Cynda could barely breathe. "Good night." She escaped into her room and released her breath in a rush.

Painting this portrait would definitely be an adventure.

* * *

Cynda had everything ready by the time Dimitri showed up in the morning—her easel in place, her pencils laid out, her nerves on overdrive. When he knocked, she let him in and showed him to a chair.

"I want you to sit there while I do some preliminary sketches."

"Why preliminary sketches?"

"To decide which pose is best for one thing. Plus I don't have a canvas large enough for a full-sized portrait, which Sophie says you must have, so Rupert is locating one for me."

He sat in the chair, his back straight. He had worn a uniform of some sort today, a red jacket with gold braid decorated with ribbons and a familiar insignia. "Is that your country's shield?" she asked.

He nodded. "All monarchs are painted in their state uniform."

Cynda studied him for several moments, then grabbed a pencil. She would sketch him sitting first, then standing, and see which looked better. After hours of drawing his face, she had no problem beginning.

Only he looked so stiff. She didn't want to capture that. Perhaps if they talked, he would loosen up. "I suppose you've always known you'd be king one day."

"As long as I can remember."

If anything, his expression grew more stony. She sighed and tried again. "What was it like as a child knowing that?"

He shrugged. "I have never known anything different, so it is difficult to say. I had lessons as any other child.''

He wasn't telling her everything. Cynda paused, searching his face. His eyes held pain. ''I imagine it was a difficult life. How could you be a normal child?''

His gaze went hazy. ''Even as a small child, I was expected to be better than the other children, to excel at everything.'' He stopped abruptly as if he hadn't expected to say that.

She frowned. No wonder he looked so grim. ''That's a heavy load for a child.''

''I am to be king.'' Dimitri lifted one shoulder in dismissal. ''My father only wished me adequately prepared.''

''Did he ever take time to play with you?'' she asked softly.

''He taught me to hunt and often checked on my studies. Sometimes we would fence together.''

''No, *play* with you. Like hide-and-seek or Parcheesi or Uno.'' Cynda had barely known her father, but her mother had always made time for her.

Dimitri stiffened. ''I was raised as all future kings are raised.''

''Alexi, too?''

''To a lesser extent. His upbringing wasn't as strict.''

She sighed. ''No wonder you two are so different. You've never had any fun.''

''While he has had too much,'' Dimitri added.

''Perhaps.'' Whoever said the life of a prince was wonderful? She much preferred the poorer but more loving life.

She worked most of the day, pausing for dinner

when she wanted to change poses. Dimitri came
to peer over her shoulder at the rough sketch. "I
am not sure I care for this one."

"Me either." He still looked stiff, though she
had tried hard to work around it. "We'll try a
different pose tomorrow." She glanced at him.
"Unless you want to keep on today."

"No. Sitting is hard work." He produced his rare
devastating smile. "I think I prefer to walk this
afternoon. Would you care to accompany me?"

Her heart gave a sudden leap. "I would enjoy
that, but what about Sophie?"

"Alexi is with her." A sudden boyishness entered
his expression. "Come with me, Cynda."

For once, his words sounded like a request rather
than an order. "Okay."

Following a simple supper in the dining room,
they sought the walking path at the rear of The
Chesterfield, which was far less populated than the
more formal gardens. The air held a nip that sig-
naled the approaching autumn, and Cynda shivered, wishing she had thought to grab a wrap.

"Cold?" Dimitri took her arm and tucked it
within his, nestling her close to his side. Her chill
instantly disappeared as the heat of his body triggered an enthusiastic response within her own.

"Better?"

"Much." In fact, she was bordering on too much
heat now, her hormones igniting to acute awareness of the handsome man beside her, her senses
drinking in his masculinity.

"Tell me about yourself, Cynda," he said suddenly. "You have drawn out my past, and I'd prefer
to know more about you. Where are you from? For
I confess, I have never met a woman like you."

The future. But she couldn't tell him that. He would cast her into the loony bin for sure. "I was born and raised outside of Boston." That much was true. "My father left when I was a child. I barely knew him. But my mother was wonderful." She smiled at the memories. "We didn't have much, but we did have each other. She worked two jobs so I could get the art training I wanted."

But Cynda couldn't sell a painting. She had wanted—so much—to prove to her mother that she had been worth all her sacrifices.

"She sounds like an amazing woman."

"She was." Cynda sighed, missing her mother yet glad the woman no longer endured the horrible pain that had ravaged her body.

"Was?" Dimitri paused in his walking. "I'm sorry."

Cynda forced a smile. "She died almost a year ago. She's at peace now."

"And the rest of your family?"

"I have no one else."

Dimitri tightened his hold on her arm and opened his mouth as if to speak, then closed it again, the words unsaid. Remaining silent, he resumed walking.

"What about your family?" she asked as the silence grew longer. "Your mother and father?"

"They are both alive."

His simple statement, though said calmly, held a tremendous amount of emotion. Cynda frowned. Why would the thought of his parents bother him? She squeezed his arm. "Are they ill?"

He hesitated, and for a moment she thought he wouldn't respond at all. "They live apart," he said finally, his tone cold. "And rarely speak to each other."

"Oh." Cynda resisted the urge to hug him. "I'm sorry."

"Father is growing weary of his responsibilities," he continued as if he hadn't spoken before. "He plans to pass over the crown next summer."

"Then all that responsibility will be yours."

"Yes." His expression remained unchanged, yet she sensed a heaviness in his voice. "I will be king."

She ached for him. "Then your life will no longer be your own."

"My life has never been my own."

As she looked up at him, she stubbed her toe, nearly falling, but he caught her in a firm grasp, holding her solidly against him. Her nipples hardened at once as her stomach knotted with anticipation.

She placed her hands against his muscular chest as their gazes locked. Fire burned in his pewter depths erasing the grimness of only a moment ago. Would he kiss her? She ached for him to do so almost as much as she feared it.

"This . . . this isn't smart," she whispered.

"I know." But he didn't release her. Instead, he ran one hand along the curve of her back, lingering at her waist. He bent toward her, then groaned, closing his eyes as he rested his forehead against hers. "Perhaps Alexi is right. Perhaps I am not worthy of being king."

"That's not true." She had never met a man more worthy.

"A king is a man of honor, and with you I am less than honorable."

She inhaled sharply, pressing her swollen breasts

even more firmly against his chest. "You're the most honorable man I've ever met." That he would hold back when she longed for him to kiss her, to touch her, when he obviously felt those same longings, went beyond honor. She reached up to touch the rough stubble on his cheek. "You will be a wonderful king, Dimitri."

He caught her hand in his, then pressed a kiss into her palm. "I must go," he said huskily. Not giving her a chance to respond, he eased away from her, then hurried down the path.

Dimitri quickened his pace. He was too weak of will. Something about this woman made him forget his duties, his responsibilities.

She looked at him as a man, not a prince, which made her unafraid to speak her mind, yet giving in nature. Too giving. The memory of their one kiss made him grow hard with need. He found it difficult to be around her and not touch her.

So why had he offered her this opportunity to paint his portrait? It meant days of sharing a room with her . . . alone. Because he owed her?

Or because he wanted to spend this time with her?

Dimitri ran his fingers through his hair. He feared Alexi was right. Dimitri wanted her in his bed with an intensity that grew daily.

But he would not—could not—marry her.

"Miss Madison, do you have a moment?" Miss Sparrow called, stopping Cynda's rush to the tower from the dining room.

Cynda smiled at her. "Of course." Though she didn't see the head housekeeper very often anymore, Cynda discovered she enjoyed the woman's company. Probably because Miss Sparrow was the only person to know the truth about her.

"I wanted to apologize." Miss Sparrow lowered her voice and drew Cynda to an isolated corner. "I could not talk the Major out of dismissing you. I did try."

"I'm sure you did." Cynda touched the woman's arm. "It actually all worked out for the best."

"Yes, I heard." Miss Sparrow beamed. "You are to paint the prince's portrait."

"It's a chance of a lifetime, so the Major actually did me a favor." Now she had painting and Dimitri—her two favorite things.

"I am so glad to hear that." The housekeeper's pleasure was genuine. "And I wish you only the best."

"Thank you." Cynda grinned. As far as she was concerned, she had that—her own suite, meals provided, and nothing to do but paint a sinfully handsome man.

They parted, and Cynda hurried upstairs. She had just rounded a corner when she heard a whimper and spotted a man twisting a young girl's arm. Cynda froze.

"Please, sir," the girl whispered, her eyes damp. "I have work to do."

"You just come with me for a little while; then I'll let you get back to work." The man pulled her after him. He was tall, well-built and passably good-looking. But the gleam of lust on his face alarmed Cynda.

The girl was a tweenie maid, one of the younger staff who helped maintain the linens, and from the looks of things, she was on the verge of being molested.

Cynda started forward, but before she had taken three steps, she heard a familiar voice.

"I suggest you release that girl at once." Dimitri stepped in front of the man, and Cynda paused. What would he do?

The man nodded at Dimitri, but didn't remove his grip. "Care to join me, Your Highness?"

Dimitri's expression hardened. "I do not. You have no business with this child. Let her go. Now."

The man jerked back in surprise, his hold loosening. At once, the girl pulled free and ran away. With a foul exclamation, the man whirled on Dimitri. "Now look what you did. She was only a servant chit."

"She was a child." Dimitri's tone was cold. "Have you no honor, sir? If you are so desperate for a woman, there are some in town very willing to accommodate you."

Cynda dropped her jaw. Dimitri was defending a servant?

"Don't want them," the man muttered.

"That is your decision. However"—Dimitri stepped closer, dark anger on his face—"you will not touch that servant or any other at The Chesterfield or I will see you removed and shamed."

The man frowned. "That's a bit much. These servants are here for us, you know."

"They are here to do their jobs, nothing more." Dimitri straightened, his disgust evident. "Perhaps it is time you left The Chesterfield."

"You can't do that."

Dimitri didn't reply, but he wore his imperial

expression that Cynda knew well. The other man didn't have a chance.

Evidently, he realized it as well, for he turned away, glowering. "Place is too crowded anyhow."

Dimitri watched the man leave, then resumed his path, coming to an abrupt halt at spotting Cynda. "How long have you been there?" he asked.

"The entire time." She smiled. The proud prince had a soft streak after all. "You're a good man, Dimitri."

He appeared flustered, an unusual state for him. "I was coming to look for you."

"Were you?" He had kept his distance since their walk in the gardens the other night.

"I have some time available now." His tone was polite . . . too polite.

Cynda sighed. "Very well, then. Let's go."

As they walked to the suites, she stole a glance at him. He continually surprised her. Just when she was convinced he held the world record for arrogance, he came to the aid of a servant. Who was Dimitri Karakov? Really?

"I like this pose better," Cynda said as she drew back from her easel. She motioned Dimitri over. "What do you think?"

He came to stand behind her, keeping a respectful distance between them yet not so much she didn't notice him. Heck, he would have to be in China for her not to notice him.

"I agree. The standing pose is more appropriate."

And more like the portrait she had been cleaning in the present. Well, it had been excellently done.

Why shouldn't she emulate it? "Good. I'll go to town and pick up the canvas and paints Rupert ordered for me so we can start tomorrow."

"Very good." Dimitri stepped farther back. "I will see you at supper, then. Grandmère is anxious to hear the end of the book."

He didn't offer to take her to town this time. Cynda bit back her disappointment. And he shouldn't. Just sharing this room had her ready to throw him down and make love to him. She needed some distance.

"Yes, until supper." She caught the train to town without even running for it. Amazing how much easier it was to be on time when she had more time to call her own.

Mr. Hadley had the pigments and canvas waiting for her at the Emporium, and she wrestled them to the train station, foregoing her usual stop at the Café of Dreams in order to return to The Chesterfield.

Sheesh, she was pathetic. Cynda closed her eyes on the train as it climbed the mountain slope. She was seriously in lust with a prince she could never have, yet knowing that didn't stop her from wanting. From hoping.

Just by imagining she could smell his unique scent, taste his potent kiss, feel the silkiness of his black hair. The man was sexiness personified. And now she was discovering he was more vulnerable, more kind-hearted than she had thought.

Damn, it had been hard enough to resist him when he was an arrogant jerk. After seeing him defend the tweenie maid, Cynda found her willpower slipping.

The train stopping at the spur jerked her back to

reality, and she stumbled toward The Chesterfield, burdened by a canvas easily as long as she was tall. Dimitri had better appreciate this.

She searched for Rupert or Jack, but naturally, neither porter was in sight. Fine, she had managed this far.

She made it as far as the hallway to the tower when she turned too sharply. The oversized canvas whirled her around, and she collided with a portly gentleman, knocking them both to the floor. He responded with a stream of curses that stunned her. What happened to the restrained behavior of this time period?

"Oops, sorry." She climbed to her feet without assistance and verified the canvas had suffered no damage. "I didn't see you."

He rose, his bald head and face red, his mustache shaking. "You, madam, are a menace to the entire hotel. You should be taken out and whipped."

"I said I was sorry." Cynda gathered her materials together again. Jeez, he was blowing it out of proportion. "It was an accident."

The man suddenly pointed a finger at her. "I know who you are. You're the prince's new whore."

The blood drained from Cynda's cheeks, then returned just as quickly. "I am an artist painting the prince's portrait."

"Ha." The man seized her arm and shook her. "You can tell that arrogant prince we don't need his kind here. Damned foreigners think they own the place."

"America wouldn't exist if not for foreigners," Cynda retorted.

He whipped his hand across her face with such force that her head snapped back and she dropped her parcels again. "Don't speak to me that way. You are nothing but trash."

Cynda doubled up her fist as she regained her footing. "And don't you hit me." Before she could plow her fist into his round face, another fist completed the task for her, knocking the man into the opposite wall.

She turned in surprise to find Dimitri facing the man, his fists raised. "If you disagree with me or my country, you may discuss that with me, but you will never insult Miss Madison again." He went to stand over the man, whose nose was bleeding profusely. "Do you understand this?"

The man spit at Dimitri. "Take your damned whore and leave this country. We don't want you here."

Dimitri's posture grew even more rigid. "I assure you I will depart at the earliest opportunity."

"Not soon enough." The man climbed to his feet, his sleeve against his nose. With a glare, he sidled down the hallway.

"The bastard," Cynda muttered. She had wanted to hit him, too.

Dimitri lowered his fists and came over to her, his hand caressing her stinging cheek. "Are you all right?"

She grimaced. "I'll live."

"Come. Let me tend to that." He searched the crowd that had gathered, nodded briefly to a horrified Miss Sparrow, and pointed at a gaping Rupert. "Bring Miss Madison's art supplies to her suite."

"Yes, Your Highness." Rupert scurried to obey as Dimitri took Cynda's elbow and led her to her suite.

Upon their arrival, Dimitri tipped Rupert generously, then went to Cynda's bathroom and dipped a cloth in cool water. Pushing her gently into a chair, he placed the cloth against her cheek. She winced despite the comfort it provided.

"He had no call to hit you," Dimitri said, his expression still clouded with anger.

"I agree." Cynda scowled. "I'm glad you punched him 'cause if you hadn't, I would've."

Dimitri suddenly grinned. "I imagine you would have, too."

"You bet. No one hits me and gets away with it." She gave him a wry smile, then winced again. Already she could feel her cheek swelling. "I'm going to be a mess later."

"I'm afraid you will be bruised." Dimitri kept the cloth pressed against her face. "Though not nearly as badly as Anya when she fell off her horse. Her eyes were swollen shut for three days." He laughed at the memory.

"Who's Anya?" Cynda had never heard him mention that name before.

His smile faded. "She is the daughter of a duke, a friend of my father's. Alexi and I have known her all our lives."

Cynda tried to dampen her rising jealously. "She's a good friend?"

Dimitri lowered the cloth and paced away from her. Only when he faced the glass doors did he speak. "She is the woman who will one day be my wife."

Chapter 10

Cynda gaped at him. She couldn't have heard correctly. "You're engaged?"

"Not officially." Dimitri turned to look at her, his expression veiled. "I expect Father will announce it after my return, but there has been an agreement between our fathers since Anya was born."

"I see." That certainly put her in her place. "Do you love her?" The words escaped before she could stop them. His answer was important.

"I like her." He didn't meet her searching gaze. "I suppose I will learn to love her."

"Will you?" If he had known Anya all his life and didn't love her yet, Cynda doubted he ever would.

"I must. My parents have an arranged marriage, and it has not been pleasant. My father spends more time with his mistress than my mother or us." He scowled. "I will *not* subject my children to that. I will honor my wife and spend time with my children."

"I'm sorry." His childhood sounded much worse than hers despite the difference in their wealth. She forced a smile. "I hope you will be very happy together."

"Thank you." Dimitri headed for the door. "I will see you at supper."

"No." She didn't want to see him any more today. She needed time to think. "Tell Sophie I'm sorry, but I'd prefer to stay in tonight."

He nodded once. "As you wish."

After he left, Cynda buried her face in her hands. At some point she had allowed herself to hope that she might have a future with Dimitri. How foolish. Such a thing was impossible.

She was here only until the solstice, to save Dimitri's life, nothing more. As much as she might desire the handsome prince, his only place in her life was in her dreams.

Within two weeks, the portrait began to take shape. Cynda finished the outlining and had started adding pigment. Dimitri came every day and posed, though he maintained a formality that added to Cynda's growing tension. They didn't speak of Anya again, but she was there—almost a physical presence in the room.

"You have dark circles under your eyes," Dimitri said abruptly. "Are you not sleeping well?"

"Well enough." She was reluctant to sleep, afraid of the dreams that made her only want the unattainable.

"Do you need a reprieve from painting? You have worked every day."

She shook her head. "I want to get it done."

"We have the entire winter before us."

Not really. She only had about two months until the solstice, and unless she figured out how Dimitri was killed, he had even less time. "I prefer to earn my sponsorship." She gave him a tentative smile and returned to the portrait.

She concentrated on the face—his sculpted, regal face with its defined cheekbones, firm chin, sensual mouth, and aristocratic nose. She could almost paint it with her eyes closed.

Only his expression presented a problem. He looked as rigid as a mannequin. "This isn't going to work, Dimitri," she said. "You need a more pleasant expression. Can you think of something nice?"

"I can try." Slowly his face changed until the passion in it made Cynda catch her breath.

"That's perfect." She worked quickly to capture the desire in his dark eyes, the slight lift of his lips, the sexuality that was Dimitri. Her hands seemed to work of their own accord, his countenance taking shape before her eyes.

This was good. This was damned good.

She painted furiously as if in a trance, not emerging until almost two hours later. Dimitri looked at her curiously. "Do you have it?" he asked.

She nodded, not trusting her tight throat to speak. The face staring back at her from the painting appeared almost alive. She could feel the passion heating her blood.

Dimitri came to peer at the canvas, but said nothing for several long moments. Did he hate it?

When she glanced up at him in question, he squeezed her shoulder. "It will do."

"What were you thinking of?" What thought created such a passionate expression?

Again, he remained silent, but his gaze fell to her mouth. "Kissing you," he said finally.

Heat rose in her cheeks, and Cynda looked away. Did he know how much she wished he would kiss her again? As she turned, a motion outside the window caught her attention, and she crossed over to it.

"I don't believe it. It's snowing. In October." Large, gentle flakes drifted to the ground, melting when they landed, but the white curtain blotted out the nearby mountains. Despite the unseasonable weather, she relaxed. "I love to watch it snow."

She sensed Dimitri when he came to stand behind her. "I find it soothing," he said.

"It makes me feel like I'm the only person in the world." She enjoyed that sensation of isolation, as if the rest of the world didn't matter.

"The only two people in the world." Dimitri wrapped his arm around her waist and pulled her gently back to rest against him. The heat of his body invaded hers, turning her bones to liquid. She should move away, but none of her muscles would cooperate.

She reveled in his nearness, his physical strength, and the possessiveness of his arm around her. For this brief moment, she could forget about everything else.

His lips brushed her hair, and her breasts swelled in response. Her heart hammered with the fierceness of a hard rock drummer. "Dimitri?"

"Hmm?" The rumble in his chest created a tickle in her own.

"What would you do if you weren't going to be king?" She wanted to imagine him as an ordinary man. As if Dimitri could be ordinary, even as a garbage collector. "Is there something you'd like to do?"

He tightened his arm around her, and she felt the hard ridge of his desire along her back. "Besides this growing obsession to make love to you?"

Her breath caught.

He bent to her neck and nibbled kisses along it until he reached her ear. "To brand you and make you mine?" He ran his tongue into her ear and around the edge, and Cynda gasped, her stomach knotting, her breasts peaking.

Still ensnaring her against him, he reached up to cup her breast. Cynda jerked within his hold as a rush of desire surged to her abdomen. "D . . . Dimitri." She wasn't sure she could remain standing much longer.

"Tell me to stop, Cynda," he groaned, even as he palmed her breast more firmly. "I have no discipline when I'm with you."

She didn't want him to stop. She wanted to turn and kiss him and strip away his clothes, but they weren't the only two people in the world, no matter how much she wanted to believe otherwise. Her future was over a hundred years away.

"Stop, please, Dimitri." She choked out the words, then closed her eyes to hold back the tears when he dropped his hands and stepped back from her. She didn't dare look around.

When he finally spoke again, his words surprised her. "I have always enjoyed carpentry."

She peeked at him to find him staring out at the already diminishing snow.

"I even have a talent for it. I made a table and chair for my mother, which she uses daily at home. I made a cabinet for Alexi."

"What is it about it that you like?" she whispered.

He held up his hands and looked at them. "Taking the wood and molding it into something useful . . . something I can do with my own hands, my own work."

"Good." Cynda blinked rapidly to ensure all her tears were gone before she turned to face him. "Then, I hereby commission you to make the frame for your portrait."

"Make the frame?" He appeared as startled as he sounded.

"Yes. How many other kings will be able to say they worked on their own portrait?"

"Besides the hours of standing?" He produced a crooked smile.

"Besides that." She smiled in return, fighting the urge to throw herself into his arms.

His gaze lingered on her mouth; then he inhaled visibly and turned for the door. "We have done enough for today."

"Yes." More than enough and yet not enough.

He paused with the door open. "Until tonight?" His expression held a hint of pleading. For forgiveness? Or her presence?

It didn't matter. She couldn't deny him. "I'll be there."

No matter how much it hurt.

* * *

She finished *The Adventures of Tom Sawyer* and grinned. After *The Prince and the Pauper*, Sophie had decided she needed to hear all of Mark Twain's works—at least the ones currently published. "We have *The Adventures of Huckleberry Finn* next."

"Excellent." Sophie leaned back against her pillows. "I do so enjoy Mr. Twain's works."

"I like Tom Sawyer," Alexi added. "Except for Injun Joe."

Cynda grinned at him. "You just wish you were Tom Sawyer."

"I think I like Huck Finn the most," Dimitri said.

Ah, the boy with no responsibilities. Cynda nodded. Evidently, the kingship was a heavy load, whether he realized it or not.

Alexi looked at his brother in surprise. "I wouldn't have expected that of you."

"I would." Cynda placed the book on the table and stood. "Now it's time for me to return to my room."

"Not yet. You must help us plan for Dimitri's birthday," Sophie said.

"Birthday?" Cynda glanced at Dimitri in surprise. "When?"

"In two days." Sophie smiled indulgently at her elder grandson. "I know we didn't expect to be here for this, so we must do something special."

"No, Grandmère." Dimitri's eyes darkened. "I wish no celebration. It is a day like any other."

"But we could hold a ball," Alexi said with enthusiasm.

"The All Hallows' Eve Ball is only a week away. That is sufficient." Dimitri rose and faced them. "I want no celebration. Is that understood?"

Sophie sighed and nodded. "As you wish, my dear."

Alexi stood and clapped his brother on the back, grinning. "You always were a spoilsport." When Dimitri glared at him, he shrugged. "But I can wait until the ball." He bowed toward Sophie and Cynda. "Good night."

Cynda followed him to the bedroom door, then paused to smile at Dimitri. "A birthday, eh?"

"I expect you to observe my wishes as well," he said, all kingly command.

"Maybe." As she left their suite, different schemes jumped through her mind. No party. Okay. But Dimitri needed something to commemorate his special day. What?

Something fun. The man had had far too little of that in his life.

An idea sprang to life and took root. She grinned.

This would be a birthday he would remember.

He should have known better than to trust Cynda. The casual indifference on her face when he entered her suite for a day's painting had provided a warning. She had worn many expressions around him, but never indifference.

He had considered foregoing his session today as it was his birthday, but the pleasure of seeing Cynda was probably the best gift he could give himself. She affected him like no other woman. He thought about her constantly and wanted her with a ferocity that surprised him. He had always prided himself on his dignity and control, yet around her, he had neither.

"No painting today," she announced, a twinkle in her eye.

"Then, I am not needed." He turned back toward the door, but as he had suspected, she hurried to grab his arm.

"Not so fast, buddy. I have other plans for you."

He assumed his sternest expression. "I told you no party."

"No party. Cross my heart." She drew an X over her chest, drawing his gaze to her high breasts. His palms tingled as he remembered their firm fullness.

"What, then?"

"You'll see." She tugged at his hand. "Just come with me."

Though wary, Dimitri allowed her to lead him downstairs until he realized they were approaching the dining room. "I am serious, Cynda."

"It's not a party." She gave him a smile that acted as a fist against his chest. "Trust me."

"I believe that would be dangerous." But he had to admit, she had him intrigued.

She took him through the dining room and into the kitchen, where Chef Sashenka was bellowing orders to his staff. When he spotted Cynda, his stern demeanor dissolved into a welcoming smile.

"Ah, Cynda, you are prompt." He executed a precise bow in Dimitri's direction. "Prince Dimitri, an honor."

Dimitri nodded once in acknowledgment. Though Sashenka was a talented chef, the man was still a servant.

"Here is the sketch per our agreement." Cynda handed the chef a drawing—a pencil sketch of Sashenka.

Sashenka beamed as he looked at it. "Excellent."
He motioned for an assistant to bring forward a
large basket. "And here is vat you requested."

"Everything I asked for is there?"

The chef straightened. "Of course."

Cynda took the basket and quickly pressed a kiss
on the older man's cheek. "Thank you, Sasha."

Dimitri tried to ignore the sudden fury that
exploded in his chest. The kiss was innocent, yet
his irrational need for this woman failed to recog-
nize that. He caught her arm. "Are we finished
here?"

"Yes." Her smile helped to ease his tight chest.
"We have to see Rupert for the next step."

She dragged him to the front entrance where
Rupert stood outside waiting by the head of a
buggy. A buggy? What did she have planned? "Get
inside," she ordered. "You're driving."

Naturally he would drive, even if he didn't know
where they were going. She spoke briefly with
Rupert, who appeared to be giving her directions
if his wild arm movements were any indication.

Eventually, she climbed up beside Dimitri and
motioned for him to leave the hotel. "Shouldn't
we have a chaperone?" he asked, dreading a third
party yet unwilling to forego proprieties.

Cynda rolled her eyes. "Pretend the horse is one.
To have anyone else would spoil the surprise. Come
on. Let's go."

Her enthusiasm was contagious. Dimitri scanned
the hotel's porch. It was still early enough that few
lingered outside to watch them leave. "Very well."

"Go left here," she said when they reached the
road.

"Left?" Away from the town?

"Left." She continued to give him directions, amusement in her voice, taking him farther away from all signs of civilization and higher up the mountain slope.

Fortunately, the warmer days of autumn had returned after the unusual brief snowfall, and the sun shone brightly, warming the air.

"Here you go," she said suddenly. "Follow this path to the end."

"What path?" Did she mean the two overgrown ruts leading into the trees?

"That path."

Apparently she did. Bringing the horse around, he followed her instructions until the trail ended in a small clearing beside a trickling brook, edged by pine trees. "This is it," she exclaimed.

Dimitri examined the area. Aside from the rustle of the wind, he heard nothing. "What?"

"Where we'll hold your picnic." She grinned at him. "I have nothing I can give you for your birthday, so I decided you needed some fun." She leapt from the buggy. "Have you ever had a picnic before?"

He climbed down slowly, amazed. "Not one like this." His picnics had been large affairs with servants to handle the food and enough people to fill The Chesterfield's dining room.

This was different—a picnic for two—yet not unwelcome. No one had ever surprised him before. "And what do I do at this picnic?"

"Eat." She spread a blanket from the buggy on the ground, then set the large basket at the edge of it. "Sasha packed us a wonderful meal." She lifted the lid. "And then some, I'd say." She waved him over. "Come on."

For a brief moment, Dimitri felt like a stranger in a strange land. This was all unfamiliar to him. But Cynda refused to let him remain so. When he knelt beside her, she proceeded to unveil the basket's contents—ham puffs, fried chicken, a crusty loaf of bread, cheese, fruit, and a bottle of champagne.

"Wow, I only asked for a bottle of wine." Cynda met his gaze, amusement dancing in her eyes. "Must be because it's your birthday."

"Then, we shan't let it go to waste." Dimitri uncorked the bottle and poured two glasses, then handed one to Cynda.

She clinked her glass against his. "Happy birthday, Dimitri."

The tightness in his chest momentarily blocked his throat. "Thank you." He couldn't have asked for a better day.

After their drink, he waited for Cynda to lay out the meal. Instead, she jumped to her feet and extended her hand to him. "Before you eat, you play."

"Play?" Dimitri climbed to his feet. His knowledge of games was limited.

"Yes. Hide-and-seek." She guided him to a tree. "Close your eyes, count to twenty, then try to find me. If you find me, you win. If I make it back here and touch the tree before you tag me, I win. Okay?"

He could do that easily enough. "Very well." He heard her progress through the trees as he counted, and he whirled in that direction when he finished.

He had only taken a few steps when he realized how to find her. Grinning, he put his plan in motion.

Introducing Ballad,
A NEW LINE OF HISTORICAL ROMANCES

*A*s a lover of historical romance, you'll adore Ballad Romances. Written by today's most popular romance authors, every book in the Ballad line is not only an individual story, but part of a two to six book series as well. You can look forward to 4 new titles each month – each taking place at a different time and place in history.

But don't take our word for how wonderful these stories are! Accept our introductory shipment of 4 Ballad Romance novels – a $23.96 value – ABSOLUTELY FREE – and see for yourself!

*O*nce you've experienced your first 4 Ballad Romances, we're sure you'll want to continue receiving these wonderful historical romance novels each month – without ever having to leave your home – using our convenient and inexpensive home subscription service. Here's what you get for joining:

- *4 BRAND NEW Ballad Romances delivered to your door each month*
- *30% off the cover price of $5.99 with your home subscription.*
- *A FREE monthly newsletter filled with author interviews, book previews, special offers, and more!*
- *No risk or obligation...you're free to cancel whenever you wish... no questions asked.*

Passion–
Adventure–
Excitement–
Romance–
Ballad!

*T*o start your membership, simply complete and return the card provided. You'll receive your Introductory Shipment of 4 FREE Ballad Romances. Then, each month, as long as your account is in good standing, you will receive the 4 newest Ballad Romances. Each shipment will be yours to examine for 10 days. If you decide to keep the books, you'll pay the preferred home subscriber's price of $16.50 – a savings of 30% off the cover price! (plus $1.50 shipping & handling) If you want us to stop sending books, just say the word...it's that simple.

A $23.96 value – **FREE** No obligation to buy anything – ever.
4 FREE BOOKS are waiting for you! Just mail in the certificate below!

If the certificate is
missing below, write to:

Ballad Romances,
c/o Zebra Home
Subscription Service Inc.

P.O. Box 5214,
Clifton, New Jersey
07015-5214

OR call TOLL FREE
1-888-345-BOOK (2665)

BOOK CERTIFICATE

Yes! Please send me 4 Ballad Romances ABSOLUTELY FREE! After my
introductory shipment, I will receive 4 new Ballad Romances each month to
preview FREE for 10 days (as long as my account is in good standing). If I decide
to keep the books, I will pay the money-saving preferred publisher's price of $16.50
plus $1.50 shipping and handling. That's 30% off the cover price. I may return the
shipment within 10 days and owe nothing, and I may cancel my subscription at any
time. The 4 FREE books will be mine to keep in any case.

Name _____

Address _____ Apt. _____

City _____ State _____ Zip _____

Telephone (___) _____

Signature _____

(If under 18, parent or guardian must sign)

All orders subject to approval by Zebra Home Subscription Service.
Terms and prices subject to change. Offer valid only in the U.S.

DN081A

Passion...
Adventure...
Excitement...
Romance...

Get 4
Ballad
Historical
Romance
Novels
FREE!

Cynda heard Dimitri come after her as she maneuvered her way around toward the clearing again. He would go in the wrong direction to find her while she came in to touch the tree.

She repressed a giggle. She hadn't played a game like this since she was a child, but it was still fun. Would Dimitri think so?

She tiptoed toward the tree. No sign of him. Great. She dashed forward, only to find herself ensnared by a muscular arm around her waist. Dimitri swung her against him as his deep laugh filled the glen. "Found you."

"Hey, that's cheating," she exclaimed through her laughter.

"How so? I call it strategy. I knew you would come this way. Therefore, I only needed to wait until you did so." He looked supremely proud of himself.

"It's still unfair." But with her body pressed against his, she found it difficult enough to think, let alone continue her protest.

She pushed against his chest, needing to free herself before she gave in to her urge to kiss him until neither of them could breathe. "Fine. I'll count now and you hide."

He nodded as he released her. She went to the tree to count and listened for him to move away. He moved stealthily, only the distant crack of a branch providing any clue to where he was hiding.

Completing her count, she whirled around, searching the nearby area. Nothing. She debated on remaining near the tree as he had done, then discounted it. He would expect her to do that.

Instead, she entered the trees, listening and looking. A blur of dark blue made her whip around to see him running toward the clearing. "I got you," she cried.

"You have to tag me first." He had a lead on her, but she hiked her dress up to her knees and ran after him. She almost had him, her hand extended to within inches of his back, when her heel caught on a stone and she stumbled forward.

He caught her in his arms, his eyes lit with mischievousness. "I won," he declared.

"What is this?" she asked with a grin. "The male ego that says you have to win everything?"

"Ego?"

"Pride."

"Precisely." He smoothed back a tendril of her hair and quickly brushed his lips over hers. "Everything."

Her heart skipped a beat. If he kissed her— *really* kissed her—she wouldn't be able to deny him anything. "I think . . ." She drew in a deep breath. "I think we should eat now."

"If you insist." His expression indicated another type of hunger, but he released her and settled on the blanket.

She remained in place for another minute, gaining control again, then joined him to serve the gourmet picnic. Dimitri insisted on more champagne, filling their glasses again.

The meal was wonderful, the company even more so. For the first time, she saw Dimitri truly relaxed. "You need to do this more often," she said. "Take time for yourself or you'll burn out."

"Burn out?" Dimitri tilted his head to look at her. "You do use peculiar expressions."

Cynda forced a smile. Being this relaxed around him had also loosened her tongue. "You'll be unable to function," she amended. "Unless you make time for fun."

"Only if you come with me."

"I wish I could." She would like nothing more than endless days with him. She downed the rest of her champagne. "But you'll be returning to your country, and I'll be going back home."

"Home?" He frowned. "You have not mentioned this before. When?"

"December twenty-first."

"You can't possibly travel in the winter. The roads will be impassable."

"The way I travel I can." All she needed was a nameplate.

"But why then? Why must you leave?"

"Because I belong there." Though lately she wondered more and more what she had to return to. Certainly not family or anyone who would miss her.

"I refuse to let you go." He issued the order like a royal decree. "You are under my sponsorship and my employ until I say otherwise."

"You can't stop me."

"Can't I?" His tone was defiant.

"No, you can't." Cynda turned away to pack the remnants of their meal in the basket, unwilling to argue with him.

After some time, Dimitri spoke. "And what does one do at a picnic now?"

"Well, we can take a walk," she suggested, then ran her hand over her full belly. "Or we can lie in the sun and sleep off our meal." Suiting her actions to her words, she stretched out on the blanket, closing her eyes against the bright sun.

Immediately, Dimitri pinned her in place, his arms on either side of her. Her eyes flew open to stare at him.

"Cynda." There was pain in his voice . . . and need. The same emotions that simmered within her.

She wasn't going to resist him, not any longer. Lifting her hand to his head, she pulled his lips toward hers. "Dimitri," she whispered, then sighed as he covered her mouth with hot passion.

His hunger matched hers, taking, giving, seducing. She wasn't sure which made her more lightheaded—Dimitri or the champagne. It didn't matter. Desire raged through her now.

When he covered her breast with his hand, she arched deeper into it, craving his touch. He caressed her swollen flesh until she moaned with need, the junction between her thighs moist and aching for him.

His kisses grew more savage, nipping at her lip, delving deep into her mouth, claiming her, spoiling her for anyone else. She clenched his hair in her fist, holding him close, while she found the buttons on his shirt with her other hand and opened them until his muscular chest was open to her exploration.

He drew away from her mouth, his eyes filled with want, his breathing ragged. Keeping his gaze on hers, he slid the sleeves of her gown down until her breasts were revealed, swollen within her corset, barely covered by her thin chemise. He eased her breasts free of the corset, then ran his hand over her swollen nipples, and she groaned, wanting more.

Lowering his mouth, he drew on her breast until her breath came in small cries. Her abdomen clenched so tightly she couldn't bear it. She needed . . . she wanted . . .

He pushed her chemise aside and suckled on her other breast while he slowly pushed her dress up along her leg, his hand gliding along her inner thigh until he reached her feminine mound. Delving beneath her pantalettes, he located her swollen nub and massaged it until her body arched with the force of her orgasm.

Tears sprang to her eyes. She had never experienced anything like this. Dimitri rolled over her, pressing his erection against her.

She lifted her hips, wanting him, wanting more. Why was he still dressed? She ached for him to fill her. He rocked against her in response while he continued to tease her breast with his hand and steal kisses from her throat, her lips, her cheeks, her eyes.

Upon encountering her damp eyes, he drew back, his face concerned. "I'm sorry, Cynda."

She shook her head fiercely. "Don't be sorry. I want you, Dimitri. Please, fill me."

He closed his eyes as a shudder ran through his body. Then he rolled to her side and gently straightened her clothing. "I can't do this. It's a mistake."

She sat up, only aware of the passion hot inside her. "That's my choice. I don't care."

"But I do." He rose to his feet and lifted the basket. "I think we should return now."

Cynda stared after him, his denial acting like a bucket of cold water. He wanted her; she knew that. But she wasn't worthy of him.

And never would be.

Chapter 11

Dimitri copped out, playing it safe by claiming business matters for the next few days, leaving Cynda to work on his portrait alone. She didn't really need him there as often now. Her memory filled in the details of his physique, the pride in his posture.

But she continued to dine with him and his family ... Sophie insisted. The elderly lady wasn't about to lose her favorite storyteller, and to be truthful, Cynda enjoyed the meals. It made her feel part of a family again, which she hadn't experienced in a long time.

If only she didn't long to touch Dimitri every time they shared a room. It was torture to sit across from him at the small intimate table and make casual chitchat while her hormones screamed for action and her heart threatened to pound right out of her chest. She tried not to look at him, but found it nearly impossible. Her gaze would drift to his where she would find an answering passion stoked in his eyes.

Cynda told herself several times all the reasons why she shouldn't get involved with the prince—she was leaving soon, he was marrying someone else, he was royalty, she wasn't and wasn't likely to be. But nothing helped. Plain and simple, she wanted this arrogant but kind-hearted prince.

He was so different from what she had first imagined him to be. Yes, he was proud, but he had been taught that at a young age. He cared about his family and tried to do what was right—at least his opinion of right—for them. And he suffered from insecurities about his pending role as king, which only endeared him to her more.

Perching on the edge of Sophie's bed, Cynda forced herself to concentrate on the pages before her. Jeez, did her reading sound as distracted as she felt? Though Alexi had left immediately after dinner, Dimitri lingered, sprawled in an overstuffed chair, his dark gaze always upon her. How was she supposed to concentrate?

"Oh, I almost forgot." Sophie caught Cynda's arm, but addressed both her and Dimitri. "I took the liberty of arranging costumes for you two for the ball."

Cynda started. The ball? Tomorrow night? "I hadn't planned on attending," she murmured, not daring to look at Dimitri.

"You must attend. I insist." Signs of the imperious queen she had once been showed. "Dimitri will take you. After all, he is sponsoring you."

"I'm not sure that's a good idea." As much as

Cynda would love an evening with Dimitri, she didn't dare.

"It is an excellent idea." Sophie glanced at her grandson. "Don't you agree?"

Dimitri hesitated before replying. "Cynda does deserve some entertainment. She has been working hard."

"It is settled." Sophie leaned back against her pillows, a satisfied smile on her lips. "I will have the costumes delivered to you tomorrow."

Cynda's pulse skipped a few beats. "What are they?"

"Ah." Sophie lifted a finger, a mischievous gleam in her eye. "That is my secret. But I do want you to come see me before you leave for the ball." She sighed. "I remember when I could dance all night. You must do it for me now."

"I haven't danced in . . . forever." High school maybe? Cynda dared a sidelong glance at Dimitri and found him watching her intently. Did he dread taking her or, like her, look forward to it with nervous anticipation?

"I am certain you will be an excellent dancer," he said.

Cynda lowered her gaze before he could see her longing for him. She had to remember he was not the man for her. Surely she could survive a simple dance and keep her hormones under control.

Maybe.

Cynda was engrossed in detailing the trim on Dimitri's jacket. He would have to pose for her some more so she could get it exactly right.

The knock at her door penetrated slowly, and

she whirled around, wiping her hands on her apron as she answered it. Rupert stood there, his arms filled with a long blue gown, his expression exasperated.

"I've been knocking for five minutes," he said.

"Sorry. I was working." She held open the door to let him in.

"Where should I put this?"

She directed him to a nearby chair. After he placed the gown there, he pulled a box out from under his arm and handed it to her.

"Mrs. Karakov said this was to go with it." He gave her an impish grin.

Cynda resisted the urge to peek, not wanting Rupert there to view her reaction. "Thank you, Rupert." She tipped him generously.

The money disappeared into his pocket in one smooth gesture. "Thank you." He started to leave, then paused before the half-completed portrait. "Hey, that's good."

She laughed. "You don't have to sound so surprised."

A flush crept up his neck. "Well, some folks were saying that the prince . . . that you and he . . . that you weren't really painting a portrait."

Cynda didn't need much imagination to conceive the stories being circulated throughout the hotel. "Well, as you can see, I am painting his portrait." She fixed him with a stern glare. "Perhaps you can set some of these folks straight."

The porter swallowed, his Adam's apple bobbing in his throat before he produced a wobbly grin. "I can do that." He almost ran from the room.

She sighed. Perhaps she shouldn't attend the ball with Dimitri if this kind of talk was going around.

Straightening, she shook her head and laughed. *Just listen to yourself.* She was beginning to sound as though she belonged in this time period. People liked to gossip. If they wanted to gossip about her and Dimitri, let them. When she presented her finished portrait, they would all see they were wrong.

She approached the chair and set the box upon it so as to examine the dress. It shimmered in a royal blue color, the flared sleeves trimmed with gold embroidery and the skirt long and full. The front had laces crisscrossing up the bodice, and the waist was a slight vee-shape forming the bottom of the laces.

What was she supposed to be? A princess? Stroking the silky material, she sighed. It was beautiful. She couldn't wait to try it on. Would it fit?

She peeked in the box next and found a silky gold chemise lying on top, evidently to wear with the dress. Beneath it lay a shimmering pair of gold-colored shoes. How could Sophie ... or even Rupert know her size?

Cynda shook her head. She would clean up and dress first, then try the shoes and see how they fit.

The dress fit as if tailored for her, the neckline curving low to reveal just a hint of her breasts, the lacing allowing some of her chemise to show through while producing impressive cleavage. The skirt skimmed over her hips and grazed the floor, the fullness of it moving with her.

She felt beautiful.

The box also contained a circlet of matching

blue cloth, caught in a roll and wound with gold strips, obviously meant for her head. She left her hair long after brushing it until it shone, then placed the crown on her head.

Now for the shoes. She slid one on with trepidation and put her weight on it gingerly. It fit well, again as if designed for her. After sliding into the mate, she walked across the room, enjoying the sensuous feel of the dress molding to her torso and caressing her hips. What would it be like to dance in this?

She would soon find out.

The final addition was a mask, blue to match her dress and trimmed with gold. Thank goodness she could see through it just fine.

A sharp rap at the door made her catch her breath in a gasp. Releasing it slowly, she went to answer it.

Dimitri stood there looking more untamed than she had ever seen him. He wore a plain white shirt, the cuffs rolled up, and over it a jerkin of dark forest green. A wide belt encircled his waist with a sword hanging in a scabbard. His muscular legs were encased in form-fitting pants of a gray-green color, and dark green boots rose to mid-thigh. A black mask covered his eyes.

If looking at him hadn't revealed his costume identity, the large bow he held in one hand and quiver of arrows thrown over one shoulder would have given it away. Cynda laughed. ''You're Robin Hood.''

He bowed, a twinkle in his gray eyes. ''At your service, Maid Marian.''

She glanced down at the dress. ''Oh, so that's

who I am." She grinned. "Sophie is a very devious woman."

"I never doubted that for a moment." His gaze lingered on her, his eyes darkening to the pewter she loved so well. "You're beautiful."

Cynda had to swallow to ease the growing tightness in her throat before she could reply. "Thank you."

He smiled, melting her bones, and extended his arm. "Shall we visit Grandmère before we depart for the ball?"

Sophie clapped her hands when they entered her room. "You are magnificent together. I knew you would be."

"Excellent choice, Grandmère." Dimitri presented a regal bow. Following suit, Cynda dropped into a curtsey, the movement of the dress around her making her feel as though she did this all the time.

"Thank you, Sophie," she added.

Sophie leaned back against her pillows. "I doubt I will be awake when you return tonight, but tomorrow I insist on hearing everything. Who dressed in what costume, the orchestra, the dances."

"I'm certain we can make arrangements to bring you down to the ball," Dimitri said. "Dr. Ziegler does have the stretcher available."

"Thank you, my dear, but I would only fall asleep after an hour. Better I stay here and imagine how grand it is." She patted her cheek. "Now give me a kiss and go on."

Dimitri kissed her cheek lightly. When Sophie glanced at Cynda and raised her eyebrows, Cynda hurried to kiss the paper-thin cheek herself. "Rest well, Sophie," she murmured.

"Have fun," the elderly woman said.

Dimitri paused in the main room to set the bow and quiver by a chair.

"Hey, that's cheating." Cynda grinned at him. She had been wondering how he would manage to dance while hanging on to a bow as long as he was tall.

"It may be more authentic, but it's also a nuisance." He winked at her. "Grandmère has seen the image she wanted to see." Taking her arm, he opened the door. "And we shall have an evening unencumbered."

The faint strains of music greeted them as they drew near the ballroom, and dancing started in Cynda's stomach as her nerves jitterbugged. Would she make a complete fool of herself? It had been ages since she had been dancing, and that hadn't been close to anything these folks were likely to do.

She hesitated. Maybe she should turn around before it was too late.

As if sensing her thoughts, Dimitri lifted her hand to his lips, the touch of his mouth affecting her nerves in a different manner. "Don't worry," he murmured, his eyes dark beneath his mask. "I won't desert you."

Her smile was shaky. "I'll hold you to that."

Tightening his hold on her arm, he led her inside the elegant ballroom. Always before it had appeared forlorn and empty when Cynda had passed it, but not tonight. Gaslight candelabras stood around the edges of the room, providing a softened light. An orchestra occupied a platform at one end, blending from one tune into the next.

Though it was early in the evening, many people

filled the room, dressed in a vast array of costumes. Evidently this time period went all out for Halloween.

Cynda cringed, remembering the year she had merely put her hair in a ponytail and declared she was Barbie. These folks knew how to party.

Pausing by the first of several tables laden with food and drink, Dimitri motioned toward a mammoth bowl of punch. "Are you thirsty?"

"Not yet." She couldn't look away from the elegance and the costumes. Though she easily recognized some of the hotel residents, she was willing to suspend disbelief and imagine them as their characters. Apollo walked by, followed by a milk maid and Caesar. And was that Miss Sparrow dressed as Athena? Cynda swung around to smile at Dimitri. "This is incredible."

His gaze didn't leave her. "Yes, it is."

Her cheeks grew warm, the touch of his eyes almost as potent as a physical touch. She dropped her gaze. She didn't dare give in to the yearning to touch him, the longing to be with him. He had made his position on that quite clear.

Several couples moved to the center of the room as the orchestra launched into a lively tune. Dimitri extended his hand. "Shall we dance?"

"I'm afraid I don't know all the steps."

He closed his hand over hers. "I will teach you." At once, the arrogant future king was in control as he pulled her onto the floor.

Despite her initial rush of panic, Cynda discovered he was a good teacher or the dances weren't as difficult as she thought. Though she made many a misstep, she enjoyed it all, and Dimitri was a great partner.

Midway through the evening, she noticed several of the older women watching her with Dimitri. Cynda didn't need to be a mind reader to know what they were thinking. Their sour expressions said it all. She tugged Dimitri off the dance floor to the side.

He immediately fetched them glasses of punch, and Cynda downed hers gratefully. "I believe we're the center of some discussion," she said quietly.

When Dimitri raised his eyebrow, she motioned toward the gossips along the wall. "Why don't you ask some of the other women to dance? It might calm them down," she added.

He looked offended at her suggestion. "But I promised not to desert you."

"I'm over my initial nervousness. I'll be fine." At the moment, she just wanted to sit down. Her feet were already swelling within the beautiful slippers. "Go on, Dimitri. You have an image to maintain. I don't."

His princely mask slid into place, and he gave her a formal bow. "As you wish." Turning, he approached a young woman standing nearby and soon led her onto the floor.

Cynda sighed. She was a fool. What did it matter what the old biddies said? It didn't matter . . . to her. But it did to Dimitri. Someone so aware of status and rank as he would hate being the center of gossip. Though Cynda doubted he could avoid it as a prince.

His new dancing partner smiled at him, all charm and grace, and Cynda turned away, not wanting to watch. These women knew how the game was played. Too bad Cynda didn't know how to be anyone but herself.

Unable to find any chairs, Cynda leaned against a pillar and closed her eyes. The night was wonderful, like being a part of a fairy tale. She scrunched her toes in her shoes. Would it all end at midnight when she once again turned into a simple artist?

Opening her eyes, she immediately sought out Dimitri on the dance floor. He had changed partners, and this woman played the coquette even better than the first one. *If she bats her eyes any harder, she'll fly away.*

"Cynda?"

She started, then smiled as she recognized Alexi in a musketeer costume. "You look very dashing, Alexi."

He bowed low with a sweep of his plumed hat. "Many thanks." Straightening, he extended his arm. "May I have the pleasure of this dance?"

When she hesitated, he produced a charming grin. "As a friend?"

"I would love to dance with a friend." She took his arm and entered the floor. As the night grew later, the orchestra played many more waltzes—the one dance Cynda did know—and this was one.

Keeping one hand on her waist, he held the other high as he whirled across the floor, his movements as smooth and elegant as Dimitri's. "You're a very good dancer," Cynda said. "No wonder all the women fall at your feet."

"Except you." He said the words with good humor, but Cynda watched him closely until she spotted Dimitri waltzing behind his brother, an attractive brunette in his arms.

Her chest tightened, but she tried to ignore it. After all, she had told him to dance.

"My brother is a very good dancer as well," Alexi said abruptly.

Cynda forced her gaze back to his face. "Yes, he is."

"Has he mentioned that he is betrothed to a childhood friend of ours?" Though Alexi spoke casually, Cynda sensed an undercurrent of emotion in his voice, almost a warning.

"As a matter of fact he has." She struggled to keep her tone even despite her inner turmoil. If only that fact could stop her from wanting Dimitri. She waited until he met her gaze. "Don't worry, Alexi. He's in no danger from me. I'm leaving in December, and you'll never see me again."

Alexi frowned. "That isn't what I want."

"What *do* you want?" Better to be direct. Would she get a direct answer?

He hesitated, his expression solemn, and turned to look at Dimitri. "I want what he has."

Cynda's heart skipped a beat. Alexi wanted the kingdom? To take Dimitri's place? "And you would do whatever it takes to get it?" she suggested softly.

Alexi stopped in mid-motion and stared at her as if he had never seen her before. "Of course not. Despite what you may think of me, Cynda, I have honor and pride as well as my brother."

"I didn't mean—"

He didn't let her finish, but escorted her off the floor and left her after a brief bow.

Well, she had blown that. But she had to know. Alexi's denial had been passionate. Would something happen to make him misdirect that passion in the future?

Before she could move away, an older man bowed before her. He wore a black cloak that covered his head and body, giving her no clue to his identity. When he offered his arm, she grimaced, but took it. After all, Dimitri was dancing with every woman in the room.

Another waltz played, and he guided her through the steps, not nearly as polished as the princes. "Who are you supposed to be?" Cynda asked. His silence unnerved her.

"Death." He gave her a leering grin that she recognized at once. He was the man Dimitri had punched.

She stiffened and tried to pull free, but he only tightened his hold, pulling her closer. "You're going to come with me," he said quietly, menace in his voice.

"Oh, am I?" Obviously, he didn't know who he was dealing with. "Then what?" Her heart pounded rapidly, but she remained calm.

"There are others who feel as I do, that these foreigners should go back where they came from." Again he presented his repulsive grin. "I believe that prince of yours will come after you and we'll have him."

Her breath caught in her throat. "What do you plan to do to him?"

"You don't need to worry about that. You'll be busy." His gaze dropped to her cleavage.

Cynda shuddered. Monet would rise from his grave before she allowed this man to follow through with his plan. She inhaled to scream, then froze as a sharp point pressed against her abdomen. The man held a small knife, using their bodies to hide it.

"I wouldn't do that." He danced toward the doors. "Come with me now."

Swallowing, she complied. Was this man the one who would kill Dimitri? Would she be an unwitting accomplice?

She had to do something.

But what?

Chapter 12

Cynda had one advantage. Her captor expected her to be a helpless female. And she didn't plan to be that.

She waited until they were near the edge of the room, then pretended to stumble. As he tried to catch her, she wrapped one foot behind his leg and pulled. He fell, his grip loosening. Not giving him a chance to react, she thrust the heel of her slipper into his groin . . . and twisted. His cry of agony permeated the ballroom as he rolled into a ball, and everyone turned their way.

Cynda backed away, the damage done. He wasn't going to move very fast for a while.

Hands came down on her shoulders, and she jumped, wresting free, then realized it was Dimitri. With a shudder, she let him pull her against his chest. "Are you all right?" he murmured.

She nodded. "He wanted to hurt you."

"Me?" Dimitri's surprise gave way to a frown as he watched the man writhe on the floor. "How? By hurting you?"

"He planned to kidnap me so you'd come after me. Then he had other plans for you." She glanced up. "He didn't say what, but I don't think he wanted to shake your hand."

Dimitri's hold tightened. "It appears I do have an enemy." He motioned toward the Major, who had just reached them. "Where is Chief Garrett? I want this man arrested."

"I'm here." Jess came up beside Dimitri, Corrie at his side. "What happened?"

Cynda quickly explained the situation, and Jess's expression grew grave. "Are you hurt, Miss Madison?"

She shook her head. "I can take care of myself."

To her surprise, Corrie gave her a thumbs-up sign.

Cynda blinked.

A thumbs-up sign?

Jess yanked the man to his feet. "Come along, Mr. Johnson. I have a cell waiting for you."

Still groaning, Johnson rose, then spat toward Cynda and Dimitri. "You'll be sorry," he shouted. "You'll both be sorry."

"Sweet guy," Corrie said, her voice dry. She paused to squeeze Cynda's arm. "Don't worry. Jess will ensure he's locked up. In fact, I plan to accompany Jess. He has this thing about not drawing his gun." She grinned wickedly. "I don't."

"Thank you." Dimitri nodded his head at Corrie before she hurried to join her husband. A crowd of people had gathered, and he addressed them

in his most majestic voice. "There is nothing more
to see here."

"Move along," the Major added. "Five minutes
until midnight."

The crowd dispersed, and Dimitri bent his head
close to Cynda's. "Do you wish to go now?"

"No." She stepped out of his hold. That crazy
old man wasn't going to spoil her magical evening.
"It's almost time to unmask. I want to see that."

He cupped the side of her face in one broad palm.
"Are you certain? I felt you shaking."

"I'm fine." She forced a smile. "More angry than
anything else. Who does he think he is?"

"Again you amaze me, Cynda. You are a unique
woman."

"You won't find another like me." *Except for,
perhaps, Corrie Garrett.*

He dropped his hand and placed it at the small
of her back. "Let me get you a drink. Champagne,
I think."

"Champagne makes me light-headed."

"All the better. Whether you want to admit it or
not, you have had a shock."

She wasn't the timid, fainting type, but after sipping a glass of champagne, she did feel better. In
fact, with Dimitri offering such devotion and
personal care, she felt downright good. "I guess I
did need a drink."

Before he could reply, the countdown began to
midnight. "Four ... three ... two ... one. Midnight."

The crowd roared in approval and removed their
masks. Dimitri reached out and gently took Cynda's
mask from her face, then smoothed her hair back
in place. "You're unmasked, Miss Madison."

"Do I turn into a pumpkin now?" she quipped.

He stuffed his own mask beneath his belt. "No, I'm not about to let you get away that easily."

The orchestra started on another piece, and Dimitri pulled her onto the floor. "This is my dance, I believe."

He kept his hand on her back, holding her close, but with Dimitri she didn't mind. It was heaven. His steps grew smaller, slower as he steered her toward a dark corner. Giving in, she rested her head against his shoulder as they moved together.

"I noticed you danced with nearly every other woman here," she murmured.

He chuckled. "You noticed?"

"They were very proper, too."

"Oh, very proper, very genteel, very adept at flirting with a prince. But they were not one thing." He stopped in the shadows, and she glanced up at him.

"What's that?" Surely they were everything Victorian women were supposed to be.

"You." His dark gaze lit with amusement. "I do believe you have ruined the prim and proper woman for me. Not one of them told me I was arrogant and proud."

Cynda grinned wryly. "Which probably meant you were behaving yourself."

"I was." He ran one hand over her hair, then cradled the back of her head. "Only with you do I want to misbehave."

She didn't reply. She couldn't. Her throat wouldn't allow words to pass through. Oh, Lord, did he know how much she wanted him to misbehave?

"I don't know what to do with you, Cynda." His

voice grew husky. "I am going to be king. I have duties, responsibilities. And you are . . ."

"A servant," she finished. He would never forget that. She tried to ease away, but he kept his hold firm.

"And more," he added. "So much more that it frightens me."

"I frighten *you*?" Wasn't it her heart she heard pounding so rapidly?

"You make me want things I can't have, imagine things that aren't possible."

"Anything is possible," she said softly. *Including time travel.*

"Perhaps in your world, but not in mine." He sighed, even as he brought his other hand up so he could capture her face between his palms. Tracing her lips with his thumb, he held her gaze, a fire banked low in his.

Cynda's breath caught in her chest. Her stomach knotted. She slid her hands over his jerkin, the feel of his tight muscles beneath her palms adding to her inner tension. The music continued, but she barely heard it.

She existed for here. Now. The scent and feel of Dimitri.

He dipped his head toward hers, their breath mingling. Just as she angled her mouth to fit his, he released her with a groan and turned away. "I can't."

Why didn't he slap her? It would hurt less. Cynda drew in a ragged breath, but didn't speak until he swiveled to look at her. "I think I would like to return to my room now."

He nodded. "Very well." He offered her his arm,

but she brushed past it and toward the doors. She didn't dare touch him.

They remained silent on the journey to the tower suites. When they reached Cynda's rooms, Dimitri unlocked the door, then gave her the key. "Good night," he whispered.

She didn't answer. She couldn't, not with unshed tears clogging her throat. Giving him a brief nod, she entered her room and pushed the door shut.

Moonlight illuminated the main room, and she paused in the middle, wrapping her arms around herself. When would she learn? Dimitri might be attracted to her, but he would never do anything to endanger his coronation and his upcoming marriage. She had to remember that.

The muted light cast a glow on her semicompleted portrait, and she found her gaze drawn to Dimitri's majestic figure. His eyes were warm, almost as if he were standing before her in life, and a hint of a smile played around his lips. Cynda blinked as a strong sense of déjà vu swept over her.

As realization dawned, she gasped and went closer to touch the face. It couldn't be. It was impossible.

But hadn't she just said anything was possible?

She had thought she was modeling this painting after the one she had restored, but that wasn't true.

This *was* the painting she had restored.

Running her fingers lightly over the brush strokes she had so painstakingly uncovered, she stared at the canvas. This was the painting that kept her awake nights, that had called to her even in her own time.

A painting so full of vitality and life that she never would have believed she had painted it.

A painting of the man she loved.

"Oh, God." Cynda groaned and turned away. It was true. She had fallen in love with this arrogant prince. How could she when she knew they had no future, when he had a kingdom to run and she a different time to which she must return?

Another thought crept up on her slowly, and she pivoted to face the portrait again.

The dented nameplate had sent her back in time. The dented nameplate belonged to this portrait. Somehow . . . someway, it played a part in Dimitri's murder.

"No!" She couldn't allow that to happen. She had to tell Dimitri, had to warn him and make him believe her.

Whirling around, she rushed for the suite door and yanked it open only to find Dimitri standing there, his hand poised to knock. She stared at him in surprise as he entered the room and closed the door.

"I need you, Cynda." The roughness of his voice tugged at her. "Tonight I am a man and you are a woman and there is nothing else."

Unable to believe her ears, she tried to speak. "Dimitri—"

He stopped her words with his lips as he pulled her into a firm embrace, one hand cradling her head, the other wrapping around her waist. He claimed, he sought, he gave . . . and Cynda forgot everything else as she responded to her rising passion.

His mouth seduced hers, his lips drinking of hers, his tongue delving inside to stroke hers. She moaned and gripped his jerkin to hold him near.

He tasted of champagne, adding to the headiness invading her body.

She wanted this, wanted him. He was right. There was nothing else.

He left her lips, his breath ragged, and nibbled his way down her neck, nipping slightly at her pounding pulse. Desire, fiery hot, shot through her. Her knees wobbled.

Locating the vee of his shirt, she slid her hands inside, over the dark curls and sculpted muscles. Heat radiated beneath her palms, the same heat that filled her.

Abruptly, Dimitri caught her hands in his and drew apart. "Tell me to stop now," he said huskily, "or I won't be able to later."

She leaned forward to nip at his chin. "Don't stop. Whatever you do, don't stop."

With a groan he released her hands and swung her into his arms and headed for her bedroom. Cynda touched his chest again with one hand, the other weaving through the hair over his collar. She had never felt as alive as at this moment.

He placed her on her feet beside the bed, steadying her with his hands on her arms, his gaze so dark she could barely see it. "I can't marry you," he murmured.

"I know." Holding his gaze, she reached down to undo his belt. It thudded to the floor, echoing in the silence.

A shudder shook his body, but he remained still as she loosened the lacings on his jerkin so that it hung loosely on his frame, allowing her easier access to the roughness of his chest. Leaning forward, she planted kisses over it, nipping at his erect nipple and reveling in his groan of pleasure. While she kissed along his throat to his chin, she ran her hands beneath the jerkin and shirt to the flat plane of his stomach, along the narrowing band of hair that led into his pants, and over the thick hardness of his erection.

"Make love to me, Dimitri," she rasped.

With a growl, he seized her head between his hands and claimed her mouth as if branding her. He drank her moans and gasps, his lips molding to hers with a hungry fierceness . . . a fierceness she echoed.

He released her head to cup her buttocks and pull her firmly against his groin. His erection rubbed against her through her petticoats, but it wasn't enough. Too many layers separated them.

Grasping the end of his jerkin and shirt, she tugged them over his head and dropped them to the floor. His chest gleamed in the moonlight, a dream come to life.

Dimitri chuckled. "You are not what I expected, Cynda."

She answered with a slow grin. "Well, I've never been called prim and proper."

"Good." Holding her away from him, he proceeded to unlace the front bindings of her dress, then eased it off her shoulders and hips until it fell around her feet. He continued by untying her petticoats so that they joined her dress.

She stood before him in her chemise, pantalettes, and corset, her breasts more revealed than covered. The tight corset threatened to rob her of the ability to breathe, and she almost sobbed with relief when he removed that next.

Cupping her breasts through the chemise, he ran his thumbs over her taut nipples, and she gasped with the arrow of desire that pierced her. Dimitri kissed her again as he continued to torment her breasts, making her squirm with frustration.

Finally he left her lips and kissed his way to her breasts, easing her chemise down ahead of his path. When he drew her nipple into his mouth, she cried out in pleasure. Nothing . . . no one had ever been like this. With each touch, she felt as if they were melting into one.

She clasped his head to her, her fingers stroking his silky hair, even as her knees grew weak. He gave each breast equal attention, bringing her blood to a boil. When she could no longer endure it, she tugged at his hair to bring his lips back to hers.

Her chemise joined the pile of clothing on the floor as her insides clenched tighter, grew hotter. "I need you, Dimitri," she whispered, running her hands over his back. She gently tickled his ear with her tongue. "I want you inside me."

"Impatient, are we?" She could hear his smile before he dropped to one knee before her and lifted her foot to remove first one slipper, then the other, his gaze never leaving hers, the heat in it enough to surpass any summer day.

With deliberate slowness, he removed her stockings, leaving her clad in only her pantalettes. Fire scorched her blood. She could barely draw a complete breath. Time stopped, waiting, as if her entire life until this moment had led to this.

She reached for the waist of her pantalettes, but he covered her hands with his and removed them. "In time."

Groaning with frustration, she swiped at his head. "Dimitri." If he didn't take her soon, she would be nothing more than a puddle on the floor.

To her surprise, he swung her into his arms again, cradling her against his chest, his flesh as hot as hers. Then, with a gentleness she hadn't expected, he lowered her to the bed. "You are exquisite." He ran his hands over her face, throat, and torso to her pantalettes and drew them off with excruciating slowness. Finally she was completely bare.

He stared at her, but she didn't feel exposed. Rather, a rightness settled over her, as if she belonged with this man forever, as if this moment was destined.

"You're still wearing too much," she said, propping up on her elbows.

"That can be remedied." In several swift movements, he removed the remainder of his clothing, and now Cynda stared.

He was magnificent, his erection jutting from between his muscular thighs. She grew even more damp, more uncomfortable with longing. "You are awesome," she told him. "Prince or no prince."

"There is no prince tonight." Joining her on the bed with a swiftness that startled her, he sought her lips again as his body covered hers, her breasts tight against his chest, his erection teasing her cleft.

She rocked her hips, wanting more, wanting him. With her palms against his back, she tried to pull him even closer. His lips drew on hers as her softness melted against his hard body.

"There is only a man," he whispered against her mouth, "desperate with wanting you."

"And a woman equally desperate," she added. "Be one with me, Dimitri."

Another shudder shook his body. "I'm afraid it may be too late for that."

"What?"

His answer was to ease their bodies apart until he could kneel between her thighs. She expected him to enter her, but instead he found her swollen nub with his hand and stroked it, watching her as she erupted in a shuddering orgasm.

Before her shudders finished, he dove into her as if claiming a new kingdom, his kingdom. Cynda cried out and lifted her hips to meet him, welcoming the feel of him inside her. Very well, let him conquer a kingdom. She would conquer the king.

He didn't move, his erection pulsing within her womb. "Are you all right?"

"I'm very all right." Clasping his back, she tugged him tighter against her, and he responded with pounding thrusts that filled her, claimed her, shattered her. Nothing in her life had prepared her for this.

As she exploded again, she bit back the words that threatened to escape. She loved him. Would always love him. But he didn't need that complication in his already complicated life.

She kissed him thoroughly as he poured his seed into her with a groan. Collapsing atop her, he supported himself on his elbows. "Cynda, sweet, sweet, Cynda."

For her, it had been a joining in every sense of the word. No matter how many decades separated them, this man would always be a part of her soul.

Easing to her side, he wrapped one arm around her to draw her close, her head on his shoulder, then smoothed her hair back from her face. "There will never be another woman like you."

No, not like her. Only his wife.

Cynda blinked back the threatening tears and buried her face against his shoulder. He stroked her hair. "Rest now," he murmured. "Rest, *mon coeur.*"

And eventually, she did.

Chapter 13

Dawn was but a promise on the horizon, yet Dimitri continued to watch the woman sleeping in his arms. She was beautiful, her long lashes fanning on her creamy cheeks, her lips swollen from his kisses.

She had been all he had wanted and more. Her passion rivaled his own and had led to a mating unlike anything in his experience. What they had shared had been more than lovemaking. It had been a bonding, a giving of more than bodies. For once in his life, he had felt treasured for himself and not his birthright.

It terrified him.

He couldn't marry her. His future was laid out for him. Yet, how could he let her go? This intriguing woman who fought him, defied him, had become important. Too damned important.

But by this time next year he would be king. He would have a wife.

Dimitri closed his eyes briefly. The thought of sharing with Anya what he had experienced with Cynda was repulsive. But Anya was the one who would have to bear the heirs to the throne.

He ran his fingertips lightly over Cynda's cheek. What if he left her with child from this night? A royal bastard. His father had many of those.

Grimacing, Dimitri drew his hand into a fist. The last thing he wanted was to be like his father.

Yet he could not imagine a future without this woman, and his father had the solution.

Dimitri would make her his mistress.

Dimitri jerked awake when Cynda stirred in his arms. Sunlight streamed through the heavy burgundy curtains to highlight the gold in her hair. He ran his hand over it, the silky tendrils as soft as the rest of her.

Cynda opened her eyes, blinked, shut them, then opened them again. "Are you really here?" she whispered.

With a chuckle, he bent forward to kiss her. "I'm here." Instantly, he grew hard with need. In fact, he had been craving her all night.

As her lips softened beneath his, sweet and pliable, he slid the comforter down to her waist to reveal her rose-tipped breasts. The nipples peaked in the morning chill, and he reached to caress them, earning a quiet moan from Cynda.

He released her lips, but continued to trace circles around her tightening crests.

Her breathing grew more ragged. "I thought you were a dream."

"A dream, eh?" Pushing her onto her back, he drew one breast into his mouth, teasing the rigid tip with his tongue, while he kept his hand busy caressing her other.

Cynda gasped and arched higher, deeper into his mouth, and he suckled more deeply, taking her into him as she would soon sheath him. She was sweet, hot, passionate. He couldn't resist her.

From the moment he had kissed her, he had known this moment would come, no matter how much he had tried to deny it. She gave him a sense of belonging he had never known. With her, he was a man, and that was all he needed to be.

He mouthed her other breast as he slid his hand lower beneath the comforter to find her wet and ready. When he gently rubbed her swollen nub, she cried out in a sound that was half pleasure and half pain.

"A dream?" he repeated.

He drew back and entered her with one swift movement, burying himself in her welcoming heat. His groan of ecstasy mixed with her gasp. Her muscles clenched around him, and he froze for a moment, afraid this wonderful sensation would end too soon.

Cynda slid her hands over his chest, then surprised him by wrapping her legs over his hips, allowing him to plunge even deeper. Heaven.

He found his rhythm and made her his. She was a part of him now. Nothing . . . no one . . . would equal this, and he would allow nothing to take her from him.

"Dimitri!" She cried out his name as she arched

against the bed, and her muscles vibrated around him, bringing him to his release.

His breathing ragged, he pinned her beneath his body as he captured her lips again, claiming her. Her passion equaled his as she returned his kiss, running her hands over his back and lower to squeeze his buttocks.

He rocked against her, growing partially erect inside her. What was it about this woman? She lacked proper upbringing and opposed him constantly, yet he wanted her more each minute.

Placing kisses over her cheeks, her nose, her eyelids, he smoothed back her tousled hair. "You are mine now," he declared.

"Oh, am I?" She sounded amused, and Dimitri frowned. He was quite serious.

"You will be my mistress." She tensed beneath him, and he hurried to reassure her. "I will find a place for you near the castle where we can be discreet. You will be well taken care of."

She pushed hard at his shoulders. "I don't think so."

Her rejection stunned him, and he allowed her to slide out from beneath him. Grabbing a sheet, she wrapped it around herself, then faced him, her blue eyes sparking. "I have no intention of being your mistress," she declared.

Dimitri stood slowly, his blood going cold. Here he had thought she was different from other women. "I will not marry you."

Rolling her eyes, she released her breath in a huff. "I don't expect you to marry me. I know that will never happen."

He blinked. Again she surprised him. "Am I

mistaken? I believe you shared my pleasure in our joining.''

Her expression softened. "Dimitri, it was wonderful. Beyond wonderful.''

Taking her shoulders, he pulled her into his arms, and she didn't resist. Instead, she leaned her head against his shoulder with a sigh. "Then, you will be my mistress.'' He had made up his mind. "For I intend to share many more nights like this with you.''

She looked up at him, sorrow in her gaze. "No, Dimitri. You've told me about your parents and their marriage. I don't intend to let your children suffer what your parents have done to you.''

Guilt poured through him like hot oil. The last thing he wanted to do was harm his future children. Painful memories of listening to the arguments between his parents filled his mind. He had wanted to help, to stop the bitter words, yet hadn't known how. He closed his eyes for a moment. How easily he could dismiss his principles for sexual gratification. She was right.

Yet after all they had shared, how could he let her go?

She withdrew from his embrace and walked to the window. "Besides, I'll be leaving soon.''

"There is no urgency.'' He spoke quickly, battling a sudden surge of panic.

"I'm afraid I have a time limit.'' She pushed her hair back, hair he longed to run his fingers through, then faced him again. "I have something I have to tell you. I doubt you'll believe me, but it's urgent that you do.''

The seriousness of her tone sent a chill along his spine. "What is it?'' Was she married?

Instead of responding, she padded into the main room and stared at his portrait. Dimitri tugged on his trousers and went to stand behind her.

"This portrait survives over a hundred years," she said. "It even makes it through a fire."

Dimitri wrapped his arms around her, pulling her back against him. She wasn't making any sense. "Cynda—"

"Dimitri, I restored this exact same portrait back to its original state."

What? He didn't understand. Was he missing something in her English?

She turned to face him, her face so solemn he ached. "I'm from the future, from the year two thousand and one." Her words tumbled out in a rush.

Dimitri stared at her. The future? Impossible. Had she hit her head? Had last night's episode at the ball upset her more than he thought? "Cynda—"

"Don't patronize me."

The firm set of her jaw indicated she meant what she said. But how could she?

"There was a nameplate that went on this portrait. When I found it, I was thrown back in time to here, to you." She bit her lip. "I think I'm here to save your life."

That again. After last night he might believe some danger existed, but that didn't make her from the future. "And you did," he said.

She shook her head. "According to an article I read in the *Hope Springs Times*, you were killed on December twelfth, here at The Chesterfield."

Just over a month away. Dimitri shrugged off the cold fingers that scraped his neck. He couldn't believe her.

Evidently she read his dismissal of her words on his face, for she grabbed his arm. "Believe me, please. The nameplate had a dent in it, like from a bullet."

"There is no nameplate." In fact, the portrait was still only about half complete.

"You have to leave here before it's too late."

The urgency of her voice created a lump in his throat. Obviously she believed this foolishness. He drew her into his arms again. If only Drake Manton, the well-known mesmerist, was visiting the resort, Dimitri could take Cynda to visit him.

"I couldn't leave Grandmère even if I wanted to." He kissed her forehead. "I'll be fine."

She trembled, and he tightened his hold. Until this moment, he never would have believed she was subject to such fantasies. Somehow he had to clear this idea from her mind.

"Come, get dressed and I'll go change. We can work on the painting."

"No." She pulled free and advanced on the portrait. "I can't finish it. I have to destroy it. If it's not here, then maybe you won't be killed."

She lifted her hand as if to smash the canvas, and Dimitri rushed to grab it. "You will not destroy this portrait." He needed it to remind him of Cynda.

As if he would ever forget her.

"This portrait could get you killed."

"Nonsense. This portrait has been commissioned, and you are obligated to finish it."

When she shook her head again, he increased the pressure of his fingers around her wrist. "If you don't finish the painting, then you no longer have need of a sponsor."

Her stunned expression revealed that she understood. Without his patronage, she would have nowhere to go.

"You would do that?" she asked in disbelief.

He fixed his gaze on her. "I would." But he trusted her common sense would not force him into such an action, for he doubted he could send her away.

Her surprise gave way to a momentary bleakness that made him yearn to hold her again. She tugged her wrist free, glaring at him. "Very well." Her voice was cold. "Then, I'll finish the damned thing."

She entered her bedroom and slammed her door. Dimitri sighed. Couldn't she see he was doing this for her own good? She needed an activity to keep her mind off these delusions, and he needed her . . . in his life, if not in his bed.

He stared at the portrait only to encounter his mocking gaze. How could she possibly be the one to paint it, then restore it a hundred years later? She might be an extraordinary woman, but she was not from the future.

Shaking his head, he headed for the suite door. Perhaps he could ask Drake Manton to make a special visit.

For now he needed to figure out how to get into his room before Alexi or his grandmother saw him.

He wanted her to finish the portrait? She would finish the portrait all right, but not until after December 12. Over a week later, Cynda was still working on the same small piece of the painting. Thrusting back memories of his delicious lovemaking, she glanced over to where Dimitri stood and returned to slowly detailing his regal jacket.

Very slowly.

But working at this pace gave her mind time to drift. This crest over his breast hid a well-muscled chest that she longed to caress again. The jacket's tailored cut disguised taut thighs and the most wonderful piece of man she had ever experienced.

Her cheeks grew warm as she remembered that wonderful night. She didn't regret it, but it made her want more. And she wouldn't be his mistress, no matter how much she longed for him.

She had heard the anguish in his voice when he had mentioned his parents and his father's mistresses. The agony of his parents' marriage had hurt him. She couldn't compound that hurt. He might want her now, but in time he would hate her for destroying his values.

Besides, she didn't belong here. She came from a world with microwaves and cell phones and Jacuzzis.

Tears stung her eyes, and she blinked them back. It didn't matter. Come the solstice, she was returning home.

"Are you all right?"

She jerked her head up to find Dimitri standing beside the easel, his gaze perceptive. "I'm fine."

She looked away quickly before he could see her desire for him and stared at the portrait, but found no relief there. The same soft pewter eyes captured her heart.

"Is that all the progress you've made?" Dimitri moved behind her. "You've been working for over a week and are still on the jacket?"

"I want to ensure I have the braids correct."

"Cynda . . ." His voice held a warning note.

She didn't look around as she picked up her rag and wiped her hands. "I think we're done for today. I need to go into town and get some more pigments."

Dimitri remained silent for several moments. "Very well," he said. "I will accompany you."

"I prefer to go by myself." The muscles in her neck ached as it was from the tension of being near him and not touching him.

"It is not proper. I *will* accompany you."

He turned toward the door, and she sighed. He was in kingly mode. Arguing wouldn't do much good. Funny how things were proper when it suited him.

Ever since she had made the mistake of telling him she was from the future, he had treated her like a child who had to be kept from running into the street. Except when their gazes met, then his passion struck Cynda with such force she could barely breathe.

He still wanted her.

And Lord knew she wanted him.

How was she ever going to survive the remaining six weeks until she could leave? And how would she ever regain the heart she would most surely leave behind?

Not many people roamed the streets of Hope Springs today. Cynda shivered within her cloak. She understood completely. The icy wind off the mountains pierced right through her clothing. Though they hadn't seen snow since that one unusual day in October, she expected more at any time. Eyeing the dark clouds tumbling over the hills, she grimaced. Maybe even today.

She didn't spend long at the Emporium. She hadn't really needed many pigments, but had wanted to escape Dimitri's presence. Glancing at him, tall and silent beside her, she sighed. Well, that hadn't worked.

"Do you wish to stop at the Café of Dreams?" he asked.

"No, I'm not—" She stopped. If her suspicions were correct, Corrie Garrett might be from the future as well. Would she confirm Cynda's story to Dimitri? Would she confirm anything at all?

Why would she, even if it was true? She was happily married with a wonderful husband, a successful business and a baby. Maybe if Cynda could talk to her alone . . . "Not today."

"Very well." Dimitri touched her elbow and turned her toward the stables where he had left the buggy.

They passed several small groups of men, most of them carrying rifles, and Cynda frowned. The sight of so many guns sent shivers of foreboding down her spine. "Why does everyone have a gun?"

"This is the time of year for hunting," Dimitri replied dryly.

"Oh." She hadn't thought of that. Still, that fact would make it very easy for someone with a gun to approach Dimitri unnoticed.

Evidently her expression gave her away, for Dimitri stopped and swung her to face him. "Cynda, I am not going to die."

She met his gaze, her heart clenching. "I hope not."

"Cynda—" His voice rose, but when a passing

couple glanced at them, he broke off and tugged her into a nearby alley instead. Deep in the dark recesses, he held her shoulders, forcing her to look at him.

"You have to give up this foolishness," he ordered. "You are as likely to be shot at as I am. Johnson is in jail. Chief Garrett has assured me he is not likely to be released any time soon."

"But I'm telling you the truth." She stomped her foot, then grimaced at the childish action. "I read the article with my own eyes. I mourned for you even before I knew you."

His expression softened, and he lifted one hand to the curve of her cheek. "I worry about you, Cynda. There is a mesmerist in Richmond. He helps people with problems like yours. I could take you to see him."

His touch only reminded her how much she wanted him and she found herself leaning into his palm. "I don't need a shrink. What can I do to convince you I am from the future?"

"Show me some proof."

Her hopes dropped. Her clothing had disappeared soon after her arrival, and her purse remained in the dirt and ruin of the future Chesterfield. "I have nothing."

Dimitri lowered his other hand to her waist and drew her closer to his warmth while he continued to caress her cheek. "Then, promise me you will mention this no more."

"I—"

He bent closer, his breath mingling with hers. "Promise me."

With her heart lodged in her throat, Cynda could barely speak. She nodded. She wouldn't mention it, but neither would she forget it. Somehow she would save Dimitri's life whether he believed her or not.

When his lips brushed hers, she sighed, as if she had received a special treat. How could she continue to deny him when she wanted him so badly?

He groaned and embraced her tightly, melding her body along his, leaving her in no doubt that his passion equaled her own. "Cynda." He deepened the kiss, his lips as commanding as his personality.

Cynda clung to him, her limbs melting with desire, her senses reeling. She even heard bells.

Wait! Cynda broke free and looked toward the alley entrance. Those *were* bells.

"What—?"

She glanced toward Dimitri, but he was already rushing into the street to look toward the sound. Hiking her skirt, she ran to his side.

People rushed past them, faces grim.

"What is it?" she asked.

"Fire." Grasping her hand, Dimitri pulled her with him, following the crowd.

Didn't they have a fire department? A truck? Cynda searched her memory for a solution. How did people handle a fire in this time period?

Coming to a halt before a blazing building, she gasped. Flames devoured the structure as if they were a living being. It was the boardinghouse if she remembered correctly.

The solution to the fire-fighting problem became quickly apparent. Townspeople formed a line and hefted buckets of water from one to the other, but they didn't appear to have much effect on the fire.

Dimitri handed Cynda his jacket, and she looked at him in surprise to find him rolling up his sleeves. "Stay here," he ordered. Before she could reply, he entered the line near the well, adding his muscular strength to those dipping buckets in the water.

For a moment she became so caught up in watching him work that she forgot about the fury behind her until part of the building crashed inside. The owner, Mrs. Zimmerman, wailed in her native German, and Cynda hurried over to her.

"It'll be all right." At a loss for words, she murmured the all-occasion platitude.

"All right?" The woman looked at Cynda as if she were crazy. "My home, my business gone. That is all right?"

Cynda cringed. "You can rebuild."

"I haf no money, no husband, no sons. How I rebuild?" Mrs. Zimmerman buried her face in her hands, and Cynda hugged her shoulders, offering what small comfort she could.

The arrival of the pump wagon pulled by horses drew Cynda's attention. The buckets now went to fill the wagon's tanks as men pumped to fill the thick hose with water. Finally, something was working. With luck, the flames would soon be under control.

The surrounding buildings were mostly brick, thank goodness. The fire shouldn't spread if they could contain it now.

Searching for Dimitri, Cynda discovered Alexi had joined his brother in the bucket brigade. The brothers worked together filling the pails and passing them on. Dimitri said something, and Alexi grinned in reply, neither pausing in their smooth movements.

Cynda's stomach clenched. That was how they should be, not feuding with each other. If she hadn't arrived at The Chesterfield, would they have shared this camaraderie or would the animosity still be there?

Watching them, she couldn't believe Alexi would harm his brother. It had to be someone else.

But who?

Johnson was in jail. Still, he had mentioned others who hated foreigners as he did.

She whirled around abruptly to face the fire. Would they also burn the business of a German woman?

Moving one step at a time, she drew closer, searching for obvious clues until the heat forced her back. Any signs of deliberate arson would be destroyed in this.

Unease seeped through her veins. She would never be able to prove it, but she would be willing to bet Johnson's friends had something to do with this.

And that they weren't finished with Dimitri Karakov either.

Chapter 14

Cynda joined the group of women preparing food and drink for the men as they fought the fire. Corrie directed the effort, heedless of the shocked glances at her pants and coolie-style jacket, and Cynda had to admire her. She had obviously made her place in this time.

But Cynda was in love with a man slated to marry another and groomed to be king of his country. There was no place for her in his life or in this time. She would be better off back in the future.

But no matter how many times she told herself that, she still couldn't make her heart believe it.

Night had fallen by the time the fire was extinguished, and with the darkness came the first flakes of snow.

"That will help," Dimitri said as he came to her side. His face, hands and shirt were streaked with soot and dirt, but his grin sent Cynda's heart into cartwheels. How could she not love him?

"I'm proud of you," she said, meeting his gaze. Spotting Alexi behind him, she amended it. "I'm proud of both of you. You must be exhausted."

"Thirsty." Dimitri took a mug from the makeshift table set up in the road and downed its contents in one swallow. Alexi followed suit.

They reached for another mug, then grinning at each other, clanked them together before again draining the ale. Alexi swiped his hand over his mouth. "Now that was good." Replacing his mug, he clapped Dimitri on the back. "I'm off to the hotel."

"You're welcome to ride with us," Dimitri offered. "I brought a buggy."

Alexi's teeth gleamed white in his sooty face. "So did I." His eyes glimmered with mischief. "Want to race?"

For a moment Dimitri looked as though he might accept; then he glanced at Cynda and shook his head. "I am transporting a lady. Perhaps another time."

"I wouldn't mind," Cynda said. A race sounded like fun.

"Perhaps not, but I cannot put you in danger."

"Even if I trust your driving?" She grinned at him and was rewarded with a smiling shake of his head.

"No, Cynda." He took his jacket, which she still had over her arm. "Let us return as well." He glanced at the smoldering remains of the boarding-house. "Tomorrow, work will begin to clean this up."

"I feel so sorry for Mrs. Zimmerman," Cynda

said as they fell into step together. "She has no money and no family to rebuild it for her."

"She will not need them. She has the good people of this town and a prince who is good with his hands."

Dimitri spoke in his imperious manner, so it took Cynda a moment to realize what he had said. She squealed with delight. "You'll pay for her to rebuild?"

"I plan to discuss it with Chief Garrett. I believe we can get a new building in place before winter is completely upon us." Reaching the buggy, he assisted Cynda up, then released the horses and swung onto the seat beside her.

She snuggled next to him despite the smoky smell. "Have I ever told you what a wonderful man you are?"

"Not that I can recall." He directed the buggy onto the road leading to The Chesterfield. "Arrogant, rude, but never wonderful."

Heat filled her cheeks. Well, he was arrogant, but she couldn't imagine him any other way. "Then, let me say it again—you are a wonderful man, Dimitri Karakov." Leaning forward, she pressed a light kiss on his cheek, then made a face at the sooty taste.

Dimitri chuckled. "Wait until I bathe and you can tell me properly." Releasing one hand from the reins, he captured hers within it, his thumb gently stroking her pulse, smearing ashy streaks on her wrist.

Had he noticed how that pulse increased at his touch? Cynda inhaled deeply. "I would think you'd want to go straight to bed."

"Excellent idea." He didn't look at her as he continued. "However, there is only one bed I want to be in."

Heat flooded her veins, and her breasts swelled in response. She wanted that as well, but couldn't. "You know we can't."

"I know we can." His voice deepened. "And I know it would be heaven on earth. But you refuse me. *You* refuse a prince."

"And you know why." Though she had to struggle to remember that point herself.

He sighed and tightened his hold on her hand. "Yes, I know why, but I am not king yet. I am not in my country. I have no wife, no children."

"Not now, but you will." *If he survives through December.* Though she hated to do it, she tugged her hand free of his. "One day you will thank me for being strong."

"I would thank you even more if you weren't."

She glanced at him in surprise, and he gave her a half smile; but the need in his eyes caught at her throat, robbing her of the ability to speak. Looking away, she closed her eyes before she weakened.

Why, when she finally found a man she could love, did it have to be this one?

After reaching the hotel, Dimitri left Cynda at her suite and proceeded to his own. Once inside her room, she sighed and sank onto the bed. It felt like days instead of hours since they had left for town.

She pulled the pins from her hair, then frowned at the aroma of smoke that surrounded her. Obviously, she needed a bath as well. Thank goodness she didn't have to go to the bathhouse; she had her own personal tub complete with hot water.

As she went to run the water, she grinned. At least now she had true appreciation for the simple things in life—like hot water and flush toilets. She stripped down to her chemise and was checking the depth of the water in the large iron tub when a knock sounded at the door.

Drat. She pulled on a robe and held it around her as she inched the door open.

Dimitri pushed his way inside, then kicked the door shut behind him. "Alexi is encamped in our tub with no sign of leaving," he said. Crossing the main room, he left clothing in his path—tie, shirt, trousers—until he stood in the bathroom doorway in nothing but his magnificent nudity. Cynda stared at him, stunned. "Ah, you've already started the water. Excellent."

He had settled himself in the tub by the time Cynda reached the doorway. "That's my bath."

"And you would deny me a chance for cleanliness?" His apologetic tone didn't match the mischief in his eyes.

"There is a bathhouse, you know."

"But why should I go all that way when I can be here with you?" He grabbed a bar of soap and proceeded to wash his hair and face while Cynda gaped at him, her insides humming with desire, while her mind struggled for reason.

After a moment, he paused and held out the soap, humor dancing in his eyes. "Would you mind doing my back?"

She released an exasperated breath but moved forward to take the soap. No sooner had she touched it, than he grabbed her waist and pulled her into the tub with him. "Why not share the bath?"

Water sloshed onto the floor as she gasped, her robe becoming heavy with water. "Are you insane?"

"Frugal," he replied with a grin. "Why waste hot water?"

"You are devious." She struggled to free herself, but the robe held her in place. Muttering beneath her breath, she tugged her arms free and dumped the sodden mess on the floor.

Pushing her hair back, she sat up, straddling his hips.

"Much better." The huskiness of his voice made her follow his gaze to her now transparent chemise, which easily revealed her pebbled nipples. He ran his hands over her back, grasping her bare buttocks to pull her forward so he could capture her breast with his mouth.

Hot need flooded Cynda, threatening the last bits of her protests. She wound her hands into his hair, holding him close, her insides clenching in time with the draw of his mouth. "D ... Dimitri ..." She struggled for words, to stop him, to restore rational thought, but he found her other breast as his hands kneaded her bottom and his erection pulsed against her open cleft.

Oh, Lord, she wanted him. Needed him.

Giving in to desire, she reached into the water to find his swollen erection, reveling in his groan of pleasure. She raised up slightly, then lowered herself onto him, sharing Dimitri's moan as he filled her. More water spilled to the floor.

He kept his grip on her hips, assisting her as she rode him, but the slippery tub made it difficult. When her knee banged the side for the third time, he let out a bellow and stood up, holding her against him so that she was forced to wrap her legs around his waist and cling to his shoulders.

"What are you doing?" she gasped, his movements adding to the tension building inside her.

"Making you mine," he growled. Holding her hips, he placed her against the cold tile wall and proceeded to finish what she had started. As she gasped, he captured her mouth, his tongue delving inside to mimic his actions.

Cynda matched his thrusts with equal passion. Each movement brought him deeper and swelled her need until she almost sobbed with desire. She climaxed once, then again, rising to meet him until finally he erupted, crying out her name.

For a moment neither of them spoke. Only the sound of their ragged breathing echoed in the small room. Dimitri leaned his forehead against Cynda's. "That was . . ."

"Incredible," she finished. A definite first for her and the most passionate sex of her life. Her insides still pulsed with the final vestiges of her climax. She started to unlock her legs, but Dimitri caught them and held her in place.

"No, not yet." He gently nipped at her lips. "I should like to spend the rest of my life buried inside you."

Her insides knotted again, the banked fires rekindling. "But won't it make it difficult to get anything done?" she asked, biting his chin.

"Nothing that matters." Holding her firmly in place, he left the bathroom and went to sit on the edge of the bed. As she brought her legs down into a kneeling position on the bed, he expertly removed her chemise, then cradled her breasts in his hands. "Now you may begin again."

"Oh, I may?" At his imperious order, she sat back to bring him more firmly inside her and grinned at the darkening of his eyes and his sharp inhale. He grew more firm, regaining new life as she wiggled her hips. "Do you think you can handle it?"

He drew his thumbs over her sensitive nipples, and she arched back, the lightest touch triggering an onslaught of need. "Do your worst," he murmured.

She tried, but bringing him to torturous ecstasy also did the same for herself. He kept his hands busy on her breasts as she rode him, made love to him, became one with him.

When her climax began, he surprised her by flipping her onto her back and plunging harder, deeper, extending her release until she cried out. Then before she could drift to earth again, he increased his rhythm, willing her body to follow, and she did. They were one. Now. Always.

He was made for her.

This was more than a blending of bodies, a sharing of pleasure so intense it rippled along her nerves. When he reached his final glory, burrowing deep within her, she knew she was lost. Her soul was his.

God help her.

You're weak, Cynda. Weak, weak, weak. Cynda berated herself yet again as she worked on Dimitri's portrait. Over a week had passed, and she had managed to avoid Dimitri, but mostly because he was so exhausted each night after spending the day rebuilding Mrs. Zimmerman's boardinghouse.

She had agreed to concentrate her efforts on his portrait while he worked in town. It provided one way she could be with him without the constant temptation of the real thing.

How could she have given in to him so easily? She eyed the portrait and pointed her brush at it. "No," she said firmly. "No, no, no." Much easier to do when he wasn't kissing her, wasn't touching her.

Just remembering those delicious moments of extreme lovemaking sent streams of liquid fire through her veins. Cynda shook her head. *Be strong. Get over him.*

Ha, easier said than done.

If she didn't remain firm in her convictions, she was in real danger of becoming his mistress, and she couldn't do that. No matter how much she loved him, she wouldn't accept just a piece of his life or risk ruining his future with Anya and their potential children.

He was going to be king, and Cynda was . . . what, a struggling artist? A woman out of time? Whatever. She most definitely wasn't royal nor likely to be. Not in any century.

She paused and set down her brush in order to examine the portrait critically. This was her best work ever. Perhaps because her love for Dimitri entered into every brush stroke, the blending of the colors, the attention to detail. He appeared almost alive, with desire glimmering in his eyes, a hint of a smile on his lips and a touch of arrogance in his stance. Very impressive and too handsome to be true.

A fairy tale prince.

With a sigh Cynda pushed back the loose strands of her hair. She would never get the knack of securing the bun on her head.

Abruptly, she glanced back at the portrait. *Oh, no.* She was nearly finished.

She had been so caught up in her dreams over the past several days, she had worked without conscious thought, letting her emotions guide the brush. Well, her emotions had just about completed the thing. The small bit left would only require a couple of days.

Smart, Cynda. This wasn't in her plan.

She cleaned up quickly. No more painting for a while . . . a long while. She didn't dare complete this before the twelfth of December. Dimitri's life depended on it.

Left with time to spend, she headed for town . . . to check on the progress of the boardinghouse. Certainly not to see Dimitri.

The site was a flurry of activity with several men busy on the structure. The exterior was already in place, and Cynda heard hammering from inside. They had made good progress.

To her surprise, Alexi was acting as the coordinator for the project. She approached him with a smile, waiting while he gave directions to two men.

Once they left, he grinned at her. "I believe we'll be done before the end of the month."

"I should think so at this rate." She glanced again at the building. "I didn't realize you knew construction."

He shrugged. "In truth, I don't, but I've helped villagers in my country with similar ventures and quickly discovered I don't have Dimitri's talent with a hammer and saw." Mischief danced in his gaze. "However, I *can* organize."

' A fine talent." With the new boardinghouse

progressing so fast, he obviously organized well. "How many are working on it?"

"I cannot name an exact number as men come and go as they have time available. Perhaps twenty, maybe more. Each contributes whatever skill he can."

"That's wonderful." Would folks in her time be so giving of their time and talents?

At hearing the distant sound of a train whistle, Alexi jerked his head around. "Train's coming."

"That's not the Chesterfield train. It won't be here for another hour."

"I know." Merriment danced in his eyes. "It's the train from New York which means it's four o'clock."

She laughed. "Now that's a unique way to tell time." She looked toward the building. "Can I take a look?"

"If you're careful." Alexi turned to answer a man's question, and Cynda slipped away.

As she drew closer to the structure, she recognized Dimitri's voice inside, but none of the words. She found him exchanging fluent German with Mrs. Zimmerman, who was fawning over him big time.

Not that Cynda could blame her. Dressed in jeans and a plain white shirt, Dimitri looked even better than in his official uniform. Strands of his dark hair fell across his forehead, and a streak of dirt highlighted one cheekbone. For once he appeared as a normal man and was all the more enticing because of it.

His slow smile when he spotted her tangled Cynda's stomach into knots. *No.* She was determined to be strict with herself. *Behave.* But her pulse leapt despite her admonishment.

"Mrs. Zimmerman, have you met Miss Madison?" Dimitri waved Cynda to his side. "She's the one I told you about."

The woman grasped Cynda's hands in hers, tears welling in her eyes. "You are one to tell Prince Karakov about me."

Cynda hesitated. "Well, I did mention it, but he—"

"You are saint." Mrs. Zimmerman squeezed Cynda's hands so tightly, Cynda fought back a wince. "I cook you dinner when I am in my house again."

"I would like that." Cynda extracted her hands while she still had feeling left in them and smiled. "Thank you."

"Thank *you.*" She bobbed her head at Dimitri, patted the package in his hands, then rushed from the structure.

Cynda raised her eyebrows. "Are you telling tales?"

"Only truth."

"Nonsense. You were here fighting the fire. I didn't tell you anything you didn't know."

He tapped her chin with one finger. "Ah, but you cared enough to ensure I knew."

Heat rose in her cheeks. Cynda quickly pointed to the package he held. "What's that?"

"Fresh cinnamon rolls. Mrs. Zimmerman is staying with Mrs. Warshoski for the present and helping out in her restaurant." His grin held an impishness that wound around Cynda's heart. "She's been bringing wonderful baked goods every day. I shall soon be as big as the house itself."

"I think you're working it off." Cynda examined

the interior. The floor for the second story was nearly completed, and the main level had walls clearly laid out. "This is impressive."

Dimitri beamed. "I'd forgotten how good it felt to do this type of thing."

"Once you're king, you'll have to create a workshop so you can do more of it."

His smile faded. "Once I am king, I will no longer have time for such frivolities."

"It's not a frivolity." Cynda touched his arm. He had to believe that. If he didn't find some kind of outlet for pleasure, he would be miserable for the rest of his life. "It's a craft. It's a gift."

"It is not necessary for a king." He looked away, surveying the building. His head lifted, his stance proud. Taking Cynda's arm, he steered her beneath some boards. "Come, let me show you what we have done."

If Cynda hadn't been impressed before, his tour confirmed her first thoughts. He was a wonderful carpenter. Boards meshed perfectly, the craftsmanship evident. Mrs. Zimmerman's boardinghouse would be even better than the original by the time it was completed.

He paused at the rear of the structure by a half-completed chimney, his gaze on Cynda as if her reaction was important.

"This is fantastic, Dimitri." Her enthusiasm was real. "I'm proud of you."

His gaze darkened. "Proud enough to reward me with a kiss?"

"Oh, no." Cynda glanced around, hoping to see other workers. Sounds of hammering reached them, but she saw no one. She put out her hand to keep him away, though he hadn't moved. "No more. I will not give in again."

"You must." As usual when he wanted his way, he spoke with imperiousness. "Memories of you intrude on all my waking moments." He displayed his hand, one fingernail half purple. "I did that when I remembered how good it felt to be inside you and the small whimpers of pleasure you made."

Desire knifed through Cynda, and she stepped back, afraid that if she didn't, she would end up in his arms. "No more, Dimitri. I mean it."

His smile was condescending. "Time will tell." He set his package on a nearby stack of boards, then approached her slowly. If he touched her . . . if he kissed her . . .

Cynda panicked. Hiking her skirt, she ran.

He caught her just outside the building, seizing her shoulders and forcing her to face him. "You cannot escape the inevitable."

"I can't do this." A sob caught in her throat, and his expression grew concerned.

"Do I not pleasure you?" He drew her closer. "Does my touch repel you?"

"You're wonderful," she admitted, "but it's wrong. Each time only makes it worse for when we have to part."

He frowned. "I have not said we will part."

"I have." She struggled to maintain control. "On the solstice, I am going back to my . . . to where I belong."

"What if you belong with me?" His voice grew cold.

"I don't." She searched his face, desperate for him to understand. "You're going to be king.

You're going to marry another woman. There's no place for me in your life, and you know that, Dimitri. You know that."

He could have been a statue for the next few moments. His face revealed nothing. He didn't move.

Finally, he closed his eyes as if in pain and dropped his hands. "We may have no future, but that does not stop me from wanting you now."

"Di—"

The shattering sound of a gunshot cut her off, and Dimitri thrust her behind him as they both turned to see Alexi throwing himself on a man with a rifle.

"Ow." A splinter dug into Cynda's arm, and she glanced over to see a hole in the boards beside her. "Oh, my God." Another couple of inches and that bullet would have hit her or Dimitri.

Dimitri faced her, trying to touch her everywhere at once. "Where are you hurt?"

"I'm okay. Just a splinter." She showed him her arm, and he plucked the sharp piece of wood from her flesh, then wrapped his handkerchief around her arm when it began to bleed slightly.

He glanced at the bullet hole, and his expression darkened even further. He swiftly covered the distance to where Alexi held the man on the ground. "Who are you?" he demanded.

The man spat on Dimitri's boots, and Alexi twisted the man's arm even tighter, his gaze blazing.

Cynda came to Dimitri's side. "He must be one of Johnson's friends." How could someone hate another person that much . . . enough to kill? "I suspect they set fire to Mrs. Zimmerman's place, too."

"We don't need no furriners here," the man declared.

Cynda curled her fists, fighting the urge to kick the man. "What we don't need is your kind," she retorted.

"All right, what's going on here?" Chief Garrett approached, his manner brisk, his gaze encompassing the entire scene.

"A friend of Johnson's, I believe." Dimitri motioned to Alexi to let the man stand. "And an attempt on my life." His tone was cold, hard. "I believe you will find a bullet in the exterior wall of Mrs. Zimmerman's boardinghouse."

"I was afraid of that. Johnson's been as communicative as a dead possum." The chief grasped the man's arm. "Come on. Maybe you'll be better at talking than your friend." He paused to nod at Dimitri. "You must lead a charmed life, Your Highness."

Dimitri released a tight smile. "I believe I do." He squeezed Cynda's hand briefly.

Now that her blood was flowing again, she frowned at him. "Now do you believe me?"

He spread his arms wide. "I am alive, Cynda."

"What if the third time does the trick?" She seized the front of his shirt. "I don't want you to die."

He dropped his hands to her back, holding her close. "I won't die." His voice grew husky. "I have far better plans than that."

She sighed. "Di—"

"Dimitri."

At Alexi's sharp tone, they both looked around. Cynda cringed. She had forgotten he was there.

Dimitri dropped his hands at once and muttered an exclamation in his native language, but his gaze went past Alexi to a woman standing nearby accompanied by an older man and woman. He went to her, still speaking in a language Cynda didn't understand.

But his meaning was clear.

The woman was young, perhaps Alexi's age, with chestnut brown hair coiled neatly atop her head. She wore a velvet cloak trimmed with fur over a gown of obvious elegance. She was lovely, her features aristocratic, her nose slender, her cheekbones clearly defined. She greeted Dimitri with a forced smile, her face revealing little, though the hand she put on his arm indicated possession.

Cynda glanced at Alexi, her chest tight, wishing she could melt into the ground. "Is that . . . ?"

He nodded, his expression grim. "That is Anya."

Chapter 15

"Anya, my dear, what a pleasant surprise." Grandmère extended her hand to draw Anya closer. "However did you get here?"

Her question echoed Dimitri's. The last person he had expected to encounter in America was Anya Vladovitcha, the woman who would be his wife.

"Once I heard of your injury and the delay in your return, I could not bear to be parted from everyone any longer." Anya pressed a kiss on Grandmère's cheek. "I have missed you." Anya glanced back at Dimitri and Alexi. "And my princes."

"You traveled here alone?" Dimitri found it difficult enough to believe she was here. Had she thrown protocol aside as well?

"Most certainly not. Count Gurieli and his wife accompanied me." She sat beside Grandmère on the bed, every bit as relaxed as Cynda when she sat there.

Dimitri chanced a glance at Cynda. He had insisted she accompany them, but her pale face gave evidence of her unease. A part of him longed to draw her into his embrace, to soothe her fears, while the responsible side realized he could no longer evade his duties.

"And you risked your life to come here?" Alexi advanced on Anya, his eyes blazing. "We chose not to return because of the dangerous winter sea, and yet you came?"

Anya gave him a gentle smile and placed her hand on his arm. "Dear Alexi, I have been in America for almost a month, but I was obligated to allow the count to conduct his business first." A gleam of mischief appeared in her brown eyes, reminding Dimitri of the young girl she had once been. "How kind of you to worry about me."

Alexi's smile was rueful. "I never stop worrying. I know your penchant for disaster."

Her laughter was light, airy, cultured, different from the fullness of Cynda's. "I am grown now and far past disasters."

"I'm not so sure about that."

Anya wrinkled her nose at him, then glanced at Dimitri. "You have been very quiet. Are you angry with me, too?"

Not angry, but stunned. "Of course not. I do not think it was wise to come here, but as you arrived safely, how can I complain?"

Anya smiled. "Ever the diplomat."

Dimitri cast a glance at Cynda in time to see the dry twist of her lips. Apparently she didn't agree with that statement.

"You will join us for supper," Grandmère said. "Dimitri, please notify the kitchen that we will have one more."

He nodded, but before he could leave to comply, Cynda stepped forward. "Miss Vladovitcha can take my place. I'll be glad to eat dinner elsewhere."

"Nonsense. Your company is appreciated as well." Grandmère nodded at Dimitri, and he left to make the change, resisting the urge to touch Cynda as he passed.

The meal was lively with Alexi and Anya providing much of the conversation. Cynda was very quiet, but watched closely, obviously absorbing all she could about Anya.

Anya was much as he remembered her from a year ago, though she displayed far more poise now. When with him, she had always seemed afraid, but in this group, she shone.

Until she focused on Cynda.

"And you are the artist?" Anya asked.

"Yes, I'm doing Dimitri's portrait."

Sitting beside Cynda, Dimitri sensed her tension. If only he could reassure her, touch her.

"How wonderful. I shall have to see it." Anya sipped at her wine, then met Dimitri's gaze, apparent innocence in hers. "How American of you to allow your servant to dine with you. I trust your father is not aware of this."

Cynda abruptly pushed back her chair. "Excuse me. I've lost my appetite." Her words were cold. She left quickly before Grandmère could stop her, and Dimitri frowned at Anya.

"That was inexcusable," he said.

"It was?"

Dimitri studied her. How much of this innocence

was real and how much was a carefully cultured performance? "Cynda is our guest at meals."

"She is a servant." Anya spoke matter-of-factly. "You have always thought little of them yourself, which is why I am so surprised you are permitting this one such liberties."

"Cynda is more than a servant." Dimitri rose to his feet, struggling to contain his rising anger. "She is a talented artist and has been accepted by Grandmère and Alexi."

Anya looked at Grandmère, who nodded. "Then, I am truly sorry. I did not mean any offense."

Yes, she had. Anya had meant to put Cynda in her place, to remind her of the difference in their positions. Not so long ago, he would have done the same thing.

But that was before he had met Cynda.

"Please sit, Dimitri, and finish your meal. Anya can make her apologies to Cynda later." Grandmère motioned him to his chair.

Feeling like a chastised child, he resumed his seat, but his appetite had fled as well.

"I do hope to see more of this village while I am here." Anya smiled at Dimitri. "Can I rely on you to escort me? As your intended, I should not need Countess Gurieli as a chaperone."

"I am afraid I will be busy with the rebuilding of the boardinghouse." He much preferred that to accompanying Anya to every shop in Hope Springs. "Alexi can take you."

"Surely you do not need to continue with such manual labor?"

"I enjoy the work." Dimitri held Anya's gaze until she looked away. "And I have promised to help."

"I will be honored to escort you, Anya," Alexi said quickly. "And Countess Gurieli as well, if necessary."

Anya gave Alexi a brilliant smile. "Thank you. I shall look forward to it."

She continued to discuss her trip across the ocean and time in New York City, but Dimitri found his mind wandering to Cynda. If Anya had not been here, he would have gone to her, comforted her. The day had held several surprises for them both.

But Anya was here. He would have to avoid Cynda from now on.

He sighed. He already missed her.

When a knock sounded at the door to Cynda's suite three days later, she ran to answer it. She hadn't seen Dimitri since Anya's arrival, and she had missed him terribly.

But Anya stood outside the door, dressed to perfection in a gown that had obviously been tailored for her. "I have come to watch you paint," she said, entering the room. She stood before the portrait, studying it. "It is a fair likeness."

She glanced around the room, focusing on the book beside the chair where Cynda had been reading. "Are you not working? I assumed that was what you did during the day." Her tone implied the night was better not discussed.

Good thing, too. She might be surprised at what Cynda could tell her.

"I was taking a break."

"I believe Dimitri sponsors you, feeds you. Would

he be willing to do so if he knew you were not painting?"

Guilt sliced through Cynda. Anya had a point. Dimitri did support her, at least while she worked on his portrait. And it appeared his future wife intended to ensure Cynda did work.

Though reluctant, Cynda tied on her apron and mixed her pigments. She had held off painting because the portrait was too close to done. As long as it wasn't finished, Dimitri couldn't die. But now she had an audience who expected her to work. "I thought you were seeing the town," she said as she moved into position before the easel.

"I saw what little there is to this village." Anya settled in a nearby chair as prim and proper as one of the women in *Godey's Lady's Book*. "Now Alexi has gone to help Dimitri with that *boarding-house.*"

Her emphasis on the building revealed her feelings. Evidently, she couldn't understand why the men would choose to work on the house instead of being with her. "It is an important project," Cynda said. "They want to get it done before the end of the month."

"I don't see what difference a few days will make."

"We haven't had a heavy snow yet, though the temperature has dropped. Mrs. Zimmerman would like to be back in her own place before we do."

"It is good they are assisting this community." Anya sounded as though she was trying to convince herself, but Cynda nodded her agreement.

"I think Mrs. Zimmerman is ready to put Dimitri in for sainthood." Cynda met his gaze in the portrait and grinned. Somehow Saint Dimitri didn't fit the simmering passion in those eyes or the way he made her feel with just a casual touch.

"Dimitri is many things, but I do not believe a saint is one of them."

Cynda glanced at Anya. Had the woman made a joke? She wasn't smiling. "I have to agree," Cynda said.

Anya narrowed her eyes as if questioning Cynda's right to know enough about Dimitri to agree. Cynda sighed. This was going to be fun—*not*.

Determined to ignore the woman, she painted. Lost in the pigments and canvas, she had no problem forgetting Dimitri's intended wife sat only a few feet away.

Unfortunately, Anya decided to visit every day for the rest of the week, sitting primly in the same chair, watching Cynda with an intensity Cynda found unnerving. Was the younger woman trying to read Cynda's thoughts, uncover all her secrets? Evidently, she suspected the attraction between Dimitri and Cynda. Was she curious as to how far it went?

Well, Cynda wasn't telling. Dimitri would have to live with Anya for many years. They certainly didn't need to start an arranged marriage with bitterness between them. After all, Cynda was leaving.

"I understand you were a waitress before Dimitri commissioned you," Anya said abruptly.

"That's right. It was a temporary position." Cynda met Anya's gaze. "Before that, I restored paintings."

Anya stood up and walked across the room. "And once you finish with this, you will return to that?"

"Yes." When she returned to her own time.

"Is that why you persist in making this commission take longer than it should? Look." She paused behind Cynda and pointed at the painting. "The portrait is completed. You are doing nothing but pretty little touches."

Cynda stared from Anya back to the painting. Dear Lord, Anya was right. It was done. By trying to keep busy in Anya's presence, Cynda had finished it, down to the last detail. Had she just signed Dimitri's death warrant?

"You're right," she murmured. "It is finished."

"Excellent." Anya headed for the door. "I will notify Dimitri at once. I suggest you begin packing."

She left as Cynda continued to stare at the painting. It was her best work ever. But did she dare give it to Dimitri?

The wind rattled the windowpane, and Cynda turned toward it. She needed to think, and the way she did that best was to sketch. Snaring her pad and pencil, she threw on a cloak and left the suite. She hadn't yet done a winter sketch of the hotel. Today was a good time to do so.

And maybe the last chance she would have.

Dimitri surveyed the completed boardinghouse with satisfaction. Every board fit perfectly, inside and out. In fact, the place was better built now than originally.

He examined his dirty hands. Not the hands of a king, but of a hard-working man. That thought filled him with pride.

One of the other men stopped by to shake his hand. "Good job, Your Highness. No offense meant, but I wouldn't have expected it."

Dimitri grinned. "I understand. To be honest, I wasn't certain I could do it."

"Well, you did, and it's a fine piece of work. In fact . . ." The man stopped, obviously hesitant to continue.

"Yes?" Dimitri offered encouragement. It had taken many days before these men relaxed around him, and he had discovered that he enjoyed their company.

"I've been needing to build on an extra room for the children, you understand? Would you be willing to help me out? I can use a man with your skill." After speaking quickly, the man waited, apprehension barely hidden on his face.

Dimitri clapped the man's shoulder. "I would consider it an honor, Hamilton."

Visible relief flowed through the man. "As would I." Hamilton grinned. "I'll contact you when I'm ready to begin."

"That would be fine. I expect we'll be here until spring."

They shook hands again, but this time with a sense of kinship. Dimitri liked the feeling. Aside from Alexi, he had never shared that before.

"Dimitri."

At hearing his name, he turned to see Anya approaching, wrapped in her fur-lined cloak. The countess was nowhere in sight. He frowned as he approached her.

"Where is your escort?" A lady did not venture out on her own.

"I could not wait for the countess." Her face was flushed, from the cold wind or excitement Dimitri couldn't tell. "Besides, I understand Miss Madison is unchaperoned most of the time."

"That's different." Yet Dimitri would be hard-pressed to put the reason into words. Cynda was more independent, less frightened of the world than any woman he had met. Crossing his arms, he fixed Anya with his gaze. "And what is so important you could not wait?"

"Miss Madison has completed your portrait." Anya announced the news with the enthusiasm of a child displaying a favorite toy.

"Has she?" Cynda had been delaying. He knew that, but he was not going to argue the point with her so long as she did not destroy the painting. "I hadn't expected her to finish yet."

"I am certain she would still be pretending to work on it if I had not made it my personal duty to sit with her every day and monitor her progress." Anya acted as if she had done him a great favor.

Dimitri swallowed a laugh. Cynda had been forced to finish and endure Anya's company as well. No doubt she wasn't in a very good mood. "Very well. Let us go see it."

Tucking Anya's arm in his, he headed for the train. "Does the painting do me justice?" he asked lightly.

"Too much so." Anya darted a glance at him from lowered lashes. "It is almost as if she knows you very well."

"Perhaps she does." Anya's hint triggered his anger, rather than guilt. Her startled expression made him relent. "After all, I sat many weeks for her."

Anya nodded and ducked back in her cloak as large snowflakes drifted from the heavy sky. "I will be glad to see her gone."

"Gone?" Dimitri had no intention of losing Cynda.

"Yes, her commission is completed. You no longer have need of her."

He stopped the words that leapt to his lips. He would always need Cynda. "We shall see."

Upon reaching The Chesterfield, he went directly to Cynda's suite. No one answered his knock, and he frowned. Where else could she be?

He glanced at Anya. "Did she say she was going anywhere?"

"No. She was here when I left."

He rapped again, harder, but still received no reply. "Cynda?"

"I recommended she pack. Perhaps she has left already."

Dimitri whirled on her. "You told her what? Who gave you that authority?"

Anya shrank back. "I . . . I only—"

Turning away from her, he hammered on the door, his chest tight. Cynda would not leave the resort. She had said many times that she had to be here on the twenty-first of December to return to her home in the future. He grimaced. "I will find someone to let us in."

Anya trailed behind him as he searched for someone—a porter, a maid. Where were all the staff? Surely in a hotel of this size and prestige they should be easier to locate. At last, he spotted an employee near the main entrance.

"Rupert." He barked the man's name as a command, hearing the edge of worry in his voice. Dimitri drew in a deep breath before he continued. "Can you let me into Miss Madison's suite? She doesn't answer her door."

"That's because she's not there," Rupert said. "I saw her leave about an hour ago with her sketch pad. Drawing again, I bet."

"Which way did she go?"

Rupert pointed to the rear of the hotel. "I don't know where she went from there."

"Thank you." Dimitri gave him a generous tip, then hurried for the back entrance, Anya running to keep up.

"I am certain she will return soon," she said. "There is no need for this fuss."

Dimitri paused by the doorway. The snowflakes were heavier, thicker now, obliterating a view of even the nearest walking path. Snow covered the ground, growing in depth.

For a moment, Dimitri couldn't breathe. This promised to be a bad storm, and Cynda was out in it. He had to find her.

Before he could open the door, Anya snagged his sleeve. "Where are you going?"

"I have to find Cynda."

"Surely she can find her own way back." Anya didn't sound very pleased with him, but he was more concerned with Cynda's safety.

"In that?" He pulled his arm from her hold. "I'm not willing to take that chance. Return to your room, Anya. I'll return shortly."

"Don't be foolish, Dimitri. You are a crown prince. You aren't responsible for finding her. Send someone else." She risked touching his arm again. "What if something happens to you?"

"Don't worry." He gave her a dry smile. "There's always Alexi."

Without waiting for her response, he dashed toward the stables. He would need a horse to search in this storm. No doubt Cynda was on the mountain slope somewhere. He knew many of her habits now. When she painted, she was oblivious to the world around her. As swiftly as this storm had moved in, she would have been caught unaware.

He had to find her . . . before it was too late.

Cynda didn't make much progress on her sketch. Her mind kept wandering. What was she going to do? Now that she had completed Dimitri's portrait, she had no reason to stay with him.

True, he had promised to introduce her to other potential sponsors in New York, but she couldn't leave here. Yet Anya would see to it that Dimitri sent Cynda away as soon as possible. What could she do to remain at the hotel for another three weeks?

The Major wasn't about to give her back her job as a waitress. Once again, Cynda would be forced to search for employment and a place to live in town.

Perhaps it was just as well. The more time she spent with Dimitri, the less she wanted to leave him. And she would have to leave him.

Her time here was short, his lifespan even shorter. Before she left the hotel, she had to convince him to believe her and the very real danger to his life. He had to leave the resort—and she had to ensure that he did.

A snowflake drifted onto her page, and she watched it melt with a wistful smile, remembering how she and Dimitri had watched that unusual October snow together. Her heart ached. They would share no more days like that.

She returned to her sketch of The Chesterfield as seen from between the black, barren trees of winter. Though only in pencil, the sketch held definite possibilities.

At least, she would take that back with her—a vast improvement in her skills and the elusive ability to instill emotion into her art.

She glanced up and blinked. Where was The Chesterfield? It had disappeared behind a sheet of driven snow. Alert now, she noticed the wind howling between the trees.

Where had this come from? She gathered her stuff together quickly. She had to get back inside.

Emerging from the thick grove, she gasped as the wind beat against her with the impact of a sledgehammer. She froze in place. The surrounding area had vanished into a blur of white. Which way was back?

Well, she wasn't going to waste time trying to decide. If she remembered correctly, she needed to go right. Without hesitation, she started walking.

Her hands grew numb despite her attempts to keep them inside her cloak, and the icy wind pierced her clothing, chilling her to the bone. Her shoes, though sturdy, did little to keep her feet dry. How did people stay warm in this time period?

Cynda shivered as she plodded through the building snow. She would give anything for a down-filled jacket and ski gloves right now.

After walking for what felt like a half hour, she paused. She should have reached The Chesterfield by now. Drat.

This was not good ... definitely not good. She needed to find shelter and soon. Already she had lost feeling in her feet as well as her hands.

How ironic, she had always worried about saving Dimitri's life. It had never occurred to her that her life might be in danger, too.

Or that she would die first.

Chapter 16

"Cynda!" The biting wind ripped the words from Dimitri's lips and carried them away in an icy blast. Fear formed a knot in his gut. How could he hope to find her in this?

Sean Quinn, the stable master, had insisted Dimitri wear his heavy coat. As the snow packed against the front of it, Dimitri murmured his gratitude. He had to keep going. He would not lose Cynda to this storm.

"Cynda!" He knew she would have stayed close to The Chesterfield. For some reason the resort fascinated her. "Cynda!"

A small cry mingled with the wind, and he reined in the horse, peering into the blowing snow. Was that dark shape in the distance her?

When the figure moved, he urged the horse forward, then slid from the saddle to gather Cynda in his arms. Her cloak was crusted with ice, and her lips were blue.

He didn't waste time with questions, but seated her on the gelding in front of him. Dropping the reins, Dimitri gave the animal its head, then nudged it into motion. The creature had a better chance of finding the stables right now than Dimitri did.

He concentrated on cuddling Cynda close, sharing his body heat. "Not much longer," he murmured, hoping he spoke the truth. She needed warmth soon.

"So c-c-cold." Her teeth chattered, and Dimitri hugged her closer, nestling her soft frame to his. The chill from her body alarmed him.

"Stay with me, Cynda." He leaned his head against hers, resisting the urge to move faster.

The horse arrived at the stables in good time. Dimitri dismounted quickly, then lifted Cynda into his arms. Quinn met them, his expression concerned.

"Thank the Good Lord, you found her, Your Highness." He frowned as he looked at her. "Is she all right?"

"She will be." Dimitri turned toward the main building. He could just make out the hotel lights through the snow. "If you'll care for the horse, I'll settle with you later."

"That's fine, Your Highness." Quinn was already removing the saddle.

Dimitri dashed into the hotel and toward the tower, calling for Rupert to follow him. He glanced at Cynda constantly. She remained still, her face pale and eyes closed. Her lashes were dark against her cheeks.

Rupert unlocked her suite for him. "She doesn't look well, Your Highness. Dr. Ziegler should look at her."

"If I feel he is needed, I will send for him." Dimitri entered the suite. "My grandmother is very knowledgeable in treating illnesses." Though he did not intend to consult her. "Thank you, Rupert." He let his tone imply dismissal, and with a sigh, Rupert turned away.

Dimitri kicked the door closed, then took Cynda into her bedroom. After placing her on the bed, he quickly removed her wet clothing, then wrapped her in the heavy quilt. He stoked the fire, then lay beside her, pulling her snug against him.

"Come, *mon coeur*. Open your eyes." He nuzzled her ear and kissed the slow pulse in her neck. "Speak to me."

Her cheeks slowly grew pink again and her breathing less strained. When her lips were no longer blue, he kissed them gently. "Open your eyes, Cynda."

She stirred, but her eyes remained closed.

He kissed her lips again, lingering, willing her to respond. At last, he felt the movement of her mouth beneath his and drew back. "Cynda?"

Her lashes fluttered, and she opened her eyes. "Dimitri?"

He brushed her cheek with his knuckles, smiling when he felt the warmth in it. "How do you feel?"

"Warmer." She shifted within his arms, then looked at him, her eyes wide. "Where are my clothes?"

"They were frozen and wet. I could not get you warm while you wore them."

She eyed him suspiciously, and he chuckled. His Cynda was back. "Don't you trust me?"

A slow smile spread across her full lips, fueling his need for her. His chest tightened. "I trust you," she replied. She slid one arm out of the quilt and touched his cheek. "You saved my life. Thank you."

Now his throat threatened to close. He had to clear it before he could speak. "I could not lose my favorite artist."

She bolted upright, the quilt slipping to reveal her full breasts before she pulled it back into place. "I finished the portrait." Dismay filled her voice.

"So Anya told me." Dimitri kept his tone neutral, sensing her fear yet uncertain why she felt it.

She gripped his arm. "Please, don't display it until after the twelfth of December."

As usual, she surprised him. He had expected her concern to be for her future, but instead it was for him and the nonsense she believed about his pending murder. "Don't worry." He cradled her cheek with his hand. "I haven't even started the frame yet."

"Good." She rested her cheek against his palm for a moment, then moved away. "I'll start packing tomorrow if that's all right."

Dimitri frowned. This was Anya's doing. "What are you talking about?"

"The portrait's done. I have to leave." She sounded so desolate, he had to struggle not to laugh.

He lifted her chin. "You're not leaving." He spoke firmly so she would know he meant every word. "Not now, not ever."

"But—"

"I told you if the portrait was satisfactory, I would continue to sponsor you."

"I thought that meant introducing me to your New York friends."

"No, it means I will continue to sponsor you while you accept other commissions." He ran his thumb over the soft skin of her throat. He had no intention of letting her go.

Cynda still looked apprehensive. "I doubt Anya will approve."

Dimitri scowled. He would be king and could sponsor an artist if he so chose. "Anya will do as I say."

"That's not a very good way to start a marriage." Cynda met his gaze, then looked away, turning her face from his touch. "Just tell her I will be gone by Christmas."

The conviction of her words acted like a punch to his gut. He couldn't lose this woman. "No."

He didn't give her a chance to protest, but claimed her mouth. Her lips were soft and pliable beneath his, and the inside of her mouth was hot— as hot as the fever in his blood.

She placed her hands against his chest in a half-hearted attempt to push him away, but the response of her lips said differently. He deepened the kiss, trying to convey his need for her, the longing she created within him. Her hands relaxed and caressed his chest instead.

The quilt drooped, and Dimitri took advantage of it to cup her breast, the soft weight filling his palm. It fit his palm perfectly, as if designed for him.

He lightly rubbed his thumb over her taut peak, and she moaned, echoing his delicious agony, then shocked him by pushing him away with surprising force. Tugging the quilt into place around her, she rolled off the bed and backed to the wall.

"No, Dimitri." Her voice trembled.

He stood and approached her slowly. She wanted him, too. Her response had equaled his passion. "I need you, Cynda." He needed to bury himself in her and share the melding of their bodies. He needed to celebrate her life.

She shook her head. "We can't do this. Anya is the one you belong with, not me."

He wasn't interested in Anya, not with his body craving Cynda's. "Anya is—"

"Anya is going to be *your wife.*" Cynda's expression was desolate, but determined. "She is going to be the one you spend your life with—the mother of your children, your mate, your queen."

Though he tried to ignore it, a twinge of guilt raised its ugly head. All the things Cynda said were true. He had known these truths for half his life, but knowing them, believing them, did not stop him from wanting Cynda.

"This is hard for me, too," Cynda continued quietly. "But remember what you told me. You intend to honor your wife and children, to be more to them than your father was to you."

He had said that and meant it, but that had been before he had known Cynda, before he had discovered the joy in his life he hadn't realized was missing. "I have changed my mind," he said.

"Not really." Her blue eyes implored him to listen, to understand. "You still want that deep down inside. You need to spend time with Anya. Learn to love her as you should."

Love? Dimitri grimaced. He had no place for

love in his life. Yet Cynda was right. Though he hated to admit it, he did need to spend more time with Anya.

"I will try." He crossed to her bedroom door, then paused to look back. Cynda remained by the wall, her quilt clutched protectively around her, her eyes wide. "You will remain under my sponsorship." He made it an order, leaving no room for argument.

"Until the solstice," she replied.

And beyond. But he did not argue the point. She was starting to shiver again.

"Take a hot bath and get into bed," he said. "I will have a tray of soup and tea delivered to you."

For a brief moment mischief gleamed in her eyes, and she gave him a half smile. "As you command, Your Highness."

Dimitri tightened his hand on the door frame. He wanted to cross to her and kiss her senseless. Fire still boiled in his blood, and the hard ache in his groin lingered.

With an effort, he left, closing the door after him, and returned to his suite.

Anya and Alexi were waiting for him, seated together on a divan while Grandmère rested in a comfortable chair. He knelt before her, concerned. "Grandmère, should you be up?"

She brushed his hair back, reminding him of similar moments in his childhood. "Dr. Ziegler has given his approval. I am to walk a little more each day."

"Did you find Cynda?" Alexi asked abruptly.

Dimitri stood again. "I found her. She was halffrozen."

"Will she recover?" Though Anya's words reflected concern, her tone did not.

Remembering the passion of Cynda's kiss as she returned to life, Dimitri schooled his features to reveal nothing. "She will be fine."

"I'm glad." Alexi did sound sincere. "Though you should not have been the one to go after her. Someone on the staff would have been more suitable."

"I knew I could find her." Dimitri couldn't explain. He had felt her presence even in the blinding snowstorm.

"You are to be king," Alexi retorted. "You cannot put your life at risk, especially for a servant. What if you had perished in the storm with Cynda?"

An icy finger drew a line along Dimitri's spine, and he stiffened. "Then you would be king, Alexi. I imagine that would make you very happy."

Anya gasped, her shock evident, while Alexi rose to his feet, glowering.

Grandmère touched Dimitri's arm. "Help me back to bed," she ordered.

Ignoring his brother, Dimitri wrapped his arm around her. She was so slight, he could have carried her entire weight with no effort at all. But he also knew her pride—a trait they shared—and allowed her to set the pace with mincing steps.

Once she reached her bed, he assisted her into it and pulled the quilts over her. The effort of her short walk showed itself in the pinched set of her lips and the paleness of her cheeks.

"You must be careful not to overdo," he said.

She smiled wanly. "Nonsense. I will be my old self very soon." She kept her grip on his arm. "You will apologize to Alexi."

Dimitri nodded. He hadn't meant to speak so bitterly to his brother, but he hadn't expected to be reprimanded for saving Cynda. He could not have left her out there.

The wind slammed against the windowpane, and Dimitri drew away to peer outside. The snow continued to fall, blanketing the ground as it erased the landscape in a sea of white.

"I am glad you found Cynda before she came to serious harm." Grandmère soothed him as she always had. "She is a most unique woman."

Dimitri smiled. "Yes, most unique." He could not imagine another like her.

"It is too bad we will have to lose her company when we return home."

He clenched his fists. "I am not so sure that we will."

"Oh?"

That single word implied a lot, and Dimitri found the tension returning to his muscles. "I have agreed to sponsor her after all."

"Yes, of course."

Though he couldn't be certain, he thought her voice held a touch of disappointment. Did she believe he should avoid Cynda?

"Are you certain she will feel comfortable in our country?"

Dimitri turned sharply to look at his grandmother. "What does that mean?"

"Only that she will not fit in at court. She was only a waitress when you met her."

"Cynda is easily equal to any of the duchesses or ladies at my court." The words escaped him before he thought, and he quickly added, "I am certain she can adjust."

Grandmère gave him an enigmatic smile. "Yes, dear. I imagine she can."

Dimitri frowned. Why did he feel as if he had just been manipulated? He stared at Grandmère; but she continued to smile at him, and his doubts intensified.

By the greatest manipulator of all?

Cynda groaned as a rap echoed at her bedroom door, and she burrowed under the quilt. Her head ached, and her throat was raw and scratchy.

She would have to die to feel better.

"Go away," she called hoarsely.

Instead, the bedroom door opened, and Sophie peeked inside. "I heard you were ill and wanted to check on you."

Cynda sat upright, wishing she could tidy her appearance. She had no doubt she looked as rotten as she felt. "Sophie, what are you doing here?"

The elderly woman hobbled inside with painfully slow steps, leaning heavily on a cane. "I am supposed to walk more," she said. "And I was worried about you."

She reached the chair beside the bed and lowered herself into it. Her strained breathing made Cynda frown.

"I'll recover," Cynda said, though she had had times when she had doubted it. "It's just a horrible cold." A cough escaped, and she buried her face in the bedcovers. "You shouldn't be here. I don't want you to get my germs."

"Germs?" Sophie cocked her head.

"I don't want you to get sick," Cynda amended.

"I won't allow myself to get sick," Sophie said

imperiously, and Cynda had to grin. She almost believed her.

"Can I do something to help?" Sophie asked. "I have a remedy which is guaranteed to cure your ailments."

"So does Dr. Ziegler." Cynda grimaced. "And he's been poisoning me with this awful concoction daily."

Sophie laughed. "Then, I will leave you in his very capable hands."

"How are *you* doing?" Cynda asked. The woman appeared thinner, less vibrant since her fall.

"As well as can be expected. Dr. Ziegler has assured me my hip is healed, but it will never be what it once was." Sophie sighed. "My nights of dancing are no more."

"I'm sorry." How unfair. If Sophie had been treated in Cynda's time, she not only would have been on her feet sooner, but regained most of her mobility, too.

Sophie shrugged. *"C'est la vie."* She leaned forward, her tone suddenly conspiratorial. "Has Dimitri been to see you?"

"No." Not once in the four days since he had saved her life. Cynda had, at the least, expected him to check on her, especially once he had learned she was ill. He must have taken her speech to heart . . . damn him.

"Well, he has been very busy." Sophie sounded as disappointed as Cynda felt. "He has been showing Anya around."

"Oh." Cynda forced herself to reveal nothing. "That's good. They haven't had much time together since she arrived."

"True, but Alexi has not found it a hardship to

escort her. I believe he spent as much time teasing her as introducing her to Hope Springs.''

Cynda had no problem picturing that. Alexi with his light-hearted manner loved to tease. "He told me they all grew up together.''

"Yes, they did. Though Anya has always been more at ease with Alexi. I believe it is because she knew from a young age that she would one day be Dimitri's bride and that knowledge has made her afraid of him.''

"Of Dimitri?" Once a person broke past his royal arrogance, Dimitri was kind-hearted and caring. "How could she be afraid of him?''

Sophie cocked her head to one side as if studying Cynda. "You must admit my grandson does have an overbearing manner at times.''

"That's just his kingly pride. Once you kick him in the butt and get past that, he's wonderful.''

Sophie's eyes widened. "You kicked him?''

"Oh, no. No." Cynda laughed. "It's a figure of speech. I let him know I wasn't afraid of him and that he couldn't bully me.''

"Ah, I suspected as much." Sophie's smile returned. "I hope Anya can do as well when they have their sleigh ride.''

"A sleigh ride?" Cynda sighed wistfully. How romantic. Anya would have no choice but to fall in love with Dimitri.

"Dimitri has been planning one for several days, but he is waiting for the snow to stop." Sophie glanced toward the window where flakes continued to drift down from a gray sky.

It had snowed off and on since the day of the sudden blizzard. Cynda had heard via the maids of a hotel guest who had been caught in it as she had. But he had died. Only Dimitri had kept Cynda from sharing that man's fate.

And here she thought she had been brought to the past to save *him*.

Seeing Sophie's intent gaze, Cynda struggled to recall their conversation. Oh, yes. The sleigh ride. "I hope they have a good time," she said with as much sincerity as she could muster.

A gleam appeared in Sophie's eyes. "I am convinced it will be an interesting ride."

Cynda frowned. Now what could the woman mean by that?

Dimitri assisted Anya into the sleigh, then took the seat beside her, arranging the furs around them. She was slight against him. When he wrapped his arm around her to draw her close to his side for warmth, she nearly disappeared.

She pushed away. "I can't breathe, Dimitri."

"My apologies." He loosened his grip. "Shall we go?"

Anya searched the darkening sky, her gaze anxious. "Will there be another blizzard?"

"No. The snow is done for now." He waved at the driver, and their sleigh glided over the frozen ground into the gathering night.

Though he had arranged this night as a chance to discuss the future with Anya, his thoughts, as usual, drifted to Cynda. She fit against his side as if sculpted to be there and had never shown the timidity he associated with Anya.

Recalling how Cynda had felt in his arms and the sweetness of her mouth, he hardened, wanting her. Dimitri closed his eyes, willing his body to listen to reason.

But it was difficult. Each day he had paused by the door to Cynda's room, needing to see her, yet realizing he didn't dare.

To see her was to want her.

When he had learned of her illness—a result of her severe chill, no doubt—he had gone as far as to enter the main room of her suite. Only Dr. Ziegler's presence had restored his sanity. Now he relied on Grandmère to provide daily reports on Cynda's health.

"You're frowning," Anya said, breaking into his thoughts. "Is there a problem?"

"No." He gave her a warm smile. "No problem."

He turned his attention to her. The gangly girl of his youth had matured into a lovely woman with doe-like brown eyes and hair the color of rich chestnut.

He should be honored to have her for his queen. Her upbringing was impeccable, her manners beyond fault. Her bloodline promised heirs of royal blood.

Yet he felt no passion for her. He found her attractive, yet experienced none of the desire just glimpsing Cynda could produce.

He found Anya's hand beneath the furs and took it in his. Her eyes widened, and she glanced nervously at the driver.

The man's attention was only for the ground before the horses. Besides, how could Dimitri compromise Anya? She was already destined to be his wife.

"You know we will be married shortly after my coronation," he said.

"Yes." Her voice was as small as the rest of her.

"I expect you to give me several sons."

"I will do my best."

Dimitri paused, staring at her, as he imagined Cynda's response to such a command. No doubt even the driver would be shocked. He sighed. "Anya, you have to stop being afraid of me."

"I'm not afraid of you." Finally a hint of defiance appeared in her manner.

He cupped the side of her face. "Then, why do I feel as if you're a frightened doe who will bolt from my presence at the first opportunity?"

"You . . . you can be intimidating."

"Yes." He acknowledged that about himself, but doubted he could change it after so many years. Visions of his future life with Anya filtered through his mind. He would always be the king, the ruler, even with his wife. He doubted Cynda would allow him to do so.

Forcing Cynda from his thoughts, he ran his thumb over Anya's trembling lips. "You are to be my wife." He lowered his mouth to a breath away from hers. "You will have to learn to accept me as I am."

He kissed her then, seeking a response, even a hint of the heat Cynda created within him. But her lips remained immobile beneath his. When, in desperation, he tried to enter her mouth, she gasped and broke away from him.

"Dimitri." She sounded shocked, but her glance went immediately to the driver.

Dimitri leaned back and ran his fingers through his hair. Damn propriety. Cynda would have returned his kiss with enthusiasm. He had felt nothing. Nothing. Not the slightest stir of desire. How could he possibly make love to this woman who would be his wife?

"Are you afraid of me, Anya, or do you find my touch repulsive?" He needed to know. This woman held a major role in his future.

"I . . . I . . ." She ducked back into her fur-lined cloak. "Perhaps in time it will be better."

"Time?" His voice rose with his frustration. "How long? A month? A year? Ten years?"

She cringed. "I cannot say. This is difficult for me."

Dimitri looked away to stare at the white-encrusted trees. How could he endure the rest of his life with a woman who barely tolerated his touch?

His resolve formed and solidified. Cynda would be his mistress. With her he could be accepted for the man he was and nothing more.

But he would not do as his father and allow his wife to learn of it through the court gossips. He owed Anya, at the very least, honesty.

He glanced at her, buried in the depths of her cloak. "Anya . . ." He paused, then started again. "Anya, as a man I have certain needs. Needs that I do not believe you can satisfy."

He drew in a deep breath, expecting a reaction yet seeing only her stare. "I plan to take a mistress."

She jerked upright. "It's her, isn't it? That artist woman."

Her sudden fury surprised him, triggering his anger and the urge to deny it. No. He would be honest. "Yes, it's Cynda."

"I suspected as much." Her tone held ice. "Very well. Then, I shall take a lover as well."

Dimitri stiffened. "My wife will not have a lover."

"Why not?" She faced him with more fire than he had ever seen before. "Is it my fault your kiss does not move me? Is it not possible that a different man could stir the passion you cannot?"

He gaped at her. This was his timid Anya? He struggled to control his anger. "Does such a man exist?"

"Yes." She lifted her chin in a show of defiance that would have amused him if not for his pride.

"And have you lain with him?" If so, she would not become his wife . . . no matter what agreement his father had made.

"No. He is an honorable man." Some of the defiance left her voice. "I come to you pure."

And he would be the one to take her virginity, an act that would pleasure neither of them. He sighed. If he intended to be with Cynda, how could he deny Anya the equal right?

He shook his head with a scowl. Damn Cynda and her sense of justice. It was affecting the way he looked at the world.

"I insist there be no doubt of my children's parentage," he said finally, certain his father would die on the spot if he could hear him.

Anya inclined her head slightly, then withdrew into her cloak again.

This ride was finished. Dimitri ordered the driver to return to The Chesterfield, thankful he and Anya had been conversing in their native tongue.

He reclined against the seat, not glancing at Anya. It appeared his marriage would imitate that of his parents', whether he wished it or not.

* * *

Cynda stood before Dimitri's portrait. She missed him, and it had only been a week since she had seen him. How would she ever survive once she returned to her own time?

She mentally kicked herself. She had survived other tragedies. She could survive this one as well.

A knock sounded, and her heart leapt into her throat. She recognized the imperiousness of that knock. Dare she answer it?

She couldn't use her cold as an excuse any longer. Though the stuff Dr. Ziegler had dosed her with tasted awful, it had worked. Aside from some body aches, she felt fine.

Dimitri pounded again, harder, his urgency making itself known.

As if of their own accord, her feet carried her over. Arguing with herself for being so weak, she opened the door.

Dimitri burst inside, pulling her into his embrace, his mouth devouring hers hungrily. He molded her body to his, the evidence of his desire hard against her thigh. The scent of the winter night clung to him, contrasting with the intense heat of his kiss.

When he lifted his mouth, his breathing ragged, he started pulling the pins from her hair. "I need you, Cynda," he growled. "I need you now."

Not now when she had been missing him so much, when her willpower was nearly gone. "Dimitri—"

She tried to protest, but he claimed her lips again with a fierceness that shattered her resistance. With a groan she wrapped her arms around his neck, holding him close. Desire burned a trail through her blood. As much as she wanted to deny it, she needed him, too.

"Damn you, Dimitri!"

At Alexi's angry exclamation, Cynda jerked free. She turned with Dimitri to face his brother. Fury blazed in Alexi's eyes as he stood inside the suite, and he held his fists tight at his side.

"Alexi, I—"

"You can't explain this away." Rage layered Alexi's words. "Anya told me you intend to keep Cynda as your mistress."

Dimitri stepped toward him. "Yes, but—"

Alexi stopped Dimitri with a solid right punch that sent his brother staggering backward. "You aren't fit to be king."

He stormed from the room, and Cynda stared after him, fear forming a hard coil in her stomach. She had never seen Alexi so enraged.

For the first time, she truly believed he could kill his brother.

Chapter 17

Cynda turned to Dimitri in alarm. He was moving his jaw as if to ensure it still worked. Meeting her gaze, he grimaced.

"And to think I was the one who taught him to fight."

His jaw would be swollen, but at the moment, Cynda was more concerned with what Alexi had said. "What did he mean you told Anya I was going to be your mistress?"

"Oh." Dimitri hesitated. "I decided it would be best to be honest with her."

Cynda jabbed her finger against his chest, the only way to get this man's attention. "I . . . am . . . not . . . going . . . to . . . be . . . your . . . mistress." How dare he tell Anya that? No matter how much Cynda wanted him, she would not accept that position in his life.

Dimitri's eyes darkened. "Yes, you will. I have tried with Anya and discovered she will not be the type of lover I need."

"You arrogant male chauvinist. *Tried?*" Cynda's voice rose with her temper. "You've barely spent a week with her. That's not trying . . . that's making a feeble attempt."

He grew deadly silent.

"And now you've told her this, you've ruined any chance of having a normal life with her." Though his desire for her was gratifying, Cynda couldn't deny her guilt. She had ruined his marriage, his life, and driven his brother to kill him. She stomped to the door and pulled it open the rest of the way. "Get out."

Dimitri reached for her. "Cynda . . ."

She backed away and glared at him in fury. "Out."

To her relief, he stepped outside, though the restrained anger in his eyes promised another encounter. She slammed the door and locked it, then leaned her back against it.

Dear Lord, what next? Dimitri would die, and it would be her fault because she had fallen in love with him.

Cynda plucked the rest of the pins from her hair and staggered toward her bedroom. Her brain refused to focus. Perhaps she could think of a solution after a good night's rest.

But her sleep was fitful. She tossed and turned, her rest broken by all-too-real dreams.

They all stood before the portrait in the main entrance of The Chesterfield—Dimitri, Cynda, Sophie, Alexi, Anya, even Miss Sparrow. A new nameplate shone on the bottom of the frame, the etched lettering filling Cynda with a sense of doom.

Abruptly a gunshot echoed in the large room, and Dimitri collapsed, blood pouring from his chest.

Cynda screamed and ran to him. She pulled his head onto her lap as she pressed against his wound in a futile attempt to stop the flow of blood.

He tried to smile. "I guess you were right."

And he died in her arms, his final breath releasing with a rattle.

"No." Cynda bolted upright in her bed, her heart hammering. She stared at her hands, half expecting to see them coated with blood. A tear slid down her cheek. No matter what, she couldn't let Dimitri die.

As the sun rose to greet a new day, she counted. What was today's date? During her illness she had lost track.

Oh, dear Lord. Her heart skipped a beat. It was already the seventh of December. She had to get Dimitri away from here. Now.

She waited for a semidecent hour before she rapped on the door to the Karakovs' suite. *Please don't let Alexi answer.* She couldn't bear to see the condemnation on his face.

Fortunately, Sophie called out from inside. "Enter."

Cynda peeked inside, not sure who she would find, but there was only Sophie, who gave her a weak smile. The elderly woman was bracing herself on the back of a chair and looked ready to fall over. "Could you assist me, dear?"

Cynda rushed to Sophie's side and guided her into an overstuffed chair before the roaring fireplace. "Thank you, dear." Sophie patted her hand.

"I'm afraid my legs did not want to cooperate this morning."

"You must be careful." Cynda would hate to see her fall again.

Sophie smiled wanly. "Now you sound like Dimitri."

Cynda's heart skipped a beat at the mention of his name. "Is he . . . is he here? I need to talk to him."

"He will be out shortly." Sophie tightened her hold on Cynda's hand when Cynda would have pulled it away. "I understand Dimitri intends to install you as his mistress."

Sophie's tone held no censorship, but Cynda flinched. Had he told everyone? "I am not going to return with him and be his mistress—no matter what he says."

A glint of humor appeared in Sophie's gaze. "I would not be so certain. Dimitri can be very persuasive."

"I know." Cynda sighed. "But I will be leaving here on the twenty-first and going to a place where he'll never find me."

"Is that what you think best?"

"It's what I have to do. He may want me now, but later he would come to hate me for destroying his dreams. I couldn't bear that."

Sophie hesitated, her observant gaze searching Cynda's face. "You must love him very much."

Cynda blinked, then smiled dryly. "I do. Too much to let him destroy his future or himself."

Releasing her surprisingly strong grip, Sophie beamed at Cynda. "Then, do as you must." She turned toward the bedrooms. "Dimitri, you have a visitor."

He emerged, fastening the cuffs of his shirt, then froze when he saw Cynda. His eyes darkened, and she swallowed the thick lump in her throat.

"I need to talk to you," she murmured.

"As you wish." His tone revealed nothing.

Sophie started to rise. "I will leave you alone."

"No, Grandmère." Dimitri touched her shoulder gently. "We will find somewhere else."

He ensnared Cynda's arm in his firm grip, then led her back to her suite. Once inside, he released her and closed the door. Crossing his arms, he faced her, his expression stony.

"You have something to say?"

Now that she actually had him in front of her, Cynda wasn't sure how to begin. She moistened her dry lips, aware his gaze followed the movement of her tongue, then lingered on her mouth. "I want you to leave here for a week."

He frowned. "And why would I want to do that?"

"Because you'll die if you stay here."

He snorted in disgust. "I told you I did not want to hear any more about that." He uncrossed his arms, but remained stiff, unbending. "If that is all you had to say . . ."

He reached for the door, and Cynda leapt at him, panic spurring her forward. She caught his arm, forcing him to look at her.

"Please, Dimitri, go away. Just for a week." When he showed no sign of weakening, she rushed ahead. "I'll go with you. I'll do anything you want."

He inhaled sharply. "Do you know what you're saying?"

Her throat went dry, but she met his gaze. "Yes. I'll do anything to save your life."

He lifted her chin, watching her closely. She

trembled, his lightest touch sending ripples of
desire through her.

"Very well. I will make the arrangements while
you pack." He tightened his fingers on her chin
and lowered his mouth to hers for a harsh kiss that
ended far too soon, but left a promise of more.

His eyes blazed as he lifted his head. "Pack
lightly. You will not need many clothes."

He left the suite, and Cynda released a shuddering breath. What had she done? At least he had
agreed to leave The Chesterfield. If she had to
share the next week with him in order to save his
life, it would be worth it.

Even if she would find it that much harder to
leave him.

"Where are we going?" Cynda asked as Dimitri
tucked her beside him on the sleigh. He nodded
to the driver to depart before he replied.

"There is a cabin a short distance up the mountain. Because of its location, it is known by few and
an excellent place for trysts. Will that be far enough
from The Chesterfield for you?"

She nodded. He wouldn't be near the portrait.
That was what mattered.

However, his description of the cabin troubled
her—a place for trysts. Her imagination immediately conceived the trappings of a gaudy bordello.
Was that what she had become?

She faced Dimitri, her heart pounding against
her ribs. "Dimitri, I'm not . . . I don't . . ."

His features gentled as he placed a finger over
her lips. "I know. If I thought for one moment

that you'd ever entered into this arrangement with another man, I would not be here."

"But what about my reputation? When we get back?" Cynda couldn't believe she was asking that question. Evidently the Victorian morals were creeping up on her. Yet she couldn't stand to see the smug or contemptuous looks from the hotel guests.

"Only three members of the hotel staff know about this, and they are sworn to secrecy." He hugged her. "I have done my best to protect you."

She nodded and snuggled against his side, unable to stop her rising nervousness. This was Dimitri—the man she loved. Why should she be nervous?

Perhaps because whatever happened this week would irrevocably change her life.

"You are very quiet." Dimitri lifted her chin until their gazes met. "Very unlike the Cynda I know."

She forced a weak smile, unable to stop her inner panic.

He frowned. "Is that fear in your eyes? Are *you* afraid of me?"

Cynda heard his disbelief and struggled to find the words to explain her trepidation. "I ... I just—"

"What are you expecting?" He chuckled. "Do you expect me to tie you to the bed and ravage you for the entire week?"

Put that way, Cynda had to laugh. For all his pride, Dimitri would never hurt her. "I'm being silly, I guess. This is so new to me."

Dimitri stole a quick kiss, then lowered his lips to her ear. "We will make love, *mon coeur*, but only because you want it as much as I."

His raspy whisper kindled hot desire through her veins, and her breasts swelled in anticipation. She met his gaze boldly with a slow seductive smile. "I am looking forward to that."

His slight inhale and abrupt shift in position told Cynda her words had their desired effect. His eyes darkened, and he tightened his arm around her shoulders. "Perhaps I *will* keep you tied to the bed," he murmured, but the humor in his voice made Cynda laugh.

They reached the cabin in an hour, and Cynda couldn't help but stare. She had pictured a cottage . . . not a chalet easily as large as her suite and Dimitri's together.

"This is roughing it?" she asked.

Dimitri frowned at her as if not quite familiar with her choice of words, but apparently he figured out her meaning, for he grinned as he helped her from the sleigh. "Why should a man suffer discomfort while seeking pleasure? Some bring servants with them."

"Servants?" Cynda eyed the cottage again. It probably had room.

"But I intend to share you with no one."

The huskiness of his voice fed the knot low in her belly, and Cynda struggled for an even breath. She turned away to open the cabin door as Dimitri made final arrangements with the driver.

Stepping inside, she had to laugh. The cabin might be less elegant than The Chesterfield, but not by much. The main room was decorated with heavy wood furniture and thick Belgian carpets. A large fireplace dominated one wall with a complete bearskin on the floor before it. The walls were wallpapered and adorned with a selection of Currier and Ives prints.

Oil lamps sat on the fireplace mantel, and thick candles in holders were placed on the ornate tables.

Cynda turned around in the middle of the room, unable to believe her eyes. They would definitely not lack for comfort.

Dimitri entered, followed by the driver, who carried two large packages. "Do you like it?" Dimitri asked her.

"This is incredible."

He grinned and directed the driver to place the packages by the wall. The shapes were so square she couldn't guess at their contents. "What are those?"

Mischief danced in Dimitri's eyes. "You'll see."

The driver paused by the door. "One week, Your Highness?"

Dimitri nodded. "One week." After the man left, Dimitri took Cynda's hand in his. "Now, *mon coeur,* let us explore. The dining room, the kitchen ... the bedroom." His voice dipped seductively low on the last word, and Cynda's senses ignited.

Oh, my.

Chapter 18

Dimitri led Cynda into a smaller adjoining room. "This must be the dining room." A large wooden table with legs as big as small trees dominated the room. This was a small, intimate hideaway? Cynda shook her head. The table easily sat ten.

"Are we expecting company?" she asked with a grin.

Dimitri answered with a sensuous glance. "No one will bother us for a week." He squeezed her fingers and led into the next room, which spanned the rear of the cottage.

The black stove hinted at the room's use. "The kitchen," Cynda said.

He nodded. "I already had provisions delivered."

Cynda examined the stove and box of wood

beside it with a grimace. "I hope you're not expecting me to cook on that thing."

"It is the only stove available." Dimitri leaned against the door frame. "Why? Don't you know how to cook?"

"Not on a woodstove." She peeked inside it. "I wasn't even a Girl Scout. I'm a firm believer in gas or electric."

"An electric stove?"

She grinned at Dimitri's incredulity. "Yep. You do have electricity now, don't you?"

"It exists, but is more used in places like New York City and then only for lighting." He came to stand beside her. "Are you saying this electricity will run stoves? Is this another of your fantasies?"

"Give it fifty years or so." She rattled the stove door. "In the meantime, we're stuck with this. Do you know how to cook on it?"

"Me?"

His astonishment made her laugh. "Yes, you, Prince Dimitri."

"I have never cooked a meal in my life."

Cynda sighed. "I was afraid of that. You'd better not expect to eat much, then."

He drew her into his embrace, humor in his eyes. "I will survive. If I become hungry, I will just nibble on you."

Suiting his actions to his words, he nibbled along her throat, lingering at her pulse which tripled its rate in a matter of seconds. He rested his lips over hers as he spoke, the movement of his mouth teasing hers. "For you satisfy my hunger far better than any food."

He seized her mouth then, taking possession, delving inside to tease her desire into full blaze.

Heat raced through her blood, her nipples hardening, and moisture pooling between her thighs.

She clung to him, wanting more, and rubbed against the hard length in his trousers. When he raised his head and clutched her shoulders to hold her away from him, she moaned in protest.

Her body needed him, wanted him, ached for fulfillment only he could provide.

His hungry gaze burned with equal fire, but he only took her hand again. "Let me show you upstairs."

He led her to a narrow staircase and up to a room that encompassed the length and width of the entire cottage. On the far end was a sitting room with chairs placed before a large window that offered a spectacular view of the evergreens and mountains. On the other end was a tub, easily large enough for three people.

Cynda stared at it, hope rising. "Does that have hot water?"

Dimitri nuzzled her ear. "Yes. I hope to try it. Perhaps we will not flood the floor this time."

Heat filled her cheeks as she recalled their last encounter in the tub. She resisted the urge to squirm, wanting to try it again now.

Standing behind her, Dimitri held her shoulders and turned her to face the room's centerpiece— a massive four-poster bed perched on a platform with steps surrounding it. Another huge fireplace filled the wall opposite it.

Cynda inhaled sharply. The only things missing were mirrors . . . thank goodness.

"If not for food, we would never have to leave here," Dimitri murmured, sliding his hands down to cup her breasts as he bent to kiss a path along her neck and shoulders.

Her earlier desire still hummed in her veins and needed little to revive it. Cynda melted against him, sensing his erection through her petticoats, giving in to his caresses.

He left her breasts to undo her buttons and remove her dress with an expertise that thrilled rather than alarmed her. He unlaced her petticoats and corset just as quickly and pulled them off.

"I forbid you to wear that contraption during the remainder of our stay."

Cynda turned to throw her arms around his neck. "Thank you. That thing is a torture device devised by a man, I'm sure."

He grinned. "I can't imagine a man being foolish enough to bar the way to a woman's breasts." Cradling the back of her head with one hand, he devoured her mouth as a man who had not eaten for a month. He teased, seduced and claimed her with lips that could easily be labeled hot and dangerous.

Cynda met him kiss for kiss, barely breathing, her hunger as ravenous as his. Her body was his, responding with passion to his touch, eager for him to fill her.

As they broke apart, gasping, she sought the buttons on his shirt and blazed a path with her lips as she peeled it back to reveal his chest. She lingered over his flat nipple, teasing it with her tongue until he shuddered.

The knowledge that she could affect him as much as he did her brought her satisfaction. Pushing his shirt aside, she followed the trail of dark hair on his chest to where it narrowed and disappeared beneath his trousers.

Unfastening his pants, she grinned. It was time Prince Dimitri learned this claiming went two ways.

She freed his rigid length and stared for a moment in awe. He gave new meaning to the word *king-size.*

"What are you doing?" he demanded in a voice not quite steady.

In reply Cynda took him in her mouth, teasing his velvet shaft with her tongue. Dimitri's groan empowered her, and she drew on him, clutching his firm buttocks with her hands.

He wove his hands in her hair, whether to pull her away or hold her fast she wasn't sure, for she chose that moment to gently scrape him with her teeth, and his entire body trembled.

If possible, he swelled even more, and Cynda suckled him with enthusiasm. He was soft yet hard with a salty masculinity that was uniquely Dimitri.

"Enough." His voice was hoarse as he yanked her to her feet. "Would you unman me, woman?"

She grinned at him. "Could I?"

With a growl he seized the neck of her chemise and tore it off.

Cynda gasped even as moist heat pulsed within her. "I only have a couple of those."

"I'll buy you more." Wrapping his arm behind her, he bent her back until he could draw her breast into his mouth. His fierceness added to Cynda's rising passion. She clutched his hair to hold him close.

He teased her breast with his tongue, his lips, his teeth, until Cynda couldn't speak, her body alive with need, small moans escaping her throat.

Yet he held her firm, releasing one sensitive peak to claim the other until Cynda could barely stand.

When he finally raised his head, triumph glittered in his eyes. Before Cynda could do more than gasp, he had them both naked and on the bed. He knelt over her, wild possession on his face, then entered her, filling her completely.

Cynda raised her hips to meet his, matching each pounding thrust with wild passion. It had never been like this before—the hunger all-consuming, the passion driving her higher to a plane she had never known existed.

Their mouths met, dueled, then moved onto each other's skin, nipping, licking, kissing. He tasted of sweat, of pure maleness, of Dimitri.

"You are mine," he murmured against her lips. "You were made for me."

He drove even deeper, taking Cynda higher. She couldn't breathe. She was dying from a pleasure so intense that every cell in her body exploded with the intensity of her climax.

She screamed his name, contracting around him, closer to fainting than she had ever been in her life.

"Cynda, *mon coeur.*" He kissed her, his body so hot against hers, she was convinced they sizzled. He pumped deep, deeper, trembling within her until he groaned and collapsed.

Cynda couldn't speak. Only ragged breaths tore from her throat. That hadn't been just sex. What they had shared surpassed that and defied words. She felt claimed, bonded, mated in an act more binding than a ceremony of words. Dear Lord, how could she ever leave him?

Dimitri rose on his elbows and kissed her with

such gentleness she had to blink back tears. "Much more of that and you will kill me far quicker than any bullet."

She smiled. "I think you're tough enough to take it."

"We will find out." He brushed over her lips, then drew back, his expression serious. "I thank whatever fates brought us together. If we hadn't met, I never would have known this ecstasy, never known that a person existed who fit me so perfectly as to be a part of me."

It was a very unDimitri-like speech, and now Cynda did cry, a tear sliding down her cheek. "I only wish circumstances were different, that I didn't have to leave."

"You don't. You won't."

She didn't reply. As difficult as it would be, she knew what she had to do when the time came.

"You won't," he repeated more firmly as if sensing her response in her silence.

She caressed his cheek, memorizing his features—his mercurial eyes, aristocratic nose and full sensual mouth. "I'm hungry," she said in an attempt to change the subject. "How about we tackle that stove?"

Dimitri remained silent, studying her, then smiled. "Very well. I will light it if you cook the meal."

Cynda managed to prepare steaks that were burnt on one side and raw on the other, but Dimitri choked down his meal without complaint.

Later, with a blazing fire set and snowflakes falling gently outside, he made love to her with such tenderness that again Cynda cried.

* * *

The next morning, following a burned breakfast, Dimitri brought out the wrapped packages, eager to see Cynda's expression as they opened them. "Are you ready for your surprise?"

"What is it?" Her excitement fed his. "How did you have time to prepare anything?"

"Ah, I am a prince." Actually he had relied on Rupert to procure the necessary items. The porter was quite adept at such services, especially when a large tip was included.

Dimitri cut the twine, then gave the package to Cynda. She tore into the brown paper with all the enthusiasm of a child, then cried out with glee at seeing the items. "You know me better than I thought you did." She clutched the sketch pad and pencils to her chest.

Her obvious pleasure warmed Dimitri. How could he not notice that she became more alive when she was sketching or painting . . . or in his bed? "I don't intend to keep you in bed *all* the time," he said.

Her eyes sparkled with mischief. "You could've fooled me."

He grinned. Waking with her in his arms this morning had generated not only desire but a soul-stirring warmth. To know she was with him and he did not have to leave brought an overwhelming sense of rightness and possession—a possession he had soon confirmed with his body.

"I also procured something for myself," he continued.

"What?" She came to his side as he tore away the paper on a large package. It was as he had ordered—four pieces of wood and a set of carving tools.

When Cynda looked at him, a question in her eyes, he touched her cheek. "I believe I was commissioned to make a portrait frame?"

A huge smile spread across her face. "Well, it's about time. I was hoping you'd get to it before I . . ." She turned away, not finishing the sentence, and Dimitri frowned.

Hadn't she yet learned that he would not let her leave him? No matter where she went he would find her. Her story about being from the future was just that—a story. Soon she would realize she belonged with him and forget her foolish fantasies.

"The light in the sitting room will be perfect." She moved toward the stairs, and Dimitri gathered his supplies together.

"Then, I will work there as well." He did not intend to let her out of sight for long. Besides, the sitting room was much closer to the bed.

But once he began working with the wood, he shifted his focus, losing track of everything but the oak beneath his hands. He knew the dimensions of the painting; however, the wood itself would determine the design.

He could not explain it, but the wood spoke to him as he worked, guided his actions to bring out the hidden beauty. Contentment swept over him. All his worries about being king faded away until all that existed was the design coming to life beneath his hands.

When he finally leaned back to ease the knots in his shoulders, he noticed the sun's angle through the large window. Was it already mid-afternoon?

He looked for Cynda, but she was gone, her sketch pad lying on the chair where she had been sitting. Panic rose within him, then ebbed when he heard her down in the kitchen muttering vile threats at the stove.

Hot need replaced panic, racing through his blood. Even a few hours were too long since he had kissed her, held her, touched her.

He headed for the staircase, then stopped beside her chair. She had left her sketch pad faceup to reveal a drawing of Dimitri as he worked.

Her talent was unmistakable. She had managed to capture every nuance of emotion in his expression. His joy with what he was doing came through clearly and made him pause.

A particularly violent threat drifted up the stairs, and Dimitri grinned. Maybe Cynda would be happier when he delayed the meal even more.

Later, as night fell, he sat beside her in the large tub, his passion momentarily sated, though he enjoyed the teasing glimpses of her breasts in the water as she breathed. He wrapped his arm around her shoulders, tucking her close to his side. With a sigh, she rested her head on his shoulder.

Here with Cynda, life was perfect. But in a few short months, he would have to return to his country and take his position as king. "I wonder if I will be a good king." He stopped abruptly, stunned to have spoken the words aloud.

Cynda sat up to meet his gaze. "I expect you will be a very good king," she replied with a sincerity that touched his heart. "You care about your people; you want to do what's best for them." She grinned. "Once you give up being stuffy and arrogant, you'll be wonderful."

"Stuffy and arrogant?" Was that how she saw him still?

She bent forward to kiss him. "Only with those who let you get away with it."

"Which you will never do?"

"Never." She returned her head to his shoulder. "What plans do you have for your country?"

"We are in desperate need of modernization, but my people are resistant to change. I will have to go slowly and allow time for acceptance before I proceed." Dimitri sighed, envisioning years of frustration. "And there is so much to be done that it will probably take more than my lifetime."

"You can do it." She drew lazy circles on his chest. "I believe in you."

He tightened his hold. Yet another reason why he couldn't let her go. "I will buy you a house near the castle where I can visit you often."

She ceased the circles and grew still, yet he continued. He had to make her understand he would not abandon her. "If there are children, I will acknowledge them and educate them with my own."

"What do you mean by 'my own'?" Tension layered her quiet words.

"The children I will have with Anya. She is obligated to provide me an heir."

"And would not any children we have be *your own* as well?"

"Certainly, but . . ." He stopped as he realized to say more was not wise, but Cynda jumped in to fill the void.

She pushed away from him and faced him from across the tub. "But they would not be legal, would they? They'd be the king's bastards."

Bleakness filled her face, reminding Dimitri of how he had treated his father's illegitimate children. He had ignored them, treated them as dirt beneath his feet, a mistake, and his attitude had determined that of the other townspeople as well. They resented his father's mistresses and their children. Dimitri did not want that for Cynda.

But what choice did he have? He was heir to the throne, his wife determined by a contract signed over a decade earlier.

He might be able to convince his father to change the contract, but not so he could marry someone like Cynda. She had no nobility in her background. She didn't even know her father. Besides, she was a waitress and an artist . . . entirely unsuitable to be queen.

No matter how much Dimitri wished it otherwise.

His future would not be as he had envisioned, but the pleasure he garnered with Cynda made the sacrifice worthwhile.

She raised one leg to step out of the tub, but he caught her wrist and pulled her back to him. The light had gone from her eyes, adding to the ache in his chest.

"I will make it work, Cynda. Somehow." He would be king. He would order the people to accept her.

Wanting now to erase her despair, he sought her lips, trying to convey how much he needed her, how important she had become in his life. Slowly, her lips softened beneath his, and he slid his hand down to cup her derriere and bring her closer.

He hardened against her belly as passion ignited, and he drew deeper on her mouth.

Perhaps he wasn't quite so sated after all.

* * *

Cynda set aside her pencil and studied Dimitri as he worked on the frame. She was wanton. She couldn't help it, though she never would have suspected it of herself. All he had to do was kiss her, touch her, and she burned with desire, wanting him with a desperation that frightened her.

The more he talked of keeping her forever, the more she weakened, wanting to stay with him. But she wouldn't. She couldn't. She could not exist in the future he described.

Dark clouds moved in, blotting out the mountain she had been drawing, so she set down her pad and walked over to stand behind Dimitri.

He had nearly completed the frame, the wood gleaming with an intricate design that awed her. Was he aware of his skill?

She massaged the stiffness in his shoulders. "This is incredible, Dimitri. You have such talented hands."

He brought her head down for a kiss that left her breathless. "Would you like me to demonstrate how talented?"

She stepped back, laughing. "You, Your Highness, are a dirty old man."

He looked momentarily puzzled, then glanced down at his hands. "Dirty, perhaps. Old, not yet. But certainly a man." His eyes darkened with passion.

"You stay." She pointed a finger at him. "I'm going to start dinner."

She scampered down the stairs. Most of their meals had been late or nonexistent due to Dimitri's raging hormones. She smiled. Not that she was complaining.

She managed to get the stove lit on the first try. After four days she was finally getting the hang of this monstrosity. Maybe by the end of the week she would be able to make a decent meal.

As she gathered ingredients for supper, she paused to place her hand over her abdomen. Dimitri's mention of children had made her wonder. With the lack of birth control in this time, she had resigned herself to fate.

But what if she was carrying his child? It was too soon to know for sure, but if she wasn't pregnant, it certainly wouldn't be for lack of trying.

She smiled sadly. At least if she were, she would have something of Dimitri to take back to her time . . . which seemed a fair trade for the heart she would leave behind.

She gasped as Dimitri rested his hands on her shoulders, breaking into her train of thought. He chuckled. "Did you think you could escape me?"

Running his fingers through her hair, he nuzzled her throat. She had taken to leaving her hair long—a state she much preferred and one that pleased Dimitri as well.

He slid his hands lower to cup her unencumbered breasts, then quickly unfastened the buttons on her bodice. After he had ripped her only remaining chemise, she had ceased to wear one and her petticoats as well.

Today she had left off her pantalettes as well, wondering how long it would take him to notice. Half the day was gone, which surprised her. She had been in a low boil all morning, feeling risqué and sinfully sexy in her nudity beneath her dress.

As he opened her bodice and bared her breasts to his very skillful hands, she moaned and leaned back against his rock-hard erection. He paused, then slid one hand over her bottom.

"Are you wearing anything under your dress?" He sounded hoarse.

"Not a thing."

He reacted as she had hoped with a passionate growl, whirling her around to find her mouth. His lips promised passion, hunger and fulfillment. She wanted all that and more.

He ground his hips against her, pushing her into the sideboard until the potatoes rolled to the floor. Cynda could barely speak. "I was . . . I was trying to make dinner."

He scooped her into his arms. "You, *mon coeur, are* dinner." Taking her into the dining room, he set her on the edge of the massive table.

With his lips sealed to hers, he gently pushed her shoulders back until she lay flat and his solid length pressed between her thighs. But her skirt was still in the way.

She rocked her hips against him. She wanted him now. But he only left her mouth and proceeded to drop kisses along her throat and exposed chest, flicking his tongue over her firm nipple, sending lightning through her.

She squirmed, aching for him, but he held her shoulders down and took her breast in his mouth, drawing on it with a fierceness that tugged at her lower muscles.

"Dimitri, please." She had been waiting for him all morning. Every touch now escalated the fever inside her.

He nipped at her taut peak, then met her gaze,

a mischievous light gleaming with the passion. "Would you deny a starving man his dinner?"

Drawing on her other breast, he feasted, suckling, then teased her nipple with his tongue before scraping his teeth over it. Cynda arched within his hold, beyond reason, only wanting, needing.

When he finally stood back and lifted her skirt to her waist, she raised her hips. Now he would fill her.

Instead, he lifted first one foot, then the other to the table edge and spread her knees wide. He parted her swollen lower lips with his thumbs, then brushed one over her throbbing nub. She reacted with a strangled cry, the tension unbearable.

Before she could predict his actions, he put his mouth and tongue to work—nuzzling, nipping, delving inside her moist heat.

She erupted, her entire body shattering, but he continued until she could not draw a breath, one orgasm melting into the next. Just when she thought she could no longer endure, he thrust into her, his male hardness giving her what she had sought.

He lifted her hips, holding her to him as he moved with long, even strokes until the passion she had thought exhausted renewed itself. When she climaxed again, he exploded with her, burying himself deep.

Cynda remained still, gasping. When Dimitri lightly brushed her nipple, she slapped his hand away. "Stop. You've killed me."

He laughed, and it rumbled through her. "Not completely." He stole a kiss.

"You are insatiable."

"Only where you're concerned." The warmth in his eyes touched her heart.

Though he would probably never admit it, he did care about her as more than good sex. The times they had snuggled together just talking had proven that.

An abrupt knock startled them both, and Dimitri frowned. He withdrew from her and turned toward the main room, fastening his pants. "Stay here."

Cynda slid off the table, buttoning her dress. "As if." They still had three days left in their week. Who could it be?

The driver from the hotel stood in the doorway, his expression grave. "Prince Alexi sent me, Your Highness. Said your grandmother is pretty ill and that you'll want to be there if . . . well, if . . ." He trailed off, clearly not wishing to finish the sentence.

Dimitri looked back at Cynda, stark fear in his eyes. Sophie had been the one stabilizing influence in his life. If anything happened to her . . .

Cynda touched Dimitri's arm as she addressed the driver. "Give us a few minutes and we'll be ready to leave."

Chapter 19

Cynda ran after Dimitri into Sophie's room to find the elderly woman sitting up in bed, sipping a cup of tea. Her eyes widened as she spotted them.

"What are you doing here? I didn't expect you back for several days."

Dimitri frowned. "Alexi sent for me. He made it sound as if you were dying."

"Dying?" Sophie's laughter dissolved into coughing and she paused before continuing. "No, my dear, I just caught Cynda's illness."

Cynda perched on the edge of the bed and took Sophie's hand. "I'm so sorry."

"Nonsense. I was the one who insisted on visiting you while you were ill. Dr. Ziegler is taking good care of me and forcing me to take that dreadful medicine."

Cynda grimaced, the horrid taste of that still lingering in her memory. "Awful stuff, isn't it?"

"Quite unpleasant, but I must admit I do feel better."

Dimitri paced the floor at the end of the bed. "I am going to kill Alexi."

Cynda shook her head. The last thing she wanted was more trouble between the brothers. "Don't be an idiot. He meant well."

"Ha." Dimitri gripped the bedpost. "He meant to ruin our week together."

Recalling the four wonderful days they had been able to share, Cynda gave him a soft smile. "No one could do that."

His expression relaxed. "You're right, of course."

"Was your interlude enjoyable?" Sophie asked.

Heat spread to every inch of Cynda's skin, but she nodded. "Very. Dimitri has been working on a magnificent frame for his portrait. Wait until you see it."

"Magnificent?" Sophie raised her eyebrows. "Then, I shall have to see it."

"It will be up shortly with the rest of our things." Dimitri hesitated for a moment. "I am moving into Cynda's room for the duration of our stay."

Cynda gaped at him. This was news to her.

"I don't believe that would be wise, my dear." Sophie's voice held a hard edge Cynda had never heard before.

"I think you should listen to your grandmother," Cynda added. As much as she wanted Dimitri's company, his outright disregard of convention would only anger Alexi more.

"I have made my decision. I will stay with Cynda."

His kingly arrogance surfaced, and Cynda stalked over to him.

She jabbed her finger against his chest. "And did you ask *me* about this?"

"I—"

"You do not own me. Not now. Not ever. I do *not* intend to share my room with you. I may not have much reputation left, but I'm not going to be treated like your pet whore."

She whirled around, pausing only briefly to kiss Sophie's cheek. "Good night. I hope you feel better soon."

She fled the suite, wanting badly to hit a certain someone. Would his arrogance never end? As she opened the outer door, she heard Sophie's voice. "I *like* that girl."

But she never heard Dimitri's reply.

Dimitri hesitated outside the door to Cynda's suite the next morning. Would she still be angry? Though he hated to admit it, she was right. He had been so concerned with his own desire that he had given no thought to her reputation or how others at the resort would treat her. He had managed to be circumspect during their trip to the cottage, but moving into her room would quickly change all the rumors into fact.

He knocked on her door, and waited. And waited.

Finally, Cynda cracked open the door. "What do you want?" She eyed him warily, as if expecting him to burst inside and carry her to bed, an idea he had considered at one point.

But he had a different plan. He held up the

gleaming frame. "I finished this and wanted to put the portrait into it."

Her expression brightened, and she held open the door. "It's wonderful." The enthusiasm that was so much a part of her bubbled to the surface. "I can't wait to see how it looks with the painting."

Dimitri swallowed his grin as he entered. Now that he had overcome her anger, he would soon have her in his arms.

But Cynda kept her distance, watching as he fitted the wooden pieces to the canvas. With that done, he replaced the portrait on the stand and moved to her side. "What do you think?"

"That frame is as much a work of art as the painting." She smiled at him, triggering the banked fire in his blood. "You'll be the only king who can say he actually helped with his own portrait."

He pulled her close, fitting her soft curves to his length. Already he was hard, needing her. Why did he constantly want this one woman? "Consider my commission satisfied." He claimed a kiss from her sweet mouth. "Now I would be satisfied as well."

Though heat clearly glimmered in her eyes, she shook her head. "No, Dimitri. Now that we're back, we can't be together like that."

"You just spent four days with me." And even that hadn't been enough.

"That was different. I only went with you to get you away from here. Now that we're back, I don't want to offend Anya and Alexi any more."

Let Alexi be offended. Dimitri wanted her. Seizing her lips again, he poured his need into her, drawing a response from her mouth, a melting of her body to his. Reaching up to cup her breast, he nearly groaned with frustration. She had taken to wearing that binding corset again. He had much preferred her with nothing beneath her dress.

Abruptly, Cynda broke the kiss and jerked from his arms, placing the width of the room between them. "No, Dimitri. It'll only make things worse." Though her chest rose and fell with her uneven breathing, she watched him as if he brandished a weapon, her eyes damp.

He shifted to ease the ache in his groin, then smiled dryly. Perhaps he did.

He stepped toward her, but she held out her hand in a halting movement. "I mean it. No. From now on, I am an artist, not just your sex toy."

Her words brought him to a stop. While he would never tire of her body, she was much more than that. She brought a light into his life that he never wanted to extinguish. Her intelligence and directness challenged his mind, made him actually *live*.

The defiant lift of her chin and set of her shoulders indicated she meant what she said. He bit back a groan. He would not be easing his ache anytime soon.

"Sophie wants to see the portrait. Why don't you take it to her?" Cynda added.

His hunger for Cynda insisted he go to her and seduce her into compliance. Dimitri clenched his fists, shuddering as he forced back that impulse. Slowly, he nodded. "As you wish."

He snatched the portrait from the easel and headed for the doorway before he lost control. After he stepped into the hallway, he heard the firm click of the lock behind him. He grimaced. Evidently Cynda didn't trust him any more than he trusted himself.

Or perhaps she didn't trust herself.

That thought provided some comfort as he headed for his suite. Before he opened the door, he paused and glanced at the portrait. It was excellent—as well painted as any artist in his country could do. He recalled her words. She wanted to be considered an artist.

And why not? She was very talented.

It was time the rest of the guests at The Chesterfield realized that. Perhaps then Cynda would not be scorned. She might even receive another commission. She deserved it.

He hesitated only a moment, then turned, determined to find Rupert. The young entrepreneur would be able to assist Dimitri on short notice. This was the right thing to do. Dimitri would hold a ceremony to reveal the portrait to the residents of The Chesterfield. Cynda would receive the honor she so richly deserved, and the gossiping patrons would discover she truly was an artist.

He would even get a nameplate made up for it and surprise her.

He grinned, excitement building. It was perfect.

Cynda awakened the next morning with a gasp, her entire body shaking with sobs. The nightmare had been so vivid, so real. She almost expected to see Dimitri's bleeding body beside her.

Burying her face in her hands, she waited for the horror of the dream to pass, but her heart continued to pound against her chest. Slowly her brain began to focus.

She and Dimitri had returned early. Today was—

Dear Lord—today was the twelfth. The day he would die.

She dressed quickly and raced to his suite. He had taken the portrait there to show Sophie. Was that where he would be shot?

Sophie answered the door and smiled at her. "I'm just having breakfast. Please join me."

Cynda followed her inside the suite. The table had been set up in the main room now that Sophie could move around. "Is Dimitri here?" Cynda asked.

"Not at the moment. He had some business to finish, but I am certain he will return soon." Sophie sat and indicated a nearby chair. "Please keep me company."

Cynda wavered, glancing from the chair to the door. Every nerve in her body danced on end as if sensing danger in the air. "I really need to talk to Dimitri."

"Wait here for him." A hint of mischief appeared in Sophie's eyes, and Cynda hesitated. What was going on?

Though reluctant, Cynda settled in a chair and accepted a cup of tea. She glanced around the suite, suddenly realizing what bothered her. "Did you see the portrait? Dimitri brought it over here yesterday."

"I believe he wanted something else done to it before I saw it."

Panic raced through Cynda. "Where is it?"

"I'm afraid I don't know."

Cynda pushed back her chair. She couldn't wait here. Not when Dimitri might be with the portrait now. At least, he hadn't yet procured the nameplate for it. But would that be enough to save his life?

A sudden thought struck her. Without the nameplate, how could she return to her own time? It didn't matter. Saving Dimitri's life was more important.

"I have to find Dimitri," Cynda said with an apologetic smile.

"Stay here, Miss Madison." The steel edge to Sophie's voice halted Cynda in mid-stride. "He will return shortly. I promise you."

"You don't understand. His life—"

The door opened, and Cynda didn't finish, swinging around. "Dimitri . . ." Any further words died as Alexi and Anya entered. Alexi's cold glare pierced her, adding to the ache in her chest. Losing his friendship hurt, but then she had hurt him as well.

"You're not welcome here," he said, his arm going around Anya's shoulders protectively.

"I was just leaving." Cynda edged toward the door.

Sophie stood, resting her hand on the head of her cane. "She is dining with me and will remain. Where are your manners, Alexi?"

"My manners? After what she's done?" He returned his cruel gaze to Cynda. "You refused all my overtures yet gave in easily enough to my brother. Why? Because he will be king?"

"That's not it at all." Cynda fought to keep her temper under control. "I didn't ask for this to happen. It's chemistry."

"I have no idea what you're talking about." Alexi led Anya to the small table and seated her. "And

I told you before, he will never marry you. Anya will be queen." He rested his hand on her shoulder.

"I don't expect him to marry me, and I have no intention of becoming his mistress, no matter what he told you." She tilted her chin defiantly. "I'm leaving here in a few days, and you'll never see me again."

"I find that difficult to believe." Alexi came to face her, his scornful expression breaking her heart. Where was the lighthearted man she liked so much? "Because of you Dimitri has sullied his reputation, the reputation of our country. He doesn't deserve to become king. He will only lead our country to ruin."

"That's a lie." She didn't bother to hold her anger any longer. "Dimitri will be a great king. He wants only the best for your country and you know it."

"I know nothing of the sort."

Cynda sighed. "Alexi, get over it."

He looked momentarily nonplussed, then reached out to grab her arm, his fingers forming an unbreakable hold. "I advise you to leave this room and this hotel as soon as you can or I will not be responsible for what happens next."

She tried to wrench free without success. "What if I don't? What do you plan to do?"

"I will—"

"Release her at once, Alexi." Dimitri's voice boomed across the suite, and Cynda turned to look at him in surprise.

She had been so engrossed in her anger at Alexi that she hadn't even noticed when the suite door opened again. Alexi glared at his brother, then pushed Cynda away and stalked to the table.

Sophie immediately rapped his knuckles with her knife. "You will apologize at once."

Alexi stiffened. "No. She is my brother's whore and deserves no respect."

Cynda gasped, the blood leaving her face, his words digging into her with all the pain of a blade. Was this the same laughing young man who had charmed every woman in his path? Had he changed so completely or had she misjudged him all along?

"Apologize, Alexi." Dimitri came to Cynda's side, vibrating with rage. "She is a lady and an artist and deserving of your respect in every way."

"Why is that?" Alexi's tone held a mocking sneer. "Because she is good in bed?"

Dimitri started toward him, intent on violence, and Cynda seized his arm to hold him back. "No, Dimitri, don't. It's not worth it."

"I cannot allow my own brother to defame you." He strained against her grip, fire blazing in his eyes.

"They're only words. They have no power to hurt me unless *I* let them." Unfortunately, Alexi's words did hurt, but she couldn't let Dimitri see that. "Please, let's leave."

Dimitri stiffened, then nodded once. "We will all leave. I have something I want to share with all of you." He glanced pointedly at his brother. "Even you, Alexi, and Anya."

"I—"

Sophie rapped Alexi's knuckles again. "You will come, and I will not hear another word from you." She turned to smile at Anya. "My dear?"

Dread filled Cynda as Dimitri took her arm. "Where are we going?"

"You will see." He led her from the room and

down to the main floor, Alexi and Anya assisting
Sophie behind them. Turning toward the main
lobby, he gave her a warm smile. "It is time people
here realized what a truly talented artist you are."

Her throat tightened, fear filling her veins. "This
is not a good idea."

"It is an excellent idea."

Rounding the corner, he paused, and she inhaled sharply when she saw the portrait on display
at the edge of the large room. His frame shone
around it, but worse—far, far worse—was the shiny
nameplate that glittered at the bottom. "Oh no."
She hurried toward it to read the finely etched
lettering . . . lettering she had seen once before on
a tarnished, dented piece of metal. *Dimitri Karakov.*

She turned to him, barely able to breathe. "Do
you realize what you've done?"

He beamed, standing proud. "I have shown The
Chesterfield that you are an excellent artist."

Dear Lord. He had arranged his own death. She
went to his side. "You must leave here now," she
murmured quietly.

"Leave?" He frowned. "Not until I have finished
with the presentation."

She dug her fingers into his arm. "You can't stay
here. It's too dangerous. You'll die."

The look he sent her held a touch of anger as
well as sympathy. "I will hear no more talk on that
subject."

"But—" What did she have to do to get him to
believe her?

"No more." Pulling away, he went to stand by
the painting and raised his voice. "May I have your
attention, please?"

A crowd quickly formed around them. Cynda

searched the faces. Was one of them the killer? Alexi glowered at his brother, obviously angry enough to give in to a murderous impulse. Anya stood by Sophie's side, her expression a mixture of resignation, polite interest and barely revealed anger.

Cynda recognized some faces, but most were new. Since she had entered Dimitri's employ, she hadn't had the daily contact with the guests. Could some of them be in cahoots with Johnson?

She spotted Miss Sparrow at the edge of the crowd and debated on waving her over and asking her for help. There were too many people.

Her palms grew cold and sweaty, and she wiped them on her dress, unable to focus on Dimitri's words. He was praising her talent and months of dedicated effort, trying to sell her as an artist in an obvious attempt to preserve her reputation. His life was more important than that.

She scanned each face and watched hands. Too many of the men held guns, evidently coming in or going hunting. In fact, they comprised the larger portion of the crowd with more entering every moment.

Her chest hurt with her inability to draw a breath. Who? When? How?

A maid rounded the corner briskly, her arms full of laundry, and smiled at Cynda. In doing so, she plowed into a man coming in from outside . . . a hunter . . . with a gun.

In an instant, realization dawned. Dimitri's death hadn't been a murder. It had been an accident. A stupid, senseless accident.

She was already moving, leaping at Dimitri, even as the gun hit the floor and a shot rang out. Fiery pain sliced into her shoulder, and she collapsed, the agony sizzling along every nerve.

Dimitri knelt beside her at once and cradled her in his arms. "Cynda, what have you done?"

"Saved your life." Blackness drifted close, promising to end the pain, and she yearned for it. "You . . . all right?"

"I'm fine."

"Good." She closed her eyes, satisfied. She had done it.

He touched her face. "Cynda." His voice was choked.

She tried to focus but couldn't. Her vision was circled with a red haze. "I'm glad . . . you're alive."

The darkness beckoned again, soothing, enticing, and with a sigh she succumbed to it.

Chapter 20

Dimitri's heart stopped for a moment when Cynda went limp in his arms, blood seeping from her shoulder. "Where is the doctor?" he roared. Someone should be here to help her, to save her. She still breathed, but barely, her chest making only a slight movement.

"I'm here." Dr. Ziegler came to kneel beside him, out of breath as if he had run the entire way. "Let me see."

Dimitri lowered Cynda to the floor and stood as the doctor examined her. Panic gripped him, a fear more devastating than any he had ever faced. She could die because he had refused to believe her ridiculous story.

He could lose her.

Dr. Ziegler looked up, his expression grave. "I have bound the wound, but I will need to remove the bullet.'' He pointed at a nearby porter. "Fetch my stretcher.'' The man fled, and the doctor stood to touch Dimitri's arm. "Have them take her to her room. I will get my equipment and meet you there.''

Dimitri could hardly breathe. She was going to die. It was there in the doctor's eyes. He seized the man's shirt, unable to hold back his rising fear. "If she dies, I'll have your head.''

Dr. Ziegler blinked in obvious surprise and then looked pointedly at Dimitri's hand. "If you'll release me, I will do my best.''

"Dimitri.'' Reprimand filled Grandmère's quiet voice as she hobbled to his side. "You forget yourself.''

Dimitri released the doctor, who hurried away.

"I can't lose her.'' He heard the pleading in his voice, as if Grandmère, who had always been there for him, could make this all a bad dream or cure Cynda with the touch of her hand.

"You won't.'' Grandmère patted his clenched fist. "Our Cynda is made of strong character.''

The porter arrived with the stretcher and laid it on the floor beside Cynda. Before he could move her onto it, Dimitri stopped him. "I will do it.''

He placed her on the stretcher with utmost gentleness, cautious of her wound. She moaned slightly, the sound wrenching his heart. He grabbed one end of the stretcher. "I will carry her.'' He glanced at the porter, expecting the man to take the other end, but Alexi lifted it instead.

"Let me help.''

At his obvious concern, Dimitri nodded. He started for her suite, as quickly as possible, yet doing his best not to jostle her.

"She saved your life," Alexi said quietly.

"I know." All because Dimitri had been too proud, too arrogant, to believe what he couldn't understand.

"It's almost as if she expected it. She moved so quickly."

"Yes." Dimitri could say no more. This was all his fault.

"I misjudged her. I'm sorry."

Dimitri looked at Alexi then and gave him a tight smile. "Yes, you did." He glanced at Cynda's pale face. "So did I."

He refused to leave the room while Dr. Ziegler performed the long, delicate surgery to remove the bullet from Cynda's shoulder, pacing in front of the window, glancing over at the operation at regular intervals. When the doctor finally straightened and began gathering his instruments, Dimitri rushed to his side.

"How is she?"

"She was lucky. The bullet missed anything vital. With some rest and barring infection, she should recover completely."

Dimitri struggled for air. "You swear it?"

"Your Highness, nothing is absolute." Dr. Ziegler lifted his bag. "I will check on Miss Madison often. Right now, she needs rest and healing. I've dosed her with laudanum, so she should sleep for quite a while."

Cynda still looked pale, her breathing shallow. Her shoulder was wrapped in a heavy bandage. Would she recover?

Remembering his manners as the doctor reached the suite door, Dimitri hurried to show him out. "Thank you, Doctor. Please forgive my earlier outburst."

The older man smiled for the first time. "It's forgotten. We all get a little irrational when someone we love is injured. Don't worry. I'll check back in a few hours."

Dimitri returned to Cynda's bedside, his thoughts in a jumble. He had never permitted love in his life. He had always known he would be king, marry Anya, and rule his country. Love made a man weak, and a king could not afford to be weak.

Yet Cynda had managed to slip into his life, into his soul, before he had even realized it. She made him laugh. She made him think. She made him delirious with wanting her. She had become as vital to him as breathing. He couldn't lose her.

He ran his fingers over her cheek. He loved her . . . had loved her even when he hadn't realized it.

And he had failed her. If he had listened to her, believed her instead of doubting her crazy story, she would not be lying here. "I'm sorry," he whispered.

She didn't move, didn't forgive him.

Clutching her hand in his, Dimitri settled into the chair placed beside her bed. He might have failed her earlier, but he wouldn't again. He would stay until she recovered . . . no matter how long it took.

He searched her face for obvious signs that she was from the future. Though her outward appearance provided no clues, he could no longer deny it. She was everything she had said she was. He closed his eyes, remembering . . . her odd choice of words, her unfamiliarity with the stove, her unrestrained passion.

"Dimitri." Cynda's soft voice crept into his dreams. "Dimitri."

He sat up, jerking awake. It wasn't a dream. Leaning forward to hear her whispered words, Dimitri rejoiced at seeing her eyes open. "What can I do for you?"

"Thirsty."

He poured a glass of water, then helped her sip it. She winced as she settled back again, but didn't complain. "How do you feel?" he asked, wishing he could take her pain on himself.

"Like a truck hit me."

He frowned. "Truck?"

She gave him a wan smile. "Not invented yet." She brought her hand up to her head. "I'm so woozy."

"The doctor gave you laudanum."

"Oh." She closed her eyes briefly, then opened them again. "Don't let me miss the solstice."

She drifted into sleep again, her chest moving rhythmically, and Dimitri sat back, a heavy weight sitting on his chest. The solstice.

Cynda had been telling him the truth about his possible death. She really was from the future, from a time beyond his comprehension. That explained her quick retorts, her independent streak, and why he found her so unique compared to every other woman of his acquaintance.

Which also meant she would not become his mistress. She had said so often, but he had refused to believe that, certain he could woo her into compliance. But she would never accept that position. He should have known that.

He groaned. It was an insult to her. She had been willing to die for him, yet he had only offered her a scrap of his life.

Rising, he paced the floor. But he was bred to be king. His life had been planned since his infancy.

And he needed Cynda in it.

Brushing his fingers through his hair, he examined every possible solution. When the solstice arrived in too few days, she would leave him. He knew it. She had told him time and again. And the future was one place he would not be able to find her.

How could he exist without her? Yet how could he ask her to be anything but a total partner in his future?

He returned to her side and gently tasted her lips. There had to be something he could do . . . some way to change his destiny.

"How is she?"

Dimitri looked around to see Alexi in the doorway. "She regained consciousness for a brief period. Dr. Ziegler says she will recover."

"I'm glad." Alexi moved to stand at the end of the bed. "I am sorry for my earlier anger. I would not wish ill on Cynda, especially when my anger was directed at you."

"I understand." Dimitri had failed his brother as well. Maybe Alexi was right. Maybe Dimitri had no right to be king.

"You love her." Alexi said the words quietly, simply, yet they reverberated within Dimitri.

He nodded and stood. Crossing to Alexi, Dimitri clapped his brother's shoulder. "Come with me. We need to talk."

His time of indecision was past. He knew what he had to do.

"I'm fine," Cynda insisted yet again. As much as she adored Sophie, she just wanted to be left alone. Ever since she had regained total consciousness, the elderly woman had been a constant presence, her solicitousness well-meaning but overbearing. "Honest."

"But you must eat. Dr. Ziegler said it is important for you to regain your strength." Sophie pushed the tray toward Cynda.

With a sigh, Cynda dug her fork into the potatoes. She had never felt less like eating in her life, but Sophie forced her to choke down every bite. "When can I see Dimitri?" Cynda asked.

She needed to see him, touch him, know in truth that he was all right. She vaguely remembered his presence earlier, but she hadn't seen him once since she awakened several days ago.

"Not too much longer." Sophie gave her the same reply.

"Where is he? Is he all right? Are you not telling me something?" Cynda leaned forward, wincing at the sharp pain in her shoulder.

"Dimitri is fine, perfectly healthy, thanks to you." Sophie smiled warmly.

"Then, why are you keeping him from me?"

"Do not excite yourself, my dear." Sophie sighed and settled in a nearby chair. "Dimitri and Alexi had to go to New York City on urgent business. I am certain they will return as soon as possible."

Cynda frowned. New York City? Dimitri just left her? Her spirits sank. He didn't even care enough to ensure she would recover? "I see," she muttered.

"They had to go. The business is very urgent."

"I'm sure it is." And with only three days left until the solstice, Cynda doubted she would ever see Dimitri again.

Perhaps this was best. She had needed all her willpower to resist him earlier. In her weakened state, he might actually succeed in convincing her to become his mistress.

She leaned back against her pillows and closed her eyes. "I'd like to rest now, Sophie, if you don't mind."

"Certainly, my dear." Sophie squeezed Cynda's hands before she approached the door. "Call if you need me. I'll sit outside."

Cynda nodded, but it wasn't Sophie she needed. It was Dimitri. Now and forever. And she couldn't have him.

Three days were all that remained until she left this time period and Dimitri Karakov's life forever.

Getting dressed by herself took forever, but Cynda managed despite the throbbing in her shoulder. However, that bone-crushing corset could rot in the corner. She wouldn't need it where she was going.

Cynda paused by the window as she fashioned a haphazard sling for her arm. Though not snowing, the day of the solstice was gray, reflecting her mood. Dimitri had still not returned, and she had to leave . . . today.

Tears welled, but she blinked them back. This was the right decision for everyone concerned. She couldn't be his mistress. No matter what he said, he would one day hate her for it. Maybe with her gone, Dimitri would at least try to make a life with Anya.

She peeked through her door into the hallway. No sign of Sophie. Great.

Cynda dashed through and hurried for the stairwell.

"Where do you think you're going?"

Caught. Cynda froze. She had said her good-bye to Sophie last night, mixing it with her good night so as to avoid suspicion. Apparently it hadn't worked. Slowly she turned to face the elderly woman.

"I'm leaving today, Sophie. You know that."

"You simply cannot leave. I forbid it."

Cynda grinned and went up to kiss Sophie's cheek. "Now I know where Dimitri gets his arrogance. I'll miss you."

Panic lined Sophie's face. "Where will you go? At least leave me an address."

"You won't be able to reach me once I leave." Cynda's throat tightened.

"Ridiculous. I know Dimitri will look for you."

"He won't be able to find me. Not where I'm going."

Sophie frowned. "I will have no more of this evasive talk. Tell me the truth now. Why are you deserting Dimitri?"

Cynda sighed, then smiled. What could telling the truth hurt now? "I'm not deserting him. I'm giving him his life back and going where I belong. Here, I'm a person out of time."

"Out of time?"

In more ways than one. "I'm going to where The

Chesterfield is a ruin and no one is forced to wear corsets and women are treated as equals."

Sophie looked at her blankly, and Cynda squeezed her hand one final time.

"I'm going to the future . . . to the year two thousand and one."

Sophie paled. "That . . . that's impossible."

"Six months ago I would've agreed with you." Cynda backed away. "Good-bye."

"Wait." Sophie called after her, but Cynda could move faster and hurried to the main part of the hotel.

Her first item of business, to locate Miss Sparrow, was successful when she found the woman leaving the dining room. "Miss Sparrow."

The head housekeeper smiled warmly. "Miss Madison, it is good to see you up. Everyone is still talking about your bravery in saving Prince Dimitri."

Heat warmed Cynda's cheeks. "I didn't think of it as brave, just necessary."

Miss Sparrow laughed. "So you would. Are you feeling better?"

"Much, thank you." Cynda drew in a deep breath. Enough pleasantries. "Today is the solstice. I came to say good-bye."

The good humor fled from Miss Sparrow's face. "You plan to leave?"

"Yes."

"I see." If anything, the woman looked distressed now. "Are you quite certain? I had thought you and Prince Dimitri . . ."

"We have no future." Cynda was abrupt. No future she could endure.

"I . . . I am so sorry." Miss Sparrow extended her hand. "Won't you reconsider?"

"I can't." She didn't dare. "Thank you." Cynda hesitated, then quickly hugged the woman. "Thank you for everything."

Miss Sparrow inclined her head. If Cynda hadn't known better, she would have thought tears watered in the woman's eyes. Or maybe it was the moisture blurring Cynda's own.

Slowing her steps, Cynda headed for the lobby. Was the portrait still there?

It was, though it had been moved to a corner. Dimitri stood there as proud and tall as in the flesh. Cynda stood before it, the ache in her chest spreading to her belly. She would always love him, even when she was a miserable old woman.

She stared at the undented nameplate, her ticket home and proof that she had changed the past. Dimitri was alive. She had achieved that. He would go on to be a wonderful king and lead his country to greatness.

She met his sensual gaze. "I will miss you so much." Her voice broke, and she swallowed hard to keep the tears from escaping.

"Cynda."

Half afraid she heard the voice as part of a dream, she turned to see Dimitri standing behind her, dressed in a thick coat, breathing heavily as if he had just run in from outside. He approached her slowly, then touched her cheek. "Don't go," he whispered.

She closed her eyes. She had to be strong. She couldn't give in now. "I have to," she whispered.

"No, you don't." Before her unbelieving gaze, he dropped to one knee and took her free hand in his. "Cynda Madison, would you do me the honor of becoming my wife?"

She hadn't heard correctly ... couldn't have heard right. "But ... but you're marrying Anya."

Humor lit his eyes. "Not any longer."

Was he serious? She didn't dare believe him. "You're going to be king. Your father will never let you marry me."

"That is not a problem."

"Why? Has your father suddenly gone senile?"

He shook his head. "I am no longer going to be king."

"What?" She felt the blood drain from her face. "That can't be."

"I have abdicated the throne in favor of Alexi. He will be the next king of our country."

Her heart skipped several beats. "You can't do that, not for me."

"Not only for you, but for me. Becoming king has become more and more a chore with each approaching year. I have dreaded it." Dimitri gave her a reassuring smile. "Alexi has the same schooling as I, he shares my goals, and even better, he has been among the people. They love him. With that, he will be able to make the necessary changes more easily."

He was serious. "You're not going to be king?"

"So I have said."

"But Anya . . ."

"Anya will marry Alexi, a much better solution for everyone concerned." His smile turned into a full-fledged grin. "Especially since I recently learned that they have been in love with each other for some time."

Alexi and Anya in love with each other? Cynda recalled the younger man's protectiveness of the woman. Of course. "No wonder he was so angry."

"I am going to stay here in America, Cynda, and make a new life for myself as a carpenter." He spoke earnestly. "And I have an inheritance of my own, not tied to my coronation, so we will not starve."

Cynda gasped. This was crazy. This was wonderful. Her head whirled as if she had stood up too quickly. "I . . . I don't believe it."

"Alexi and I have spent the past several days sending telegrams to our father. It took a great deal of persuasion, but he finally agreed, especially when I made him understand I had no life without you. I love you."

The solemnness of his words brought tears to her eyes. "I love you," she whispered.

He smiled up at her so gently, her heart contracted. "Cynda, I am still waiting for your answer, and I am developing a cramp in my leg."

With a laugh, she tugged him to his feet. "My answer is yes. I would love to be your wife."

Careful of her shoulder, he drew her close and claimed her lips in an extremely possessive kiss that sent shocks to her very core. "We will be married right away," he announced.

Cynda raised her eyebrow, and he grinned, adding, "If you agree, of course."

"I completely agree."

"Excellent." He kissed her again, and Cynda dimly heard the sound of applause surrounding them. Glancing behind Dimitri, she found the lobby filled with people cheering enthusiastically. Miss Sparrow stood at the edge, wiping a tear from her eye, but her face was beaming.

Sophie tottered over to them, her smile wide. "You have made the right decision, my dear." She kissed Dimitri's cheek, then Cynda's. "Alexi is much better suited to be king, and you will be far happier, I believe."

Dimitri narrowed his eyes. "Why do I feel as if you planned this entire thing?"

Bringing her hand to her chest, Sophie presented indignation. "*Moi?*"

Cynda laughed. They had both been set up, and she couldn't be happier. From now on, her future would include Dimitri. "I still intend to paint," she told him.

His familiar scowl returned. "No wife of mine is going . . ." He broke off and sighed. "You are going to be difficult to manage, aren't you?"

She kissed him softly. "Perhaps, but who else would put up with your arrogance?"

"Only you, *mon coeur*. Only you."

Epilogue

Esme Sparrow polished the nameplate against her sleeve before she placed it inside her hope chest beside the shiny dueling pistol and the gleaming badge. For a short while she had been afraid this match would not reach fruition, but Dimitri had made the right choice.

At his Christmas wedding to Cynda, he had looked more relaxed and far happier than the young man who had visited The Chesterfield in past years. Cynda had glowed with love, making the occasion even more bittersweet for Esme. They were so involved with each other, it would be some time before either of them realized the nameplate was missing from the portrait.

The grand duchess Sophie had beamed with pride, certain she had been the one to make the match. Esme would not disillusion her. Her assistance in uniting the couple had been invaluable.

A final touch to the wonderful day had been Chief Garrett's update on Johnson and his friends. Johnson's friend had confessed, revealing that only he and Johnson had plotted to kill Dimitri, and both men were safely locked away for many years to come. Dimitri would have nothing to fear from them.

Miss Sparrow closed the chest with trembling fingers. This had to work. Only two more couples remained. But the next match would be the most difficult yet.

Would young Emily know how to catch a thief?

To the Reader,

Thank you for sharing my first time-travel adventure into the past. I loved exploring the differences in the two time periods and watching the arrogant Prince Dimitri soften into a man in love.

I especially enjoyed the chance to write with the other members of my critique group on this series. We shared in the development of The Chesterfield and its assortment of staff—the Major, Rupert, Jack O'Riley, and of course, Miss Sparrow. If you've missed the first two books in this series, they are *Enchantment* by Pam McCutcheon and *Fire With Fire* by Paula Gill.

Be sure to read the next stories of time travelers at the Chesterfield, *Stolen Hearts* by Laura Hayden, and *At Midnight* by Maureen McKenzie, to learn more about why Miss Sparrow is so determined to match these special couples.

I love hearing from readers. You can write to me at P.O. Box 31541, Colorado Springs, CO 80931-1541 or e-mail me at *karen@karenafox.com*. To discover what other books I have coming out, visit my web site at *http://www.karenafox.com*.

See you between the pages.

Karen Fox

COMING IN SEPTEMBER 2001 FROM
ZEBRA BALLAD ROMANCES